THINGS

THINGS

FRANCINE GARSON

ANT COLONY PRESS

Ant Colony Press, a division of Olive Group, LLC,
P.O. Box 1577, Belton, MO 64012

ISBN-13: 978-1726311380

Ant Colony Press 1st edition August 2018

10 9 8 7 6 5 4 3 2 1

Manufactured in the United States of America

For information regarding special discounts for bulk purchases, please
contact Ant Colony Press at antcolonypress@gmail.com.

www.antcolonypress.com

It's never too late to have a happy childhood.
–Tom Robbins, *Still Life with Woodpecker*

So we beat on, boats against the current, borne back cease-
lessly into the past.
–F. Scott Fitzgerald, *The Great Gatsby*

She never mentions the word addiction
In certain company
Yes, she'll tell you she's an orphan
After you meet her family.
–The Black Crowes, *She Talks to Angels*

1

The day after my neighbor moves out, I rent her vacant apartment. It's small, and one of the bathroom tiles is cracked, but the studio floor plan gives me the square of open space I need.

"But you're still keeping your current apartment, 1E?" Mrs. Thornton, the property manager, points a red-nailed finger at me. "And you want to rent the one next door as well?"

"That's right." I nod.

"If you're thinking about breaking through the wall, making it into one big—"

"No, I'll just be renting the two *individual* apartments. 1E and 1F in Building A."

"Okay, Jenny. Just remember we don't allow separate apartments to be combined into one."

"That's fine." I sign the lease and slide two checks made out to Sea Grove Gardens across her desk. One month's rent and the security deposit.

Mrs. Thornton squints as she peers over her glasses at me. "I notice on the rental agreement that you're a self-employed college counselor. These are garden apartments. We're not zoned for commercial, you know. You won't be using the second apartment for business, will you?"

"No. I have an office in the Clayton Professional Building. That's where I meet clients, and I keep all my business files there, too. I can give you my card." I dig into my bag.

"No, that's okay. Don't bother." Mrs. Thornton shakes her head, but her blonde-from-a-box hair doesn't move. "I have your office contact information on your application." She pauses. "It's my job to make sure our tenants comply with the rules. And I just wondered, if you don't mind me asking, why are you renting two apartments next to each other?"

"For…uh…storage," I stammer, looking into her carefully penciled eyes. "I need some extra room. For my… things." I glance down at my watch. "So, if that's it—"

"That's it, but just so I understand, you'll be paying rent on a second apartment for storage? That sounds like an expensive proposition."

"Maybe 'storage' isn't exactly the right word then. I… uh…I like to live in an uncluttered area, so I still have some things in boxes. I guess it might be more accurate to say I just want the extra living space," I explain, feeling a tiny pulse above my right eye. "Is that a problem?"

"No. It's not a problem. Not a problem at all. It's just unusual, but wait a minute…" She tilts her head, and her eyes narrow into suspicious slits. "You're not planning to sublet, are you? Because we have rules about that. You can't—"

"I'm not going to sublet. I just would like more room." I shrug as nonchalantly as I can. "That's all."

"Okay." She sighs and lays a silver-toned key in my palm. "Enjoy *both* of your apartments, then."

I smile weakly. "Thank you, Mrs. Thornton," I say and drop the key into the pocket of my leather jacket.

Apartment 1F. *Mine.*

I walk toward the closest of the three-story ivory brick buildings across from the management office, breathing in the smell of freshly cut grass sparked with the salty tang of the nearby ocean. An island of small evergreens decorates the lawn surrounding the building, and evenly trimmed hedges flank its newly painted front door. Stepping into the foyer, I pass my current apartment and fit my new key into the adjacent door.

Chloe, the previous tenant of 1F and a thirty-something-year-old woman with springy red curls and paint-splattered jeans, had accessorized her 'creative space', as she called it, with unfinished paintings and floor pillows. She explained her philosophy of living *with* and *through* her art to me one night over a bottle of merlot and a bowl of artichoke dip. But after a year in Sea Grove Gardens, she packed up her brushes and unsold canvases and moved into her parents' basement. I called Mrs. Thornton.

The apartment looks like a ballet studio without the mirrors. Just one large wood-floored square bracketed by a small kitchen with tall cabinets and a tiny bathroom. A set of double doors along the side wall leads into a huge walk-in closet outfitted with a modular shelving system. Plenty of room.

Moving from Manhattan to New Jersey was a good idea. A very good idea. The apartments are so much larger here. And this new one will give me even more space.

Apartment 1E for living, Apartment 1F for…things.

I close the door to my new apartment, jiggling the knob to make sure it locks behind me, and feel for the New Jersey-shaped key ring in my bag. Kitschy maybe, but I like it anyway. I slide my new key onto the ring, walk the six steps to my original apartment, and unlock the door.

After hanging my jacket in its usual spot between my navy pea coat and a hooded sweatshirt, I move into the living room. A textured area rug sits under a leather sofa flanked by a pair of matching floor lamps, and an arrangement of white roses rests on the glass coffee table. Tall columns of cardboard boxes occupy the corners of the room, and a lower wall of cartons stands behind the sofa, reaching up to the sill of the picture window. A light oak wall unit hosts a motley conglomeration of boxes and books. Hunching my shoulders and crossing my arms against my chest, I slide sideways between the walls of boxes that narrow the hallway leading to my bedroom.

Like the rest of the apartment, my room is neat. Crowded, but neat. A cream-colored comforter, corners tucked in, stretches across my queen size bed. Two large pillows are positioned diagonally below my headboard, which is stacked with piles of to-be-read books organized by size. My silver hand mirror with its matching comb and brush lay centered on my dresser, and my armoire stands in the corner of the room. The towers of cardboard boxes that line the walls are neatly labeled and evenly spaced.

After living in a cramped New York apartment, this space had seemed huge. Enormous. Certainly big enough. I remember humming Bruce Springsteen's song about traveling to the 'Jersey side' and skipping through the empty apartment just before I moved in, smiling as my voice ricocheted off the bare walls. I thought I had room to unpack. But that was more than a year ago.

I don't tell anyone about renting the second apartment. Not my mother. Not my friends. No one. I know what they would say.

Why do you want two apartments? Wouldn't it be easier just to rent a bigger one? One apartment would be cheaper than two, right? And then, a sigh, a rolling of the eyes, a shaking of the head. The boxes? Is that what this is about? Didn't you unpack yet? Do you need help? Don't you think it's time to…? Jenny?

The furniture for Apartment 1F arrives at two, exactly midway through the four-hour window I scheduled with the delivery service. I hand one of the two movers the room map I drafted on graph paper and watch as they place everything according to the diagram. I give each of them a bottle of cold water and a crisp new bill.

"I hope you don't mind if I check the spacing," I say as I pull a tape measure out of the top kitchen drawer. When I bend to measure the space between the dresser and the bookcase, I feel my shirt ride up over the waistband of my jeans.

"Knock yourself out, honey." I hear a whisper and a low whistle.

My face grows hot, but I move from the bookcase to the night table and continue to measure. Straightening up, I look at the men, one with a scraggly blonde ponytail, the other with a tattooed bicep. "I'm sorry to bother you, but the dresser needs to be moved two inches to the right."

The men lift the dresser and carry it the two inches.

I measure again and nod at them. "And the desk? Can you move it to the left?" I ask. "An inch and a half?"

They exchange a glance and move the desk.

I bend down to measure the distance between the desk and the wall and feel two pairs of eyes lasering into my back. Pulling myself upright, I turn toward the movers. "I think it's still a half inch off," I say quietly. "I'm sorry."

"Are you kidding?" the ponytailed man grumbles.

"Not really." I shake my head. "I know I've got issues." I smile and shrug.

The men move the desk, and I measure the space. Again. "It's good now. Thank you." I breathe out, feeling my shoulders relax.

"Good thing the bed was in the right place," the pony-tailed man mutters.

As the movers walk to the door, the tattooed man turns and laughs. "You're a crazy chick," he says, winking as he leaves the apartment.

They have no idea.

Queen size bed, night table, dresser, armoire, desk with padded rolling chair, and large bookcase. The white wood furniture seems to float along the walls that with the help of a large sea sponge and a concoction of blue paint and white glaze, I've turned into a make-believe sky.

It's a good start.

I step into the hallway between my two apartments. It's a late afternoon kind of quiet, just as I expected. The occupants of the four other apartments on my floor will be at work for at least another couple of hours. Using two of my kitchen chairs, I prop open the doors to both apartments. One by one, I carry each of the labeled cardboard boxes from my original apartment into my new one, stacking them into vertical piles wedged among pieces of my just-delivered furniture.

Locking the door behind me, I go back to 1E. Without the piles of boxes around, I can finally give it a good cleaning. I pull out my vacuum and grabbing a rag, begin to clear a film of accumulated dust from the newly exposed floors and moldings. And my boxes are just next door, I remind myself as I work.

After I finish, I stow the cleaning supplies in a closet and stroll through the apartment. So nice in here. So much room. And I still have everything I need right in the next apartment. *My* apartment. Wrapping my arms around myself, I smile.

Back in the living room, I lift the pleated blind covering the window and admire the blue glint of the ocean sparkling above the weathered gray boardwalk. At the start of each fiscal year, the town planning board considers replacing the ancient boardwalk. And each year, after a perfunctory discussion, the board members vote in favor of preserving the aging wooden planks of Jersey shore history. It's a money issue, really. But anyway, the bleached gray boards look good against the whitish tan beach sand.

My apartment complex is a short walk to the beach. So, from Memorial Day weekend through Labor Day, I tuck a chair under my arm, throw a bag over my shoulder, and head over on foot, happy not to deal with the summertime scramble for the limited number of parking spots near the ocean. Since I've got an office in a professional building just a few miles inland, I head to the beach after work during the off-season too. Bundled up in a sweatshirt and jeans, I review my clients' college applications or read novels to the sound of squawking seagulls and breaking waves, my own personal seaside soundtrack.

One apartment to live in, another to set up, and a nearby office. I'm getting there.

I snatch up the key to my new apartment and pull a pair of scissors from a desk drawer. Now for the boxes…

2

Where do I begin? I stare at the cardboard skyline decorating 1F, my newly rented apartment. Scanning the columns of boxes, I read through the dozens of labels carefully lettered in my own neat print. Names, places, and years. The story of my life entombed in cardboard. I stop at a box labeled *Dad 2009*. Just three years ago.

Do the hardest things first, my father always said. In this case, that means starting with the end.

"Your father's going in for some tests. Nothing to worry about," my mother told me that spring.

The following week, just a year after he had retired from the Army and joined a small accounting firm in Florida, and only months after he and my mother had purchased a condo in Boynton Beach, my father was diagnosed with pancreatic cancer. Terminal.

"Don't come down here, Jenny. I mean it." My father's words were delivered as orders.

"Dad, I—"

"Jenny, you heard me. Stay in New York."

Daring to disobey my father, I took a four-week leave of absence from my job at Columbia and flew to Florida. Just three months after his diagnosis, I didn't recognize the shrunken man staring at the television as my wide-shouldered, perfectly-postured father. The man whose entrance into a room had made everyone stand up straighter had shriveled into a newly bald stick figure buried under a rumpled blanket.

"Look a little different, don't I?" he muttered.

Don't cry, I told myself, pressing a finger against the bridge of my nose. Be a good little soldier. "It's only hair, Dad. It'll grow back," I said.

"I'm not going to be around long enough for that to happen, Jenny." He lifted a skinny arm.

"Don't say that. You're a fighter. You—"

"I'm not a fighter." He shook his head. "I worked with numbers in offices not guns on battlefields. And that was by choice, something that I was lucky enough to have had. Not everyone in the Army is a fighter. You know that."

"You're right. 'Fighter' is the wrong word. But you've always made the rules, and you can do it now. Dad, you can beat this."

"I didn't *make* the rules, Jenny. I followed them."

A series of choking coughs engulfed him, and I handed him a glass of water. Closing his eyes, he sipped and swallowed until the coughing subsided. I looked at the row of pill bottles, arranged in size order, parading across the table next to his bed while the TV droned. The screen's image of a dark house filled with toppling mounds of clothing, boxes, and bags cut to a commercial.

During this last summer of his life, my father had become fascinated with the reality TV series featuring compulsive hoarders. From the hospital bed that had replaced the dining room table in the Florida condo he shared with my mother, he watched back-to-back episodes of the show on a small flat screen. He followed the progress of professional organizers and cleaning specialists as they waded through heaps of unworn clothing, boxes stuffed with used envelopes and plastic bags, stacks of crumpled newspapers, and piles of trash.

"Do you still have those stacks of boxes in your apartment, Jenny?" My father's voice came out in a hoarse whisper.

"I've unpacked some of them."

"Unpacked? I thought you were going to get rid of them. The stuff you don't need," he said. "It makes the whole place look messy. Sloppy."

"It's not messy, Dad. Everything's organized. You know I'm not sloppy."

"But why do you need all that stuff? I hope you're not becoming a hoarder." He wrinkled his nose and blinked, his face twisting into a grimace.

"You just get well. And the next time you visit me, the boxes will be gone." I arranged my mouth into what I hoped looked like a smile. "Okay?"

I think about that promise as I cut through a wide band of packaging tape and spread the flaps of the cardboard box I had sealed three years ago, uncovering the large white envelope that has been buried inside. I unwind its string closure and pull out a jumble of sympathy cards and the funeral home's guest book. Opening a manila folder, I thumb through a clutter of lab reports, post-surgical instructions, scrawled directions to doctors' offices, and hospital maps. I remember my mother's quizzical look and slow nod when I asked to keep my father's files. The cancer files.

"Just to have," I had told her.

I replace the contents of the box and reseal it, not wanting to hold on to those memories. I should throw it out, I think as I shove the box into the bottom of the hall closet. I'll do it later. Maybe. Enough for today.

Turning the key in the lock next door, I go back to 1E where I pop a frozen dinner entrée into the microwave, grab a bag of ready-made salad from the refrigerator, and empty it into a bowl. A handful of nuts and a squirt of dressing, and I'm good to go. I carry my food into the living room with its ocean view and set it down on the coffee table. Opening my laptop, I click on a pale blue folder-shaped icon and read through my newest client's file.

Megan Campbell is number five in her class, has taken a string of honors and AP courses, and has earned nearly perfect SAT scores. Like me, Megan's parents had gone to Columbia, both of them. They want their daughter, currently a high school junior, to follow in their academic footsteps. Columbia? Coincidence? And what about Megan, is that what she wants? I have lots of questions about this one. The initial appointment with Megan and her mother is scheduled for tomorrow at my office. Should be interesting, I think, poking a fork into my salad.

"From what I see on paper, Megan, we can put together a very strong college application." I lean toward the shiny-haired girl sitting across from me. "Tell me what you do in your spare time."

"I like to—" Megan begins.

"Megan, I think Ms. Gilbert wants to know more about your extracurriculars." Mrs. Campbell directs a tight-lipped smile toward her daughter. "You are vice-president of your class, student council secretary, a chemistry tutor, and you're on the tennis team," she continues, counting on the fingers of her left hand. One, two, three, four. "And don't forget about your volunteer work at the food pantry last year." Five.

I glance at Megan, letting my eyes drift down to the bitten thumbnails capping each of her clenched hands. I've never been a nail biter myself. My own specialty is a slight twitch in my right eyelid. Annoying, but rarely noticed by others.

"I only worked at the food pantry for a few days," Megan murmurs.

"But still," her mother says, "it counts, Megan. It counts."

The kind of girl who has no idea how pretty she is. The phrase pops into my head as I study Megan's large green eyes and glossy hair, that streaky blend of dark blonde and light brown that celebrities pay lots of money to get just right. But Megan's hair is natural. Just like mine.

I remember being her age. The whispers I heard coming from my parents' bedroom ring in my ears.

My mother's voice... *Jenny...beautiful...like a young Cindy Crawford...probably get married young.*

And from my father...*Not if I can help it.*

"Let's back up a little," I say, my eyes on Megan. "Have you decided on Columbia as your first choice?"

"Not really. I don't—"

"Ms. Gilbert, Megan seems to have some sort of irrational bias against Columbia. I know from the bio on your website that you're an alum too. Maybe you could tell her a little about your experience. Give her another perspective."

Mrs. Campbell's pointed toe shoe taps a sharp staccato rhythm on the wood floor.

I smile. "First of all, I'd like you both to call me Jenny."

Mrs. Campbell nods, and Megan bites her lip.

So, it's not only her nails.

"And yes, I'd be happy to tell you about my college experience," I say. "For me, Columbia was a good fit. I moved around a lot when I was growing up, but I'd never lived in a city. New York seemed like an interesting place to spend four years, and I was attracted to the idea of being in an environment where everyone seemed to be from somewhere else. A place where I wouldn't be the only new kid. I also liked the core curriculum at Columbia, the idea of everyone taking the same courses initially. I liked the structure. I was used to it."

I still like it.

Stop talking, I tell myself, breathing in slowly. That's way too much information about yourself. Get back on track. My shoulders drop as I exhale.

"Of course, there are lots of highly competitive, prestigious schools out there," I say, hoping my statement registers with Mrs. Campbell. Focusing my gaze on Megan, I continue. "You have a very impressive academic and extracurricular record. There are a lot of colleges you might want to consider, and you're only a junior. Meeting now, before summer starts, gives us plenty of time to come up with a list of schools. Is there a particular field of study that interests you?"

"I-I'm not sure. I like to sew, to make things. Clothing and accessories mostly. I know that's not a major. Sewing, I mean. But—"

"No, sewing is not a major." Mrs. Campbell sighs.

"You're right, Mrs. Campbell. Sewing is not a major," I say. "But I would like to know more about Megan's interests and hobbies. So," I smile at Megan. "what do you like to make?"

Reaching down, Megan lifts a brightly colored tote bag from the floor and places it on my desk. "Well, I made this," she mumbles as a pink flush travels from her neck to her forehead.

The woven-handled bag was created from hand-sewn strips of jewel-toned fabric, ribbon, and mesh. The combination of colors makes me think of one of the Matisse paintings I had to identify years ago on an art history exam. I peer inside the bag and run my finger along the finished edges of the sturdy lining, equipped with a zippered inner pocket, that surround Megan's jumble of books, notepads, and pencils.

"This is very, very impressive, Megan," I say. "You certainly do have a talent and an artistic eye too."

Megan's pink face deepens to red as she tugs on one of the braided drawstrings dangling from the neckline of her peasant-style top.

"And your shirt?" I ask.

"Uh huh." A slow smile lifts Megan's cheeks.

"She also does blazers," Mrs. Campbell says, patting the lapel of her dark gray jacket. "My daughter is very talented. That's true. But fashion?" She shakes her head. "I don't know that that's an academic pursuit or a career path for someone like Megan."

"Someone like Megan?" I repeat her words.

"Someone with her abilities," she says. "Her credentials."

"I agree with you, Mrs. Campbell." I nod. "Megan certainly does seem to have a wonderful combination of talents and abilities," I say and then turn toward Megan. "And what are your plans for the summer?"

"I'm going to be a camp counselor, and—"

"Head counselor," Mrs. Campbell interrupts.

"Yes, head counselor, Mom," Megan says. "And I'll also be doing a couple of introductory sewing workshops for a fabric store in my town."

"Good. Sounds like you have some great plans." I smile and clap my hands together. "So, let's talk about what comes next."

Mother and daughter lean forward, and I describe how I use Megan's paper credentials, my interview notes, and my files of research on colleges to develop an initial list of target schools. We schedule our next session. The unveiling of 'the list'. Most parents do choose to attend that meeting, but I already know it won't be easy to get Mrs. Campbell to look beyond Columbia.

After they leave, I close the door behind them, and gaze around my clean, minimally decorated office. One of my mother's paintings, a simple seascape that somehow survived each of my family's moves, hangs above the credenza, and a large window pours natural light onto the polished wood desk. I grab my laptop, head to the door, and snap off the light.

3

*M*y eyes travel up and down the rows of boxes neatly stacked along the walls of my newly rented apartment, 1F. This might actually be fun, I think, reading through the carefully lettered labels affixed to the cartons. Boxes of toys, marked as *Baby*, *Preschool*, or *Childhood*, and books, categorized by reading level and genre, are piled alongside containers marked *Stuffed Animals*, *Dolls*, *Cards and Letters*, *School Records*, and *Official Documents*.

A collection of artifacts and relics. Manufactured memories. A shrine of cardboard.

It would probably be easiest to start with the books. They've already been sorted and just need to be arranged on the shelves. Not too complicated.

I lift the top two boxes from the pile next to my bed, uncovering a carton marked *Book Series*, and cut through the wide strip of tape securing its flaps. A collection of Nancy Drew books, numbers one through ten, their yellow spines bright and familiar, nestle against the first three Harry Potters. A border of soft-covers chronicling the adventures of Amelia Bedelia and the girls of the Baby-Sitters Club outline the inside perimeter of the box. Keeping each series together and in order, I move the books to the second shelf in my bookcase. I open another box and fill the top shelf with *Goodnight Moon*, *Where the Wild Things Are*, and a row of Little Golden Books. Before I add my Dr. Seuss collection to the shelf, I flip through the shiny, blue-covered book about a cat and a hat. I love the pictures and the words. I love the story.

"What a stupid book," I remember my father saying. "Why would a cat come into a house, mess it all up, and then clean it?'

I run my finger along the book's smooth edge, crack it open, and inhale its new book smell. Like most of the things my father said I didn't need anymore, my first copy of *The Cat in the Hat* was left behind in the wake of one of our moves. But books, like toys and games, are easy enough to replace. And old or new, they still smell good.

From *Lord of the Flies* to *Fahrenheit 451*, I squeeze my high school favorites onto a single shelf. One more box, and that'll be it for today. *Reference Books*. My scissors slice through another band of tape, and I sift through an assortment of dictionaries, atlases, and thesauruses, an SAT study guide, and my mother's old handbook for military parents.

Opening the handbook, I begin to read. "*Your positive attitude toward the move is crucial for your children's successful adjustment to a new home.*"

"Look at it as an adventure," my mother would say. "Living in other parts of the country. How many people get to do that?"

The parental script, repeated each time we were relocated, stressed the immediate acceptance of newcomers by military families and the importance of fostering independence in children.

"You'll make new friends, Jenny. You always do. You know that."

I continue reading from the handbook, enunciating each word as clearly as a kindergarten teacher speaking to a class of five-year-olds. "*Let the children say good-bye to their friends. Get them involved. Let them make as many decisions as possible. Try to give them a sense of control.*"

Before each of our moves, my mother rented movies, ordered in pizza, and planned a farewell sleepover party for my friends. Using my best penmanship, I recorded their names, phone numbers, and addresses in a shiny white book decorated with a U.S. map. I was allowed to dismantle my own room, and label and number my own boxes. *Jenny's Room #1 Stuffed Animals, Jenny's Room #2 Books A-M, Jenny's Room #3 Books N-Z.*

Every time we set off to make our home on a new base in a new state, my mother would grip my shoulders and look into my eyes. "Be thankful your father is in financial management and doesn't get deployed to a combat zone." And then she would shudder. "We're lucky he's not in danger and that we all get to stay together."

But I didn't feel lucky. Still, I refused to cry and acted the 'good little soldier' as my mother flew into a frenzy of sorting and discarding. Sorting and discarding.

When my father asked why there were so many boxes labeled *Jenny*, my mother would respond. "Her things are light. Don't worry. We won't be over the weight limit."

Then he would grumble. "I'm not paying extra."

So, I watched my mother give away her own salad bowls, coffee mugs, and vases to friends and neighbors so that I could take a stack of thumbed-through magazines and an outgrown doll collection to the next new place I would be told to call *home*. We never did have to pay extra, but each time my family settled into that new home, I would discover that a toy, a book, or one of my bedraggled stuffed animals had been left behind.

I arrange my reference books along the bottom shelf and step back, surveying the nearly full bookshelf and glancing at the columns of still unopened boxes. I've spent a long time, a very long time, hunting for just the right 'things'. Replacements, substitutions, and copies of the missing bits of my life, the many pieces that were thrown away or lost as my family moved from state to state, base to base. I haven't rushed my search for the exact objects I need, and I won't rush the process of unpacking them.

"A place for everything, everything in its place," my father used to say, quoting Benjamin Franklin.

As a child, I hung my clothes, arranged by color, on carefully spaced white plastic hangers, lining my shoes in a neat row along the closet floor. Now, still my father's daughter, I'm going to put away each of the things I've so carefully collected exactly where it belongs. I have the space, and I'll make the time. I fling the military handbook into one of the empty cartons and gather up the rest. Balancing the pile of empty boxes, I lock the door behind me and head over to the outside dumpster.

I bought the first item in my collection soon after moving from my parents' home on an army base in New Jersey to a Columbia University dorm in New York City. I remember walking into a crowded secondhand store downtown. Its dark interior was packed with cast-off toys, dog-eared paperbacks, and no-longer-stylish costume jewelry. I combed through its collection of discarded treasures and stumbled upon a gently used, tired-looking gray and brown Pound Puppy.

"What are you going to do with that?" My roommate laughed when I brought the stuffed animal back to the dorm.

"I had a Pound Puppy just like this one. Same exact colors," I said, stroking the toy dog's floppy ear.

"So?"

"I just thought it would be nice to have something from…Never mind. It's stupid."

"It's your money." My roommate shrugged. "Going to the library. See you later."

Leaving the toy in the store's pale yellow bag, I placed it on the top shelf of my closet.

A year later I had my own bedroom in another apartment that I shared with a different roommate. I had a tiny closet, deeper than it was wide. Plenty of room to stash a few cardboard boxes where the treasures I planned to accumulate could be hidden and housed. Temporarily. Just until I could afford a bigger space.

I scoured flea markets and garage sales, and I navigated through eBay and craigslist, amassing a hoard of books, Barbie dolls, and board games. Sorting and categorizing my finds, I stored them in boxes salvaged from the back rooms of local supermarkets. But even after I graduated, landing a job in Columbia's Admissions Office, and could afford to live alone in a studio apartment in the city and later in a spacious one bedroom in New Jersey, I kept my collection sealed up in cardboard boxes.

Imagine the apartment of a young professional decorated with stuffed animals and a Backstreet Boys poster.

Better to have kept everything packed away until I was able to rent another space. *This* space.

It's hard to believe, but it's been only just over a year since I moved from New York to New Jersey and rented an apartment and nearby office space. Now, in that short time, I can afford a second apartment. Setting goals, planning, and working hard—I guess I did learn a lot from my father. But, unlike him, I'm going to settle into a place of my own choosing. Create a home. And no one can ever order me to relocate.

When I did decide to give up my New York apartment and look for a place in New Jersey, I called my mother. I pictured her in a sleeveless cover-up over a black bathing suit, her hair pulled into a ponytail, its chestnut brown threaded with a few silvery stands. At nine-thirty in the morning, she would be gulping down a glass of orange juice in the sunny kitchen of her Florida condo before grabbing a towel and heading down to her ten o'clock water aerobics class. After a quick shower and lunch, she would spend the afternoon sketching or painting, finding her inspiration along the nearby shoreline.

"I'm going to start looking for an apartment in New Jersey, Mom," I began.

"You want to move to New Jersey?" she asked. "From the city?"

I imagined the unspoken questions ricocheting through her mind.

Why? Is something wrong? What twenty-something wouldn't want to live in New York?

The Big Apple. The City That Never Sleeps. Bars filled with young professionals, museums and galleries, the theatre, Central Park, and a patchwork of ethnic neighborhoods jigsawed together on an island of less than twenty-three square miles. Manhattan air bubbled with opportunity and promise. After graduating from Columbia, I had been over-the-moon excited about staying in New York. Parlaying a work-study experience in the registrar's office and a stint as a campus tour guide into a job as an admissions counselor for my alma mater, I had started my own practice as an independent college counselor. And finally, I was able to afford my own tiny apartment, decorated with pillar candles and IKEA furniture, on the eighth floor of a doorman building.

"But what about your business, Jenny? How will you get clients in New Jersey?"

"I've gotten lots of clients through word of mouth." I pressed the phone to my ear. "I've even had to turn a few of them away."

"In New Jersey?"

"Yes, in New Jersey. I got them through referrals and from the internet."

"I don't understand," my mother said slowly. "I thought you loved the city."

"New York just doesn't feel like home to me, and that's what I need. A home," I said softly.

Home was the place where the inside of your closet door was striped with pencil marks recording your growth from first grade to eighth. It was where you knew the history of every ding in the wall and every stain on the carpet. It was where your friends still remembered you as a pigtailed girl with two missing front teeth.

I knew my mother had had a home and that she had tried to make one for me. She had driven carpools, baked brownies for school fundraisers, and hosted pajama parties and sleepovers. She bought me the jeans that *everyone* had and helped me sponge paint the walls of my room.

Each time we moved to a new house in a new state, my mother planted a white rose bush outside the front door and brought the familiar smells of freshly washed laundry, lemony furniture polish, and homemade apple pie into our new home. As a military brat, I knew the drill. I understood that my father's 'permanent change of station' assignments were never *permanent*, and I didn't cry whenever a dinnertime conversation began with "I have orders." My father was proud of his good little soldier, but my mother sprouted an itchy, red rash on her forehead every time I had to walk into a strange classroom in a new town or on an unfamiliar base. I knew that with each dab of cortisone cream, my mother prayed that this time we had settled into what would be a place-to-grow-up-in kind of home for me.

"What about moving down to Florida instead?" My mother's words tumbled out in a breathy gush. "I'm sure there are plenty of people down here who would hire you to help their kids with college applications. You have experience, and you graduated from an Ivy League school. If you're tired of New York, you could live with me. Temporarily. Or even permanently." She paused. "If you want to, that is."

I chose my words carefully. "You know I love to visit you in Florida, Mom. You have a great life there."

"But?"

"I think you know what the 'but' is. New Jersey just feels like home to me. I want to move back there."

I could hear a soft whoosh as my mother exhaled. "We didn't live there that long, Jenny. You were a baby the first time. We moved back for a few years, but—"

"I know. But I was born in New Jersey, and I went to kindergarten there. First grade and most of second too. The school was on the base, all military kids. Just like me. And I did my last two years of high school in New Jersey. I—"

'But your high school wasn't on the base, Jenny. You went to Pemberton. It was mostly civilian. Kids who'd lived there forever."

"Mom, Pemberton High was twenty percent military. I remember the statistic. Twenty percent. Do you realize what that meant?" I didn't wait for her answer. "There were lots of army brats there who'd moved around, and the civilians were used to new kids. It was so…normal."

"Normal," my mother repeated the word. "Yes, I guess it was."

I winced, imagining my mother pressing an index finger into her upper lip, her eyes drifting to the floor. "I'm not saying our life wasn't normal, Mom. And you did everything right. I was always allowed to have friends over, and you helped me clean up the mess before Dad got home. And how many times did you pack my Sunny Bear even when Dad said I was too old for stuffed animals?"

"Sunny Bear! Boy, did you love that bear!" She laughed. "You got it as a birthday gift from the girl who sat next to you in second grade. Or was it third? Hmmm…I don't remember."

"It was second. I got it from Amy. Right before we moved."

"That's right. Amy. Now I remember. She had blonde hair. Curly, right?"

"Yup, that was her. She gave me the bear when I turned eight. Dad had just gotten orders, and we were getting ready to move, boxes everywhere. But you still made me a party in the house. Five or six girls. You helped us make friendship bracelets, and then you polished our nails. You were great, Mom." I swallowed. "You *are* great."

"Oh Jen, you're gonna make me cry, and I have to get to the pool. Aerobics starts in fifteen minutes."

"Mwah." I blew a kiss into the phone. "Hup two three four."

As I clicked off the phone, I remembered the spoon I had left in the kitchen drying rack. Pulling a checkered towel from the stack of meticulously folded squares under the sink, I wiped the spoon and placed it in the cutlery tray, careful to align it with the pile below. I grabbed a bottle of water from the refrigerator, walked through the apartment's narrow living room, and turned the knob of my bedroom door. Running a finger down the first column of boxes lining the wall next to my bed, I stopped halfway toward the floor and traced the black letters I had neatly printed on a press-on label. *Stuffed Animals.* I stared at the box, knowing that a button-eyed dog with a torn left ear, a soft purple elephant, a fleecy white lamb, and Sunny Bear rested inside. My eyes followed the cardboard landscape bordering the perimeter of the room. My time in New York had been special and meaningful, but I needed more. I needed a home. I needed space.

Starting over again in New Jersey hadn't scared me. My New York clients referred their New Jersey relatives and friends, and after presenting complimentary workshops at local venues, I picked up a few more. Still, I knew that getting back to New Jersey would involve more than clicking my heels three times and chanting "There's no place like home." And after nine years in Manhattan, four as a college student and five as a young professional, I wasn't ready to settle into the picket fence suburbia I had dreamed of as a child.

New Jersey map. I typed the words into my search bar and clicked on an image of the squiggly-bordered state that looked like a misshapen S. Scanning the map's yellow, red, and green patchwork of counties, my gaze drifted toward the large blue area marking the state's east coast, the Atlantic Ocean. The Jersey Shore.

During the two and a half years I lived in New Jersey as a child, my family had headed to the shore on summer weekends, our car packed with a striped umbrella, a cooler, a stack of beach towels, and an array of plastic buckets and shovels. Years later, after postings in Missouri and Colorado, when my father was relocated to New Jersey again, I made the one-hour drive from Pemberton to the beach with friends whenever one of our parents would agree to loan us a car for the day.

Be careful. Eyes on the road. Call when you get there. The warnings and instructions were always the same.

My parents had grown up in a small New Jersey town a half hour's drive from the beach. My mother had spent her summers filling dry, sugary cones with rainbow-colored ice cream that dripped onto sun bleached t-shirts while my father manned boardwalk games, collecting coins from ball tossing and water squirting kids. I treasure the faded pictures and souvenirs-of-living that my mother saved from those days. A cracked spine yearbook, a dried-out prom corsage, and photos of my father with hair trailing over his collar and my mother in hip hugger jeans hibernated in one of my boxes.

My mother called me 'the family archivist'.

'Hoarder' had been my father's word.

After months of scrolling through craigslist, trekking through buildings, and negotiating with rental agents, I moved into a spacious, sunny apartment, big enough to accommodate my growing collection of boxes. I rented a furnished office nearby and began to build my home in Sea Grove.

Now, just over a year since my move to New Jersey, I have a waiting list of clients and can afford to rent the second apartment I need. Right next door. It will be a work in progress.

And my original apartment, stripped of the stacks of cardboard that have been hiding its walls and swallowing its space, looks like the tastefully decorated home of a successful, practical, and well-adjusted young professional. A beautiful, airy space that I can be proud to call *home*.

4

One loud rap followed by two softer ones. Lauren's knock. From inside Apartment 1E, the only one Lauren knows about, I open the door.

"O-mi-god, this place looks great!" she squeals from the doorway.

"You haven't even seen it yet." I hug my friend and pull her inside. "Not since I've redecorated."

Moving into the center of the living room, she turns her body with a series of small steps, surveying the sleek, yet comfortable, furniture that floats in the open space. Her mouth drops open and spreads into a wide smile.

"I'm speechless," she says.

"Speechless? You?" I laugh.

She wraps her arms across her chest and narrows her eyes. "Let me see your bedroom."

"C'mon," I say, wagging my finger and leading her down the short hallway.

Inside, the late morning sun filters through ivory window blinds and pours onto a golden oak bedroom set, cream-colored comforter, and fluffy rug the color of beach sand. The room shimmers with light and air. And space.

"Okay, I give up." Lauren holds out her hands, palms up. "Where are they?"

"Where are what?" I ask, my mouth shaped into an O, my eyes widened in mock innocence.

"The boxes? The ones holding your Nancy Drew books, your Barbie dolls, and all the other stuff you've been stockpiling? The ones you've moved from apartment to apartment? The ones you've never unpacked?"

"Well, I did unpack them. I sorted through everything and got rid of a lot." I shrug. "I just kept a few things."

"And where are those 'few things', may I ask?"

"The apartment complex has a storage area. The fee is minimal, so I keep a few boxes there."

"Jenny Gilbert, we've been friends since high school." Lauren shakes her head, fighting back a smile. "And I know you didn't get rid of all that stuff. But honestly, whatever you did with it, I don't care. Your apartment looks so normal now." She grins. "But seriously, it looks *great*. Just great."

"Gee, thanks for your seal of approval." I laugh.

"I know this couldn't have been easy for you," Lauren says slowly. "You've been collecting those things forever, and it seemed like every time I visited you, you had even more boxes. I had to walk through a maze to use your bathroom. I'm proud of you, Jen." She pauses. "However you managed it."

My heart thumps against the sudden tightness in my chest. I want to grab Lauren's hand and pull her into the apartment next door.

Look, I want to say, showing her the home I've created a few steps down the hall. *All the things I've had to leave behind. I worked so hard to find them again, but I've had to keep them packed away for such a long time. And now, finally, I have a place for them. A place for me. A place where I can surround myself with all the things that were taken away from me. A place that feels like home.*

My mouth opens and then closes. I swallow the shiny pebbles of the words I will not say, feeling their edges fit together into the hard rock of a secret. Stepping into Lauren's outstretched arms, I hug my best friend.

"I'm proud of you, Jen," she repeats, squeezing my shoulder. She steps back and winks. "Now, let's head down to the beach."

After spending the day with Lauren enjoying the sun, the ocean, and each other's company, I hug her and say good-bye. I wave as she makes a left turn out of the Sea Grove Gardens parking lot and head back into the apartment I just showed her, my original one.

I'm so proud of you. It's beautiful. It looks so normal now. Her words had made me smile, although the last one had stung a bit. *Normal.* Lauren hadn't meant to hurt me. I know that. But to her, an account executive for a pharmaceutical firm, a 'normal' home for a young professional is clean, uncluttered, and grown-up. Like her own apartment. But Lauren's outgrown dolls and favorite childhood books are stashed in her parents' basement. The collage of friends' photos that she made in high school still hangs in her teenage bedroom where she stays when she visits her family back in Pemberton. She has always been surrounded by things. *Her* things.

Dropping the key to the apartment next door into my pocket, I lock the door behind me. I smile as I look around the large single room that is Apartment 1F. A cloud-patterned comforter, a Walmart find that is just a shade darker than the one I had as a teenager, covers the bed, and Sunny Bear leans against the matching sky blue pillows. On my dresser, a collection of sticky lip glosses and drugstore perfumes ring the lighted make-up mirror that I found on eBay. A Trapper Keeper notebook and a hot pink pencil cup filled with Bic pens and yellow number twos rest on my desk.

I pull the closet door open and look up. Candy Land, Chutes and Ladders, Clue, and Twister. The game boxes are stacked neatly on the top shelf. I'm not done with those yet, I think, squeezing my eyes shut as I try to remember the names of the other games that I was forced to abandon before each of our moves. Tiddlywinks, Chinese Checkers, and a tin of dominoes. They shouldn't be too hard to find. I open my Trapper Keeper and start a list.

It's been six weeks since I rented 1F. Six weeks of opening boxes, sifting through the treasure trove of items I've amassed over the years, and meticulously arranging them in my new space. Now, from the towering columns of cardboard that I stacked along the apartment walls just weeks earlier, only two sealed cartons remain. I hoist the one marked *Yearbooks and Photos* onto the bed and cut through the tape stretched across its flaps. Reaching inside, I pull out an oversized dark green book. *Pemberton Township High School 2002*. I trace the embossed gold letters with my index finger and sit on the edge of the bed, opening my high school yearbook onto my lap. I flip through the pages of photos of teachers standing at blackboards and sitting behind desks and students cheering at football games, pulling books from lockers, and dozing in classrooms. Turning the pages more slowly when I reach the *Seniors* section, I stop at the professionally photographed portrait of my younger self. The eighteen-year-old girl with smooth blondish-brown hair wears a half-smile aimed at the camera and an uncertain look that gazes beyond it. The end of high school meant moving. Again. I read the caption printed below my picture.

Jenny Gilbert
Debate Team Captain, National Honor Society President, Yearbook Editor
Voted 'Most Likely to Succeed'

That list, combined with my almost-perfect SAT scores and selection as class valedictorian, translated into an acceptance letter from Columbia University. It would have been simpler to go to Rutgers. A lot of my friends from Pemberton were going there, and I had already enrolled in a Rutgers summer course. It still would have been a move, but a smaller one, an easier one. But I couldn't say no to Columbia, especially with a scholarship offer.

I close the yearbook and place it on the single shelf above my desk. Returning to the open box on my bed, I look down at the navy blue cover of another oversized book. *Howell High School 1981.* I turn the pages to my father's senior portrait. Bruce Gilbert, the guy with the Tom Sawyer grin and the thick brown hair that flopped into smiling gray eyes, the man who had married my mother during their sophomore year of college, had grown into my father.

"It was different back then," my mother had tried to explain. "I met your father in ninth grade algebra. And besides being the cutest boy in the class, he was good in math. Quadratic equations, scientific notation, polynomials.

He just… got it. Science too, especially when we did the unit on weather. And luckily, I sat next to him."

"So, he did your homework?" I asked.

"No, he didn't *do* my homework, but he explained it to me. Your father was a born teacher. A natural. He could break things down simply. Make them easy to understand. And he was always so patient."

"Patient? Dad?"

"Yes. Patient. Dad."

"So why didn't he finish college and become a meteorologist or a science teacher like he planned?"

"We got married, and he joined the army. He could have been a military meteorologist, but he wasn't interested in…"

"In what?"

"In analyzing the weather's effects on launching missiles or firing artillery weapons. So, he went into the army's financial management program. It was a good career path with a lot of opportunity." At this point, my mother would sigh. "You already know the story, Jenny."

Over the years my mother and I had variations of the same conversation again and again. And again. But I still don't understand. Not really.

My father was a smart and popular high school athlete who, unlike his many friends planning to major in business and earn the big bucks, dreamed of tracking hurricanes or getting a classroom of teenagers excited about relative humidity and the formation of rain.

I flip the yearbook pages back to my mother's senior portrait. Donna Randall was a darker-haired Stevie Nicks lookalike. She struggled with algebra, wore flowery peasant shirts, and turned her own visions of the sky, the ocean, and the sand into light-filled, painted canvases. She had never been to a professional baseball game, didn't understand football, and listened to the weather report only when there was a possibility of a school snow day. But somehow, after months of lessons on solving for x, my parents became best friends, high school sweethearts, and soulmates. They both went to Rutgers, my mother as an art major and my father wavering between meteorology and secondary education.

"You know there are a lot of cute girls in education classes?" he would tease her.

But they both knew that from the time he had been a fourteen-year-old high school freshman, Bruce Gilbert was totally smitten, besotted, and absolutely in love with Donna Randall. And she felt the same way. I can recite the exact words of my mother's story.

"It was one of those perfect Florida nights, just a light wind and the sky was navy blue. The moon…"

Sophomore year in college, spring break in Florida, a romantic night on the beach, my father's proposal with a beer can flip top slipped onto my mother's finger, and their barefoot Ft. Lauderdale wedding.

That May, as she studied for her final exams, my mother battled morning nausea and gave in to nightly cravings for pickles and pizza. In August, my father enlisted in the army in order to support what would become his new family. I was born in January. A honeymoon baby, and a New Year's gift.

Another piece of history, I think as I position my parents' high school yearbook on the shelf next to my own.

Digging into the box, I pull out five magnetic page photo albums, still in their original cellophane wrappings, and a stack of large manila envelopes. I spread the envelopes across my bed and scan their neatly printed labels. *Donna and Bruce: Pre-Army, My High School Years, My College Years, Post-College.* Sliding a finger under the taped flap of the first envelope, I turn it upside down. A cascade of photographs, black and white and color, some of them yellowed with age, spill out, and I thumb through the sheaf of pictures documenting my parents' childhoods. Long ago moments captured on film. My mother gripping a terrycloth giraffe and my father peeking through the rails of his crib, my mother wearing a Girl Scout Brownie uniform and my father dressed as a Halloween pirate. I spot the portrait of my parents at their senior prom. My shaggy-haired father in a dark tuxedo and my mother, her beautiful face framed by a crinkly perm, in a pale pink puffy-sleeved dress. My father is clasping my mother's small hand and looking into her eyes. Even then, as eighteen-year-olds, they shared a love that radiated out from a routinely photographed five-by-seven inch picture taken at a high school prom. I peel the cellophane wrapping from one of the albums and lift the clear plastic overlays, pressing the pictures onto the self-adhering pages. Closing the book, I label its spine. *Donna and Bruce: Pre-Army.*

I open the second envelope and flip through pictures of my father in his Army greens, my mother with a bulging belly, and myself as a baby. I glance through nine of my class photos, from kindergarten through eighth grade. My childishly rounded cheeks disappeared between fourth and fifth grade, and my eighth grade picture shows a hint of mascara and lip gloss. But in each photo, I wear a practiced smile, mouth stretched wide, cheeks lifted, and serious eyes focused on a spot above the camera. I riffle through photos of myself reading the newspaper with my father, baking with my mother, playing board games with my friends, and riding my first two-wheeler. The pictures were taken in New Jersey, South Carolina, Missouri, New York, and Colorado.

"The average military family moves six to nine times between its children's kindergarten and high school years," my mother told me. "We're lucky."

I arrange the pictures in another album, label it, and open the third envelope. I spent my freshman and sophomore years of high school in Colorado, my junior and senior years back in New Jersey. Only one move during high school, and that was lucky? I shake my head and position a picture of my first boyfriend, a quiet guy from Colorado who taught me to play *Imagine* on the piano, onto a page in a new album and sort through photos of myself in a blue cap and gown surrounded by friends, arms slung about each other's shoulders, and snapshots of my smiling parents.

I fill my fourth album with photos of white pillared buildings, gated archways, cramped apartment interiors, open air plazas, New York streets, smiling friends, a couple of short-term boyfriends, and a blue and white tiled subway sign spelling out Columbia University. My fifth envelope holds three pictures. A photo of Columbia's Admissions Office, one of my office in New Jersey, and a shot of the door to my first apartment in Sea Grove, 1E. I place them in my last album and label it. *Post-College*.

Plenty of empty pages left, I think as I gather the albums and place them next to the yearbooks on the shelf above my desk, and only one more box to unpack. I look at the sealed carton resting on the floor next to my desk. It's labeled *Ryan*. I exhale, blowing a stream of air out of my mouth.

"I'll do that one next time," I say aloud as I slide the box along the floor, pushing it into a corner of the closet.

5

*T*he days pass, and late spring turns to early summer. My graduating seniors have all submitted college applications, received responses, and made plans for the upcoming fall. One will be going to Yale, one to Princeton, one to Duke, and one to Northwestern. The others will be joining the freshman classes at NYU, BU, GW, and Michigan. It's been a good year. In another month, I'll send them each a Starbucks gift card and a personalized letter filled with good wishes.

I operate in rhythm with the seasons. I always have. My September through June school years were filled with assignments, tests, and extracurricular activities, and my summers were for swimming at military base pools, long bike rides, babysitting, waitressing jobs, and reading. Lots of reading. As a college counselor, I live by the same schedule. Right now, Megan is my only active client. The others will scramble to hire me in late August or early September. So, my summer stretches out ahead, long and free, and I live without the threatened disruption of 'permanent change of station' assignments.

In Sea Grove, summer unofficially starts on Memorial Day weekend. Beginning that Friday afternoon, cars race to the Garden State Parkway where they join the slow-moving line of traffic creeping south and eastward toward the Jersey Shore. From that evening until the first Monday in September, Sea Grove's population swells with 'bennies', as the locals call the visitors from Bayonne, Elizabeth, Newark, New York, and all parts inland who swarm into town each summer.

Benny. Another word for *outsider.* Over the past year, I've built a home at the shore, inhaling the salty air and pushing my roots deep into Sea Grove's grainy sand. And for the three months of hot, sunny days between Memorial Day weekend and Labor Day Monday, I'm happy to share my adopted town, its beach, and its boardwalk with tourists, visitors, day-trippers, bennies, or anyone else not lucky enough to live here year-round.

I wake up early on summer mornings just because I want to. On weekdays, armed with a chair and a woven straw bag, I walk to one of the less crowded areas of beach and wade into the still-cold ocean, plucking seashells from the water's edge. Then I settle into my chair, open a sand-filled book, and bask in the sun's slanted rays, looking up from my reading to watch quarreling seagulls squabble over day-old French fries. Later in the morning, teenagers packing iPods and Frisbees unfurl their towels under the sun as mothers lugging sandwiches and toys follow galloping toddlers onto the sand. Wearing one-piece bathing suits and sunglasses, the mothers plant umbrellas, slather sunscreen, and watch vigilantly as their children run toward the ocean. That's my signal for lunch. I stuff my book and latest seashell keepsakes into my bag and fold up my chair. Trudging through the sand, I cross Ocean Avenue and head back to my apartment.

I've got a different routine on summer weekends. I still wake up early, but steering clear of the crowded beach, I hunt down local garage sales, mapquesting addresses listed in the PennySaver and following signs tacked onto telephone poles. I feel a racing heart kind of excitement when my trek leads me to a stockpile of discarded treasures displayed on an aluminum table set up on a suburban driveway. I sift through mounds of unwanted, no-longer-needed relics of other people's lives in search of the missing pieces of my own. Last month, I found a black plastic CD tower and the June 1999 issue of Seventeen Magazine on one of those driveways. As I paid the sunburned woman standing behind the table, I spotted a soft doll, its face framed with red yarn hair, clad in a white apron and striped stockings. Raggedy Ann.

"I'll take this too," I said.

"That'll be another five dollars." Sliding a scrunchie down her wrist, she scooped her limp hair into a ponytail.

"No, Mommy, she's—" A sad-eyed girl tugged at the woman's shirt.

"I told you, Amanda," her mother hissed. "We need to sell this stuff."

"But I sleep with her." The child whimpered as her eyes filled.

I pressed a five-dollar bill into the woman's palm and handed the doll to the little girl. "Can you let her keep it?" I asked the mother.

The woman nodded and looked away from me.

Carrying the CD tower and magazine, I walked down the driveway and opened the trunk of my car. After stashing my finds, I looked up toward the top of the driveway and spotted Amanda hugging her doll to her chest.

The Englishtown Flea Market is another of my favorite weekend haunts. I bypass the main buildings and permanent outdoor stands stocked with new clothing, home furnishings, and electronics and head toward the perimeter of the market. There, I wander through the large dusty sand lot dotted with folding tables and open-backed trucks packed with motley collections of cast-off odds and ends. From a set of multiplication flash cards to my Birthday Bear Beanie Baby, I've found an assortment of treasures in that hot, gravelly market.

After spending the morning on one of my shopping expeditions or at the beach, I shower and fix myself a quick lunch of leftovers stuffed into a pita pocket. Then I sink into the leather couch in my living room and move the vase of white roses resting in the center of the glass coffee table to the side. Nice to be able to work from home this time of year. I open my laptop and update my spreadsheets with the latest college statistics and demographic information. When I finish, I close my laptop, move the vase of roses back to the center of the table, and reach for my keys.

As soon as I open the door to 1F, I see the books, games, toys, and a smorgasbord of odds and ends I remember from my childhood. My mouth stretches into a grin. Renting this second apartment was a good idea. It's turned into so much more than just a space to unpack my boxes. It's become a home. I flop onto the cloud blue comforter covering my bed and cradle Sunny Bear against my chest. This is what it must feel like to go back to the place where you grew up. Always warm, familiar, unchanged. A forever kind of home. Propping a pillow behind my head, I close my eyes. Just for a few minutes.

When I wake up, the yellow bear is still in my arms. The room is darker, and the air-conditioned chill prickles my exposed arm. Turning my wrist, I check my watch. Seven p.m. How did that happen? What time did I come in here?

Four o'clock? Five? I sit up, pressing my hands into the mattress. It's thick and firm with just the right amount of give. Comfortable. Very comfortable. As comfortable as my own bed. I shake my head. But this is my bed too. Isn't it?

I cross the room to my desk, open my Trapper Keeper, and read through the neatly printed list of things I still need for this apartment.

Tiddlywinks

Chinese Checkers

Dominoes

Purple Koosh ball

Etch A Sketch

Mr. Potato Head

Plucking a pen from the cup on the desk, I add one more thing.

Alarm clock!

6

*I*n the small entrance hall of my building, I turn the key in the silver box marked *1E* and pull out a bundle of mail. As I leaf through the pile of bills and advertising circulars, a green card marked *Delivery Notice* flutters to the floor. Picking it up, I walk over to the management office. When I step inside, I see Mrs. Thornton seated behind her desk, her eyes focused inside the brightly colored paperback that she holds open between her outstretched hands.

"Excuse me," I say softly.

She closes the book and quickly turns it facedown, but not before I glimpse the cover drawing of a bare-chested man staring down at a reclining woman whose blouse has slipped below her shoulders.

"Yes, Jenny, what can I do for you?" Resting her elbows on the desk, she leans forward.

"I have a delivery notice." I hand her the card.

"Another package?" She sighs. "I'll check the back," she says, shoving her book into a desk drawer and slowly rising from her chair.

While I wait for her to return, I study the framed photograph hanging on the wall behind her desk. A large arched sign, supported on each side by an ivory stone pillar, dominates the picture. *Welcome to Sea Grove*, it beckons, spanning the road leading to the main beach entrance. In the background, a long jetty separates the clear blue sky from a stretch of sun-dappled sand and reaches into the sea.

I usually avoid the main entrance to the beach, preferring instead to use a lesser-known access road, but I do recognize the rocky jetty, although I've never seen the sign.

Mrs. Thornton returns to the office, a red mug gripped in her right hand and a brown-wrapped box tucked under her left arm. "Only one package this time?" She sets the mug and the box on her desk and squints at me.

I wonder if she bought that mug to match her nail polish. Or was it the other way around? I swallow the tickle in my throat, willing myself not to giggle. "That's it for today," I say. "Thank you."

Mrs. Thornton presses her lips, colored to match her nails and the mug, into a thin line. She lifts the box and, without loosening her grip on it, places it in my open hand. "You get an awful lot of packages, Jenny."

"I've been redecorating." My face grows warm. "I hope I'm not inconveniencing you."

"No. No inconvenience," she says, releasing her hold on the box. "As long as you're not using that second apartment for business."

"I'm not using it for business," I say slowly. "I meet with clients in my office in the—"

"Yes, I'm aware of that." She nods. "Just making sure that you're following the rules. Now if you'll excuse me…" She reaches for a pen.

"Just one more thing, Mrs. Thornton. I noticed the picture above your desk. It's beautiful. The composition, the light…"

She swivels her chair around and looks at the photograph. Turning back toward me, she says, "Thank you. My brother took it back in the nineties. He's quite the photographer."

"Yes, he is." I nod. "I was wondering about it because I've never seen a sign like that near the beach."

"It was destroyed by a tropical storm a few years after my brother shot the picture." Mrs. Thornton clicks her tongue, shaking her head. "They never replaced it. Too dangerous, I guess." She shrugs. "We've been lucky since then. Even Hurricane Irene last year didn't do much damage to Sea Grove. You were living here then, weren't you?"

"I moved in a few months earlier. And yes, we were lucky. A few trees down, some power outages, but no permanent damage."

"Well, it's a good thing we don't get hit that often, and it's never *direct*. Usually Florida gets the brunt of it."

"That's true." I gulp, thinking of my mother's sunny condo. "Anyway, thank you for the package."

I head straight to 1F, open the door, and kicking off my sandals, grab a scissors from the desk and plop onto the bed, still holding my package. I cut through the tape and pull the box open.

Stars 'n Stripes Army Barbie. In a tan camouflage uniform with green canvas bags crisscrossed over her chest, white-blonde hair topped with a jaunty red beret, the doll lies encased within a pink box behind a film of clear plastic. With large blue eyes, and an incongruous painted red smile, her arm is raised in a perpetual salute.

I was eight when Santa left Army Barbie under the tree. My list that year had included a copy of *Harriet the Spy*, a 300-piece jigsaw puzzle, and a new Barbie doll. *Not in a bathing suit or a fancy dress*, I had written, underlining the words with a pair of pencil lines, dark and thick. I bounced out of bed early that Christmas morning and raced to the tree in our living room. Scooping up the gifts marked with my name, I gathered them into a small pile, placing the Barbie-sized rectangular box at the bottom of the heap. My parents, smiling, watched as I ripped off the wrapping paper and tore into the largest packages first.

I remember the neon pink sweatshirt and black leggings I got that year. I held them against my body and jumped up to hug my mother. "Omigod, I love it!" I think I might have screamed. Then, I pecked my father's cheek and moved into his loose embrace. "Oh, and thanks, Dad," I said.

I hadn't even thought to ask for a sweatshirt and leggings combination like the ones the other third grade girls on the Missouri base wore. Leave it to Mom, I remember thinking at the time. Another relocation had meant unfamiliar accents and slightly different clothing. I told myself it didn't matter, that I was used to it.

As I opened the rest of my presents, my father smoothed the sheets of torn wrapping paper into flattened pieces, minimizing the space they would need in the trash can. *Harriet the Spy*, a Nancy Drew book, a map-shaped puzzle of the fifty states, Clue, a Magic 8 Ball, and a gray and brown Pound Puppy. A carefully curated assortment of presents, some that could be shared with newly made friends and some that would entertain a quick-minded only child. Even at eight, I sensed my mother's sharp intuition behind my Christmas booty.

Surrounded by gifts, I sat cross-legged on the floor and reached for the last unopened package marked with my name. I already owned two Barbies. One had come in a swimsuit, the other in a dress, both traditional Barbie attire. I had a few other outfits, but I wanted a new doll in order to expand my playtime storylines beyond 'Barbie Goes to Work in an Office', 'Barbie Gets Ready for a Date', and 'Barbie Goes Out to Dinner'. I'd seen the possibilities at friends' houses and on TV. Ski Fun, Teen Talk, Rollerblade,

Doctor, even Barbie Love-to-Read. Jittery with excitement, I pulled the paper from the rectangular box.

Stars 'n Stripes Army Barbie.

"It was your father's idea!" my mother exclaimed, clapping her hands together.

Fighting back a wet tingle in my nose, I inhaled sharply and blinked. I forced my mouth into a smile and turned to my father. "It's great. I love it," I heard myself say as I hugged and kissed him.

"I saw it in the PX, and I knew you'd like it." He grinned. "Guess I know my little girl."

I never did come up with a playtime scenario for Army Barbie. Stripping the doll out of its camouflage uniform, I dressed it in a series of outfits from evening gowns to workout wear, but nothing looked quite right, and Army Barbie got left behind the next time my family was relocated. Still, it was a part of my childhood, and when I saw the doll on Amazon, I clicked *Add to Cart*. I slide it, still in its box, onto the top shelf of the closet before pushing the door closed.

7

The sound of fuzzy static, like a radio dial set between two stations, drifts into my ears, nudging me awake. Rolling onto my stomach, I lift my head from the pillow and stick my finger between the slats of the blinds. A steady rain falls through the pale gray sky. Early July, and it's a wet day at the Jersey shore. I burrow deeper into bed, wrapping the cloud-patterned comforter around me. It's not that this bed is more comfortable than my *real* bed, the one in my first apartment. I just like to sleep here sometimes, that's all. Why shouldn't I? I ask myself and close my eyes, willing the gentle sound of the falling rain to pull me back into a doze. I turn onto my side and try to empty my mind. But my father's words, *Wake up, Jenny. Don't waste the day*, echo in my ears. I slide out of bed, smooth the sheets, and arrange the comforter, checking that the edges hang evenly. Looking through the door's peephole and seeing that the hallway is clear, I dart next door into 1E. No reason for anyone to know that I no longer sleep there.

I start the day with a bowl of oatmeal, a glass of orange juice, the *New York Times*, and the *Sea Grove Sentinel*, both online. The staticky sound of the rainfall that roused me from sleep earlier has morphed into a pounding drumbeat that tells me, *No beach today*. I shower and slip into a sundress, although the sun has gone missing today, and carry my laptop and cell phone into the living room. Settling onto the sofa, I place my laptop on the glass coffee table and begin to work.

I have a preliminary list of schools for Megan. Columbia, of course, Yale, Penn, and Johns Hopkins, the usual picks for students with her credentials who are looking for an urban environment within a three-hour drive from home. But those are all 'reach' schools, even for Megan. I'll need to explain that to her mother. NYU and GW would be good 'safe' schools, and so would BU, if she'd go that far. We also need to talk about some of the more competitive smaller colleges. But the school I really want them to look at is Cornell. It's a four-hour drive, and the campus is suburban-slash-rural, but it has a Fiber Science and Apparel Design program. It's not Columbia, so Mrs. Campbell won't be happy. But maybe Megan will, I think, smiling as I press her name on my cell phone.

She answers, and we schedule an appointment for next week.

"Would it be okay if my mom comes?" Megan's voice becomes a soft whisper. "She'll probably want to."

"Sure. That would be fine." I say. "See you then."

It might even be better this way, I think as I hang up. Megan will need my help convincing her mother that Columbia is not the *only*, or necessarily the *best*, college choice for her daughter.

I close my laptop and stand up, rotating my shoulders as I lean backward, arching my body. Maybe I should buy a desk for this apartment instead of doing my work hunched over a coffee table. Now that the boxes are unpacked, I actually have the room. But then again, I do have a desk. Just next door in 1F. Crossing into the kitchen, I slide a thick black folder out of the narrow cabinet that serves as my makeshift home filing system. *Unpaid Bills*, the label says. I pull my keys from a drawer, gather my laptop and phone, and slip into my other apartment, making a beeline for my desk.. This will work just fine. I open the folder and stack my statements into a neat pile, scanning each of them for the balance due and punching the amounts into the vintage Texas Instruments calculator I found at a garage sale last year.

How could I have spent so much? I stare down at my calculator. I must have entered something wrong. I clear the display screen and slowly page through the pile of statements on my desk, carefully re-entering the total amounts due into my calculator. The same series of black numbers appear. I don't understand it.

Before I even considered renting a second apartment, I anticipated the expenses and budgeted for them. Rent for both apartments and my office, utilities, cable, cell phone, miscellaneous. I ran the numbers so many times. I should be able to do this. Leaning on my elbows, I drop my forehead onto my clasped hands and shake my head as I realize what the problem is.

Miscellaneous.

I've spent almost a decade hunting down and collecting the abandoned, left-behind keepsakes of my childhood. Now that I have the space to take them out and recreate the memories of all the homes I was forced to leave, I notice the things that are still missing. Toys, games, books, pieces of my past. And I've been buying them, spending cash at garage sales and flea markets in addition to racking up credit card bills.

Renting two apartments has been a financial drain for me. That's true. But it was an important move. A *necessary* move. Now my original apartment, 1E, is uncluttered and tasteful. I'm proud of it and finally feel comfortable inviting friends over. The boxes are gone, and with them is my need to explain. And my second apartment has become a sort of cocoon. It feels warm and safe, and I've found myself spending more and more time here. Like now, I think, looking up from the mound of bills piled on the white wood desk resembling the one I had as a teenager in Colorado and later in New Jersey. Books, dolls, posters of the Backstreet Boys and 'N Sync, the start of a Beanie Babies collection, and an Easy-Bake Oven, still in its box. I remember sliding a pan of lumpy beige dough balls into my own toy oven while my mother pulled a hot apple pie out of hers. We did the dishes together, breathing in the cinnamon apple smell of the warm kitchen.

I get up from my chair and lift the Easy-Bake Oven out of its box, placing it on the kitchen counter. A cinnamon apple scented candle would be nice in here. And maybe a set of stoneware dishes like the ones my mother used to have. Even just a single place setting would be fine. That can't be too expensive. I still have so many more things to buy…

Feeling the beginning of a tiny pulse in my right eyelid, I inhale deeply and then breathe out slowly. I can work out the money issues. I know I can. I'm not too busy with clients now. Summers are always slow. I have time to do something else, maybe get another job. I'll figure it out. I know I will. But for now, I just need to relax.

I pick up the oven's instruction manual and begin to read. *"Preheat the oven for 15 minutes. Pour contents of cake mix into bowl and stir to break up any lumps."*

8

I always do my grocery shopping on Wednesdays, usually in the late afternoon. I don't have a particular reason. It's just the way I've always done it. Habit, I suppose. That, and growing up in a military family. A day for the supermarket, a day for laundry, a day for vacuuming and dusting, a day for cleaning the bathrooms.

Standing on the checkout line, I watch the curly-haired woman in front of me plunk a box of sugary cereal, a bag of potato chips, and a stack of TV dinners onto the conveyor belt. Positioning a divider behind her purchases, I unload my cart. The cashier scans my groceries. I bag, swipe my credit card, and thank her. Pushing my cart toward the automatic glass doors, I stop to check the flyers and advertisements tacked onto the store's bulletin board. *For Sale: Dining Room Furniture-Like New*, *Babysitter Available-Mature and Responsible*, *Cleaning Service-References Provided*. No garage sales this weekend, I guess. I scan the board one more time and spot a small white index card half-hidden behind a color photo of a patio set for sale. I read the card's neat black print. *SAT Tutor-Reasonable Rates*.

SAT tutor? Hmmm…Why not? I wonder if Mr. Freeman still runs Academic Edge. Would he remember me?

"We usually only consider people who have completed at least one year of college," Mr. Freeman had said during my interview for my first post-high school job as an SAT tutor. "But in your case…" he said, looking down at my official SAT report, "perfect scores, accepted by Columbia…" He seemed to be thinking aloud.

And luckily for me, he did consider, and then hire me after I graduated from high school. That summer I tutored and prepped high school students for the SAT and took a class at Rutgers. I saved some money and earned three credits toward my degree at Columbia. A win-win situation.

I feel an optimistic ripple run up my spine as I steer my shopping cart into the parking lot and head for my car.

Now, ten years later, Mr. Freeman is retired, and Academic Edge has expanded beyond individual tutoring to offering SAT prep classes. After two telephone conversations, an interview, and an all-day training session on the current version of the exam, I'm ready to start. I'll be teaching classes for just the verbal sections because the task of relearning high school math would have been a deal breaker for me.

So far, I've committed to running the late afternoon classes during the summer session Monday through Thursday for six weeks.

I drive northwest on Route 18, heading from the shore to New Brunswick, home of Academic Edge and Rutgers University. The road is familiar, and traffic in this direction is light. Still, I left Sea Grove early. *If you're early, you're on time. If you're on time, you're late.* Shades of my father.

I zip along a stretch of open highway bordered by trees until it turns into a traffic-light-dotted roadway flanked by strip malls. Turning into a municipal lot, I park my car and grab the bag containing my tutoring manual and packet of practice tests from the passenger seat. I look down at my watch. Academic Edge is less than a block away, and my workshop isn't scheduled to begin for another forty-five minutes. Even I can't be *that* early, I think as I step onto the hot sidewalk.

The heavy summer air presses down on my shoulders, and I squint against the sun. A cup of iced coffee would be nice, I think as I scan the storefronts lining the street. Spotting the familiar green awning offering an oasis of shade on the white-hot concrete, I cross the street and head into Starbucks. Five minutes and four dollars later, I carry my iced latte to a small round table and pull out my phone, tapping the calculator icon. With the extra money I'll be earning from Academic Edge and the clients I'll be taking on later in the summer, I should be able to...

From the counter, I hear the barista ask, "The usual?"

I look up and glimpse the back of a tall man, slim and broad-shouldered, his dark brown hair grazing the top of his collar. With a paper cup in his hand, he turns, peering around the room until his eyes focus on the empty table next to mine. As he moves toward it, and me, I realize where I've met him before.

Nick Russo sets his drink on the table and looks up, his eyes meeting mine. He tilts his head, and his mouth spreads into a smile. Lifting his cup, he walks toward me. I feel my face grow warm.

"*Military Brat*, right?" His mouth closes, and then opens. "Just give me a minute. I'll get it." He looks down, tapping a hand against his thigh. "Jessica?" He looks at me and shakes his head. "No, not Jessica."

"Not Jessica," I repeat, feeling my mouth stretch into a smile.

"Jennifer?"

"Technically, yes. My name is Jennifer. But everyone calls me Jenny."

"Okay then, Jenny. May I join you?" He points to the chair across from me.

"Mm hmm." I nod, a tingle of nervous happiness creeping up my arms.

Nick Russo was the teaching assistant for the course I took at Rutgers the summer before I entered Columbia, the same summer I worked for Academic Edge. For someone like me, a girl who had filled faux leather diaries with soul-baring pages of neat cursive handwriting, a girl who devoured books and never begged for a TV in her room, a girl who found solace in imaginary worlds, a creative writing class was a natural choice. Four papers, a couple of quizzes, and three credits for the in-state tuition price.

"Sounds like a good way to get a head start on your coursework," my father had said. "Just make sure Columbia accepts the credits."

"You'll love it!" my mother had whispered.

And 'love it', I did. Professor Lindstrom, a small man with a large red face and a trim white beard, appeared for the first class and the last, turning over the bulk of his teaching responsibilities to a graduate student in the English department.

On that second day of class, Nick Russo stepped in front of his desk and said, "Welcome to Creative Writing 101. And please," he said, pausing to make eye contact with each of us, "call me Nick." Then he grinned, his eyes crinkling at the corners.

Nick? In my thirteen years as a student in countless different classrooms across five different states, my teachers had been *Mr.*, *Ms.*, or the occasional *Mrs.* Staring at the too-young-to-be-a-professor teaching assistant running my first college class, I pressed my lips together, suppressing a smile.

He needs a haircut, my father would have said.

Welcome to college, would have been my mother's giggling response.

And now, ten years later, my first college instructor is sitting across from me at a Starbucks just blocks away from the small Rutgers classroom where he had asked the eighteen students enrolled in the 2002 summer session of Creative Writing 101 to 'please call him Nick'.

"What are you doing here?" Nick and I ask each other in unison.

"Ladies first," he says, laughing as he dips his head in a mock bow.

"I'm on my way over to Academic Edge to teach an SAT prep class. I tutored for them ten years ago." I lift my shoulders in a quick shrug. "The summer I took your class," I say more quietly.

"Ten years?" He squints. "You took my writing class *ten* years ago?"

I nod. "The summer after I graduated from high school."

"Yes, I do remember that," he says slowly. "You were heading off to Yale, weren't you?"

"Columbia," I say.

"Ivy League school in the city." Grinning, he extends his hands, palms up, in a gesture of mock surrender. "I was close, wasn't I?"

"Yes, you were close," I say, mirroring his smile.

"It's been so many years, but I still remember your final essay for that class. It was for the creative non-fiction assignment. You called it *Military Brat*. It was…" He pauses, "remarkable. Your writing was so true. So real. Not only the actual details of your life. Moving around like that. But also your relationship with your brother. How close you were despite the age difference. How he was the only one who could make your father laugh. I don't remember all the details." He taps the table. "What was his name again?"

"Ryan." I say, feeling a slight twitch in my right eyelid.

"Yes, Ryan," he repeats. "And so? Tell me the rest. What's your story?"

"'What's your story?'" I repeat his words. "You used to say that in class."

"You're right. I probably did." He picks up his cup and takes a sip. "Not too creative for a former writing teacher, huh?"

"Former?"

"Yes, former. I only taught that class when I was in grad school. Ted Lindstrom was my advisor, and he offered me a teaching assistantship. In fact, I had just completed my first year of the program when he asked me to take over your class."

I did the math in my head. That would make Nick Russo thirty-three. "So, what do you do now?" I ask.

"I'm an English professor at Rutgers. Contemporary American Lit. But hey…" He points a finger at me. "didn't I ask what *you've* been doing?" Again, that smile. "For the last ten years?"

"After college, I worked in the Admissions Office. Now, I'm an independent college counselor. I moved back to New Jersey."

"That seems like a very short version of your story."

I laugh.

"I want to hear the rest of it, but I have to run. I've got an appointment on campus." Nick checks his watch and looks up. "Can I call you?" he asks, his soft brown eyes locking with mine.

I nod, feeling…something. Something good.

He pulls out his phone and enters my number. "I'm really happy I ran into you, Jenny." He grins and nods. "Really happy."

And I'm really happy, too. I sling my bag over my shoulder, toss my almost full latte into the trash can, and head out to the street.

In the familiar red brick building, home of Academic Edge, I greet the receptionist and climb the stairs to Room

2, first door on the left. I introduce myself to the twelve students enrolled in my SAT class and hand out the mini practice tests. The first session always starts this way. While they work, I open my instructor's manual. I stare down at the page, but I can't concentrate on *Super Strategies for Critical Reading.*

Closing my eyes, I squeeze my hands together. I hope he calls. But my mind jumps from thoughts of Nick to a vision of the sealed box still stashed at the bottom of the closet in my second apartment. I've stared at its label a hundred times.

Ryan.

9

The next morning, perched on the edge of my bed, I clasp my only unopened box to my chest. The room overflows with books, toys, games, and replacements of the left behind pieces of my life. It is the sort of room that I imagine my friends return to when they talk about going home for the holidays. But this is not my childhood bedroom decorated in colors chosen by my teenaged self in my parents' house. It's my own creation, a sort of sanctuary in the second apartment that has become my home. I've put off the task of opening my last box, the one marked *Ryan*. But I know it's time. Those memories belong in this room.

I open the flaps of the box and look down at the collection of items inside. One by one, I lift them out and carefully arrange them in an evenly spaced row across my bed. A blue and yellow knitted baby blanket, a floppy-eared stuffed elephant, my white t-shirt decorated with pink rhinestones spelling out *Big Sister*, and a teddy bear-patterned crib sheet entombed within its original cellophane.

Twenty years have passed and still, I feel my eyes water.

My parents, my mother's belly swollen with the promise of my new baby brother, left for the hospital on a hot July evening. We had finished dinner—funny that I still can't stand meat loaf and mashed potatoes—and my mother had just opened the freezer.

"Who wants ice cream? I have mint choc…" Suddenly she moaned, bending forward, her arms wrapped around her stomach.

"Mom!" I yelled as my father sprang out of his chair.

"It's okay," my mother said calmly. "We have time."

But within the hour, Mrs. D'Angelo, a neighbor whose husband had been deployed, was scooping mint chocolate chip ice cream into two bowls, and my parents were headed to the hospital. I beat Mrs. D. at checkers twice before letting her win the third game. We watched *Full House* and *Murder, She Wrote*, and the night dragged on until the telephone finally rang. I jumped off the couch, but Mrs. D. had already been in the kitchen, sliding a pitcher of lemonade out of the refrigerator.

"Bruce?" she answered the phone with my father's name.

I stood in front of her, bouncing on my toes as I looked up into her face. I could hear the muffled baritone of my father's voice through the phone, but I couldn't make out his words.

"W-What?" Mrs. D. gasped as her fingers gripped the phone. The color drained from the center of her face, leaving two bright circles of pink blush on her cheeks.

Mrs. D. spent that night on the corduroy couch in our den. I slept with my arms wrapped around the blue stuffed elephant that I had taken from the crib my father had assembled a few weeks earlier.

My parents came home the next day. My father, his mouth curved downward into a sad parenthesis, held my mother's trembling hand as he told me what had happened in the hospital delivery room. While my mother was panting and pushing, Ryan's shoulders had gotten stuck in the birth canal, restricting his flow of oxygen. *Shoulder dystocia.* That's what the doctors had called it. My mother had already had two miscarriages, but her stomach had never bulged with those babies. Their feet had never kicked. They hadn't made her belly ripple. They hadn't had names. I immediately understood that I would never be a big sister. Not Ryan's. Not anyone's.

Over the next few days, the dark wood crib and chest of drawers disappeared from the room that would have been Ryan's. A mobile, festooned with brightly colored circus animals, and a box of diapers stashed in the corner of the closet vanished too. Before the room was converted into a home office for my father, I snatched a knitted baby blanket, a stuffed elephant, and an unopened crib sheet from a packed box destined for the Salvation Army. I hid them, mementos of the brother I didn't have, along with the *Big Sister* t-shirt I was wearing the night my parents went to the hospital underneath a stack of pajamas in my bottom drawer. And each time we moved during the ten years from that summer until I left for college, I smuggled those precious few keepsakes in a suitcase stuffed with clothing. It wasn't until I rented my first apartment in the city that I preserved them within a single box neatly labeled *Ryan*.

I gather up the physical reminders of the brother I almost had and pile them on the top shelf of my closet. Breaking down the empty box, I fold it into a thick square. As I drop it into the trash can, my cell phone rings.

An unfamiliar number appears on the screen.

"Hello?"

"Hi Jenny, it's Nick."

10

*I*t's just dinner. It might not even be a date. Maybe he's only interested in me because I'm his former student. Maybe he wants to learn more about college counseling. Or jobs at Academic Edge. Maybe he just wants to take a ride to the shore. Maybe he…I shake my head no.

It's a date. Definitely. So? That doesn't explain why my heart is racing like I've just come off a treadmill. I'm not a middle school kid going to a movie on a military base with the boy down the street. I'm a grown woman having dinner with a grown man. It's true that Nick is a very attractive grown man. It's true that he's my former teacher. And it's also true that based on an essay I wrote ten years ago, he might have a misconception about my family. Maybe even a big misconception. But still…

I look at the mound of clothing piled on my bed. I don't remember the last time I tried on and rejected so many outfits while getting ready for a date. In high school? I fold each of my not-quite-right shirts and replace them in a dresser drawer. Then I hang the three pairs of pants that I've decided against in my closet. Wearing a simple sleeveless black dress, I check my reflection in the mirror. Not too dressy, not too casual. Should be fine.

He said seven-thirty. That gives me another twenty minutes. At least. It wasn't until I went away to college that I learned that seven-thirty could mean seven-thirty-five or even seven-forty and still be considered on time. In my family, dinner was served at six-thirty. Not six-twenty-five. Not six-thirty-five. Six-thirty. I came home from school at three-thirty when we lived in Missouri, and at four when we lived in Colorado. When I entered high school and began to stay after for extracurricular activities, I hung a copy of my weekly schedule inside the pantry door. Any tardiness always required an explanation. A good one.

I close the closet door and glance around my bedroom. The bed is neatly made, and I've left a book on my night table and a pair of slippers in the corner. No one would suspect that I no longer sleep here. Nick won't be in my bedroom, but I've gotten used to being careful.

I was surprised he wanted to pick me up here. I haven't dated much since I moved to New Jersey, but back in New York, meeting dates at restaurants was the norm. So, when Nick asked me to recommend a place for dinner in Sea Grove, I suggested meeting at the Ocean Grill, a popular spot on the boardwalk.

"The Ocean Grill is a good idea," he said. "But meeting there? That's not the way I do things, Jenny."

I could hear a smile in his voice.

I've been independent for a long time. Maybe always.

Don't ask for help if you can do it yourself, my father had told me.

Don't ever let yourself become dependent on a man, was my mother's advice. *No matter how much you love him.*

Still, it isn't a big deal to let Nick pick me up. It might even be kind of nice. And maybe I do want to see how he 'does things'. The soft tickle of a giggle escaping from my mouth surprises me.

I move into the living room. A vase filled with the white roses I bought today rests in the center of the glass coffee table, and I've left my laptop on the sofa. I don't spend much time here anymore. The space next door, 1F, feels so much more like home. I've thought about giving up *this* apartment. Financially, it would be a wise move, but part of my identity lives here. This space, my original apartment, is an anchor, the home of a successful, young professional. And as long as I rent, maintain, and spend at least some of my time here, I feel grounded, attached to the outside world. Besides, how could I invite someone like Nick, or anyone, into my second apartment, a space filled with the books and toys of my childhood and decorated with posters from 1995?

The doorbell rings. I check my watch. Seven-thirty-four. Not bad. I press my lips together, turning my smile into a more neutral expression, and open the door.

Nick holds a single yellow tulip in his outstretched hand. "Hi, Jenny."

"Hi," I feel my mouth stretch back into a smile. "And thank you," I say quietly, accepting the flower and lowering my head to breathe in its faint green scent. "Come in."

I step back and watch as Nick, in an untucked button-down shirt and jeans, walks into my living room. He stops in front of the coffee table and turns his head, nodding as his eyes sweep the room. I follow his gaze. Leather sofa flanked by two floor lamps, large area rug, book-filled wall unit.

"This is a great apartment. How long have you lived here?"

"About a year and a half."

"It's so neat. Orderly. There's no extra stuff lying around." He scans the perimeter of the room again, more slowly this time. "How do you do that?" He chuckles. "And can you teach me?"

No extra stuff lying around. His words echo in my head as I visualize my stash of memorabilia next door.

My mouth goes dry, and I swallow and wet my lips. "Guess it's just part of growing up military." I force my shoulders up in a casual shrug and stroke the smooth petals of the single flower in my hand. "Let me put this in water, okay?" I say, lifting a 'just a minute' finger.

Without waiting for Nick's answer, I duck into the kitchen. I slide a glass vase from the cabinet, fill it with water, slip the long-stemmed tulip inside, and head back into the living room.

Nick, arms across his chest and head tilted, stands in front of my wall unit, scanning the rows of books that fill its shelves. "Small TV, lots of books." He turns toward me, his eyes smiling along with his mouth. "I like your priorities."

"Good," I say, laughing. "I'm glad."

"But right now, my priority is dinner." His arm sweeps toward the door in an 'after you' gesture. "Ready?"

We leave the apartment, stepping onto the concrete walkway shimmering in the pale light of the early summer evening. I breathe in the familiar brew of ocean air spiked with freshly cut grass and watch Nick's nostrils flare as he inhales slowly.

"This is a nice place to live," he says.

"Yeah, it is." I stop and turn toward him. "Do you want to walk to the Grill? It's just across the street and a block down."

"I'd love to," he says, touching my elbow lightly. "Let's go."

We walk through the parking lot, cross Ocean Avenue, and climb the three shallow steps leading up to the board-walk. The air is cooler here, and I feel the warmth radiating from Nick's body as we walk together, not touching. The ocean breeze tickles my bare arm. Ahead of us, a ponytailed young woman in denim shorts chases a laughing toddler.

Three teenage boys duck into an arcade, and a gray-haired couple, their thin arms linked, strolls along the boardwalk.

"Summer at the shore," Nick says with a slow nod. "Brings back memories."

"Yeah?"

"Yeah." He smiles, nodding again. "When I was a kid, going down to Point Pleasant was a treat. The ocean, the rides, the boardwalk. I loved it. In high school, my friends and I would go to Belmar or Manasquan when we could. I've spent some time down here over the years. Not as much as I would have liked, but I've got some great memories."

We stop in front of a large windowed building ringed with outdoor tables. Groups of friends, families, and couples, suntanned and smiling, fill the seats. White letters underscored with the repeating *u* of a wave pattern decorate the turquoise awning that hangs over the restaurant's front entrance. *The Ocean Grill.* Nick checks our reservation with the hostess, and she leads us through the crowded restaurant to a table on the back verandah overlooking the beach.

"How did you get *this* table on a Saturday night? In July?" I ask after we are seated.

"I don't know." He shrugs. "I made a reservation."

"It's almost impossible to get an ocean view table here on the weekend in the summer. Who do you know?" I laugh.

"I guess I got lucky," he says, opening his menu.

We order. The calamari appetizer to share, swordfish for Nick, and salmon for me.

I glance to my left. Beyond the restaurant's wooden railing the ocean waves sweep over the edge of the beach. A seagull glides across the orange streaked early evening sky. I turn back to Nick.

"So, where did we leave off at Starbucks?" he asks, lifting his water glass and taking a long drink.

"You were telling me that you were an English professor at Rutgers and—"

Tilting his head and arranging his face into an 'I'm trying to look serious' expression, Nick raises his palm like a security guard at a school crossing. "Just a minute, Jenny. I remember it a little differently."

I feel my eyebrows arching.

Our waitress approaches. "Your calamari," she says, setting the platter between us.

"Saved by the squid." Nick deadpans.

We thank the waitress, and she hurries toward the sound of an "Excuse me, miss" coming from a neighboring table.

Nick fills a plate with a generous portion of calamari and hands it to me. Then he serves himself. "As I remember it, I was trying to find out what *you've* been doing for the last ten years."

My face grows warm, a good kind of warm. "Well, I already told you that after I graduated, I worked in the Admissions Office at Columbia. I started there part-time as a student, and as a psych major without definite plans, I was thrilled when they offered me a job after I graduated. One day the mother of a prospective student asked me if I would consider advising her younger son."

"Wouldn't that have been a conflict of interest?"

"I was afraid of that, so I checked with the director. But he didn't see it as a problem as long as my private clients weren't applying to Columbia."

"And from that one client you built a business?"

"Uh huh." I nod.

"Hmmm, now I'm really interested." Nick spears a piece of calamari and dips it into marinara sauce. "Tell me more," he says, popping the squid into his mouth.

"There's not much to tell. I printed up some business cards and developed an informational program. Then I called libraries, churches, synagogues, even coffee shops and presented free intro sessions." I shrug. "The clients came."

"You are quite the entrepreneur." He leans back in his chair. "And your presentations? Did you know that public speaking is the average American's number one fear?"

"I've heard that. But I guess moving around so much and being 'the new girl' so many times…" An almost-laugh escapes my throat. "I'm fearless."

"Fearless?" Nick drums his fingers in a slow roll along the edge of the table.

"In some ways."

He nods. "So, what *are* you afraid of?"

You. I close my mouth over the word, not saying it. Instead, I smile and dig my fork into a piece of calamari. "I'll have to think about that one, but now it's your turn. All I know about you is that you're an English professor at Rutgers, and you have fond memories of the shore. So, what's *your* story?"

"My story? Not that interesting really. I'm from New Jersey. Small town. Big Italian family. Grandparents, aunts, uncles, cousins. We've been here for a couple of generations. My parents are in the restaurant business, and to them," he says, pointing to the last piece of calamari on his plate, "this is *cal-ah-mar.* Not *calamar-i.*" He grins. "It's a New Jersey Italian thing."

"But you called it 'calamari' when you ordered it."

"One of the many things I learned in college."

"But didn't you go to school in New Jersey? Rutgers?"

"I didn't do my undergrad work at Rutgers."

"No?"

"No, I went to school in California."

"California?"

A young man removes the empty appetizing platter and dishes from our table, and our waitress delivers our dinner orders.

Nick leans over his plate and inhales. "Smells delicious." He looks up at me. "Bon appétit."

"Bon appétit," I repeat, ignoring my food. "So... California?"

He nods. "I had a tough time convincing my father. Sending his son to school across the country to study English—not what he thought of as a practical major—was a little out of his comfort zone. But my mother understood that I needed to go. And she knew I'd come back." He lifts his shoulders in an exaggerated shrug. "I'm a Jersey guy."

"What school did you go to?"

"I went to Cal Berkeley," he says slowly. "I applied there on a whim. I'd never been to California. In fact, I'd never even been beyond the east coast." He shakes his head, his lips pressed into a thin line. "I was feeling a little adventurous. Rebellious maybe. Then, when I was accepted, I couldn't say no."

My college counseling antennae perk up. "Where else did you apply?" I ask quickly. Too quickly. "I'm sorry. Am I being nosy?"

"No, you're not being nosy." He chuckles, shaking his head. "But you're not going to understand this."

"Try me."

"I only applied to three schools. Rutgers, Princeton, and Cal Berkeley."

"And?"

"I was accepted by all of them."

"You got into Princeton, and—"

"Mm hmm," he says with a nod as he cuts into his swordfish.

I stare at him for what feels like a long moment. "You know, Princeton was my first-choice school. I wanted to stay in New Jersey." I shake my head. "But I didn't get in."

"Jenny, you went to Columbia. That's one of the best schools in the country," he says, his warm eyes finding mine. "And you're in New Jersey now."

But the handsome man sitting across from me gave up Princeton and left his family and his home to go to college in California. He's right. I don't understand.

"You look confused," he says.

"Yes, 'confused' is a good word."

"My family's in the restaurant business. I told you that. It's hard to explain, but that lifestyle is all-consuming. The nights, the weekends, the long, long hours…They can suck the life out of you." Nick stares at a spot above my head, conjuring up an image of something. Something I can't see and don't understand. "I grew up in the restaurant. When I was a kid, too young to be left alone, my mother would pack a bag with toys and books and set me up in a corner of the back office where she worked. When I got older, I bussed tables. Then I became a waiter. Soon I was taking reservations, helping out with the payroll, ordering supplies, scheduling employees. My parents worked there, and so did my sister and her future husband. They chose that life, but I wanted something different." He looks at me, his brown eyes turning a shade darker. "I knew that if I went to school in New Jersey, whether Princeton or Rutgers, every weekend they would call on me. An employee would be sick, or quit, or just not show up. And I would never say no." He pauses. "I needed to leave."

I open my mouth and then close it, not sure what to say.

"So, what are you thinking?" Nick smiles as he brings his fork to his lips.

"I'm thinking that there's more to your story, and I want to hear it."

While we eat, I ask the questions, and Nick answers. He came back to New Jersey during his college summers and worked in the restaurant. That was part of his deal with his father. He applied to graduate programs at Berkeley, Princeton, and Rutgers. This time Princeton rejected him. But soon after he sent his deposit to Cal Berkeley, his father had a heart attack. Nick returned to New Jersey and the restaurant. His father slowly recovered, and Nick enrolled at Rutgers. As a teaching assistant for Professor Lindstrom the following year, he ran the summer session of Creative Writing 101.

"And now Jenny, what's *your* story?" he asks.

I tell him about a childhood in motion. Packing, moving, unpacking, and then doing it all over again. Making new friends in South Carolina, New Jersey, Missouri, New York, and Colorado only to leave them behind each time my father received another 'permanent change of station' order. Dropping people and things in a trail of breadcrumbs that could never lead me back home. And later, my father's retirement from the army, my parents' move to Florida, my father's death, and my own move to New Jersey. Finally… home.

So far, so good, I think as Nick listens, stroking his chin. But then…

"What about your brother?" he asks. "What's he doing now?"

Your brother. Nick's words wash over me. A gentle wave with a hidden undertow. I want to tell him the truth. I want to tell him that the younger brother I wrote about ten years ago, the little boy who had looked at each of our moves as an exciting adventure and taught me to do the same, was a fantasy, a wish, a dream. Ryan Gilbert, the child who died in my mother's belly, lived only on paper, his existence confined to that one creative *non-fiction* essay I had written in Nick's class. I want to tell him. But instead, I inhale, swallow, and continue my invented story, trying to ignore the tiny quiver beginning to tickle my right eyelid.

"Ryan's in college. At…" I hesitate, thinking of a school far enough away. "Duke. In North Carolina."

"Great school!" is Nick's response. And then, he smiles. "Maybe I'll get to meet him some time."

"Yeah, maybe," I force myself to say.

After dinner, we walk back to my apartment complex, our bodies swaying toward and away from each other, as we stroll along the boardwalk. I feel Nick's hand on my back as we move down the stairs and onto the street. When we reach my building, he kisses me softly, watching as I turn the key and walk into my original apartment, the one he knows as my home.

I sit on the sofa and close my eyes. I told Nick a lie about my brother, and I did *not* tell him about my second apartment. A lie and a secret. Probably not the best way to begin whatever it is that we're beginning. But there's no other way. He'd never understand. No one would.

Fifteen minutes later, enough time for Nick to be out of Sea Grove, I leave the apartment, holding the vase containing the long-stemmed tulip against my chest, and walk the six steps to the space next door. To sleep, to dream.

11

*T*hrough my closed eyes, I feel the morning sun seep into the room that is my second apartment. Still cocooned beneath my cloud-patterned comforter, I roll onto my back. Stretching my arms, I extend my legs, pointing my toes, and glance over my shoulder at the alarm clock on my night table. Nine-fifteen a.m. A late start for a summer Sunday. I tick off my mental to-do list.

Check out two garage sales and the flea market, prepare for tomorrow's meeting with Megan Campbell and her mother, review the materials for my Academic Edge class.

I swing my legs over the edge of the bed and coax my body into a standing position. As I bend backward, easing myself into one more stretch, my cell phone rings.

Nick wants to see me again. Soon. Windmilling my arms in two happy arcs, I head to the shower.

Monday morning, and I'm in my office, my laptop and
Megan's file on my desk. I lean back in the padded swivel
chair and survey the room. Two comfortable chairs face the
cherry wood desk. A credenza bookended with a leafy floor
plant and an extra chair is centered on the opposite wall. My
mother's painting of a bluish-white sky reflected in a mirror
smooth sea, bubble wrapped each time we moved, and my
college diploma decorate the walls.

It's a good place. And each month, I pay a hefty rent
to keep it.

But do I need this office? *Need*? No, I don't *need* it.
When I lived in New York, I met clients in library conference rooms, empty classrooms, and vacant offices at
Columbia. I even met one student in his home, turning his
family's rarely used dining room table into a makeshift desk
and filing system. He went to Georgetown, accepted off
the waiting list. It wasn't until I moved to Sea Grove a year
and a half ago that I signed a rental agreement for my own
office in the Clayton Professional Building, spreading my
roots wider and deeper into the New Jersey soil.

Chewing on a fingernail, I think about the things I
bought yesterday. A Ouija board, a Magic 8 Ball, a box of
Crayola Gem Tones crayons, and the Electronic Dream
Phone game. But my big purchase of the day was a vintage
Cabbage Patch doll, its beige yarn hair tied into a single high
ponytail. Still in its original box, it could have been a twin

to the one I left behind when we moved from New York to Colorado.

"You're too old for that," my father had said when he tossed the doll into a box marked *Donations*.

No matter. I have it now.

Two sharp knocks rattle the door, and before I have a chance to answer, it swings open. Mrs. Campbell—I know she doesn't want me to call her Brenda—steps into my office wearing a pasted-on smile. Megan follows her.

"Come in," I say unnecessarily, directing my own smile toward Megan. "Sit down."

Mother and daughter settle into the chairs across from my desk. Megan, her arms loosely crossed in her lap, leans toward me, her lips slightly parted. Hopeful.

"So, Megan tells me you've come up with a list of colleges," Mrs. Campbell says, her tone frosty. "I suppose we do need a list, but as you know, she's aiming at Columbia."

"Yes, you'd mentioned that, Mrs. Campbell. But I wouldn't be doing my job if I didn't come up with some other schools that might interest your daughter. Right?" My eyebrows arch, but I force my shoulders to relax.

Mrs. Campbell clears her throat. "Yes, that's true. But Megan is planning to apply to Columbia Early Decision. She'll need to get her application in by November first, and she'll have an answer by mid-December." She presses her lips together and nods. "Then she can relax and enjoy the rest of her senior year."

I turn toward Megan. Her mouth is closed, and her posture is rigid. Her hands grip the edges of her chair. "You know that an Early Decision acceptance would be binding?" I pause, my words hanging in the air. "You would be making a commitment to attend Columbia if you're accepted."

"I know, but we don't have to decide about Early Decision now, do we? I-I'd like to see the other schools on your list." Her eyes lock with mine.

"Yes, of course," Mrs. Campbell says, lightly tapping her fingers against the arms of her chair. "We'll take a look at the list."

I hand each of them a stapled sheaf of papers. "Based on our previous meeting, the questionnaire you filled out for me, and your credentials," I direct my words toward Megan with a quick glance to include her mother, "the top sheet is a list of colleges you might want to consider. The other pages give more detailed information about each of the individual schools."

In an almost synchronized motion, their heads— Megan's, a natural brownish-blonde and Mrs. Campbell's, a hairstylist's interpretation of the same color, bend over the top page of their packets.

"I'll give you a few minutes to look everything over," I say, "and then we'll discuss it."

Leaning back in my chair, I scan my own copy of the list I've already memorized. Columbia, Yale, Penn, Johns Hopkins, NYU, GW, BU, and Cornell, which is the school I really want to talk to Megan about.

Glancing up, I see Mrs. Campbell's gaze fixed on a spot above my head and Megan's eyes focused downward on the packet in her lap as she turns a page.

"Thank you for preparing this, Jenny," Mrs. Campbell says, "but we don't really need it. I feel fairly certain that Megan will be headed off to Columbia next fall."

"But then..." I pause, careful to keep my face neutral. "Why did you hire me?"

"*Everyone* hires a college advisor," she says, tilting her head and lifting her chin. "We need someone to help Megan with her essays and make sure all the paperwork is in order and submitted on time. Plus, I checked your credentials. You went to Columbia, and I thought you could conv...I mean...*talk* to Megan about your own experience there."

Everyone hires a college advisor. That's probably true—in Mrs. Campbell's world.

I look over at Megan, her head still bent over one of the sheets in her lap. Craning my neck, I can see the bold strokes of my own yellow marker. The highlighted section of black type springs off the white page.

"Cornell..." she says slowly, raising her head.

"Yes, Cornell," I say. Shifting my gaze back and forth between Megan and her mother, I tell them about the school's Fiber Science and Apparel Design program, a unique combination of science and art offered at a top university.

Megan's head bobs up and down, her eyes wide and the edge of her lip caught between her teeth. Mrs. Campbell, her expression stony, listens in silence.

"Would you consider visiting Cornell, Mrs. Campbell?" I ask.

She sighs softly before answering. "I guess we *could* do that," she says slowly.

We schedule another appointment, and I walk them to the door. Megan follows her mother out of the office, turning back to me with a quick smile.

A good start, I think, although I know the rest of the process won't be easy.

I slip my laptop and Megan's file into my leather tote bag, moving from the air-conditioned coolness of my office into the hot heaviness of the outside air. Squinting against the brightness of the day, I hurry to my car, opening the windows and turning on the air conditioner before I slide onto the seat. It's only noon, and my SAT workshop doesn't begin until four. It's too hot for the beach, and I don't feel like changing anyway. The afternoon stretches out, long and free.

Standing at the kitchen counter in 1E, I devour half a turkey sandwich and down a can of diet soda. I lock the door behind me and scoot next door.

Stepping inside, I take in the room. Rows of books with brightly colored spines fill a tall bookcase, and piles of games stacked into size-ordered pyramids rest on the wall shelves I've just had installed. The dresser is decorated with a parade of drugstore perfume bottles and a Lucite organizer housing a collection of lip glosses and nail polishes in the bubblegum colors of my adolescence. A make-believe zoo of stuffed animals lives inside the large plastic bin stashed under my desk. I'm home. The room overflows with things. All meaningful, all valuable. But somehow, I need to make space for the recent finds I've left arranged in a neat row across my bed.

I prop my new Cabbage Patch doll up against my pillow, smoothing her white embroidered apron over her pink flowered dress. She looks good there. Then I stash my newest box of Crayolas in a desk drawer and grab my Magic 8 Ball.

"Does Nick like me?" I ask, giggling as I shake the smooth black ball and turn it over. *Signs point to yes.* "Glad I asked," I whisper as I position it on top of a stack of games.

That leaves the Ouija board and the Dream Phone. Rubbing the back of my neck, I look around the room and shake my head. I need another storage unit. More shelves? Another bookcase?

"What about a set of stackable plastic crates?" I say out loud. My bedrooms in Missouri and New York had setups like that.

White plastic crates. They'd fit, and they wouldn't be expensive. I can pick some up later in the week or order them online. I walk the perimeter of the apartment, stopping in front of the wall shelves. If I rearrange some of the games stacked on them, I might be able to squeeze in the Ouija board and the Dream Phone. And I could get a toy hammock for my stuffed animals. That would free up even more space. Organizing, reorganizing, and straightening up a room that doesn't need it—Yes, I really do feel like I'm home. I move a pile of boxed games onto my bed.

Music. That's the only thing missing. I close my eyes and conjure up an image of my younger self singing along with Hootie and the Blowfish while folding my laundry. I scan the column of plastic jewel cases alphabetically arranged in my black CD tower. No Hootie. Whitney Houston will have to do. I pull one of her CDs from the tower and load it into my boombox, and while she sings about wanting to 'dance with somebody', I move to my desk and add *Hootie and the Blowfish CD* to the running list I keep there. Bopping my head to the music, I dance over to the shelves and grab another pile of boxed games.

Rap-thump-thump. The door vibrates with three loud knocks.

I freeze, the stack of boxes balanced in my outstretched arms.

Rap-thump-thump. Again.

I tiptoe over to the bed and gently place the games next to the others.

"Hello? Anybody home?" A vaguely familiar male voice calls. "I want to introduce myself. My cousin, Chloe, used to live in this apartment." A pause. "I know somebody's there. I hear music."

"Damn," I mutter as Whitney sings. Moving to the door, I look through the peephole. Tall guy in skinny jeans, the kind who knows he's good-looking. *Greg.*

I don't have a choice. He knows someone's here. I yank the door open.

Greg's head jerks back in surprise. "Jenny?"

"Greg?"

"Hey, babe," he says, his eyes traveling from my face down my body and back to my face. He flashes his trademark grin.

That grin didn't work on me when Chloe lived here, and it doesn't work on me now. Neither does 'babe'. I stand in the doorway, blocking his view of the apartment.

"Don't you live next door?" he asks.

"Uh huh." I nod.

"Then who lives here? I asked the dragon lady in the management office, but she wouldn't tell me. 'Confidential', she said."

"Mrs. Thornton?"

"Yeah, that's her name. Blonde hair, red fingernails. Rarrr!" he growls, extending his fingers, clawlike.

"If it's confidential, why are you asking me?"

"Well, what are *you* doing here?"

"I'm taking care of the apartment while the tenant is away," I say evenly.

"What does 'taking care of' mean? Watering the plants?"

"Yes, watering the plants and…other stuff."

"Like what other stuff?" he asks, slouching against the doorjamb.

"Like none of your business."

"Getting a little testy, aren't you? Never knew you to be so feisty, Jenny. Actually, I kinda like it." He winks.

That doesn't work on me either. "Well, don't."

"Can I come in?"

"No, you can't," I say, closing the door behind me and stepping into the hallway.

"Why not?"

"Because I can't just let you into someone else's apartment." The not-exactly-a-lie comes out smoothly. "Why are you here, Greg? Chloe doesn't live here anymore."

"I know she doesn't. I'm here because I wanted to rent her old apartment. This one," he says, his index fingers aimed like twin pistols at the closed door behind me. "But Mrs. T. told me it wasn't available."

"Don't you live in North Jersey? Aren't you in real estate up there?"

"I can be in real estate anywhere, babe." He smirks. "Thought I'd try living down the shore."

"Well, I'm sorry it didn't work out for you," I say, fighting off the smile tickling the edges of my mouth.

"Oh, but it did." He nods. "There was a vacant apartment upstairs. I rented that one."

"Good for you, Greg." I swallow. "Good for you."

"So, I guess I'll be seeing you, Jenny." He grins. Again. "Gotta run." He winks. Again.

I watch him strut down the hallway and disappear around the corner. Then, I duck back into the apartment. I need to take a shower.

12

*F*lipping through the hangers in my closet, I realize that I have no idea what to wear for 'a drive'. Those were Nick's words when he asked me to be ready at three. "I want to take you for a drive," he'd said on the phone.

"A drive? Where?" I asked.

"Never mind where." He laughed. "Just dress comfortably."

"But, I don't know—"

"There's nothing you have to know. Is three okay?"

"Yes, but—"

Another laugh. Warm and kind. I could feel it wash over me through the phone. "I'll see you Sunday at three then," Nick said. "Gotta run now."

I scan my wardrobe, organized by type of clothing and color, arranged on evenly spaced plastic hangers. A sundress? No, I wore one on our first date. Jeans? Too warm for an August afternoon. Flipping through the hangers, I settle on a pair of white rolled-cuff cropped pants and pull out a black tank top with a light jacket for evening. I return the hangers to their correct spots and slip into my clothes.

"So, are you going to tell me where we're going?" I ask as we pull out of my building complex.

"No, I wasn't planning on it." Nick answers, his eyes on the road ahead and his lips pressed together, fighting off a smile. "I just want you to sit back and enjoy the ride." He taps the wheel. "Can you do that?" he asks with a sidelong glance at me.

"Enjoy the ride," I repeat his words.

But rather than delighting in the journey, I've always focused on getting to the destination. And *knowing* the destination. Career, geographic location, financial security, and now the replacement of lost things. Maybe it's because I've taken too many *rides*, set out on too many journeys, made too many moves. All into the unknown. And somehow, the kind, interesting, and perceptive man in the driver's seat next to me has already begun to figure that out—by our second date.

"Yes," I say, sliding my hips forward and leaning back into the seat, "Actually, I think I can."

As we travel west, the numbered highways give way to narrower roads cutting through summer green woodlands and rolling pastures dotted with horses and cows. Pointing to a hand lettered sign advertising lemonade at fifty cents a glass, Nick pulls over and hands a dollar bill to one of the two pigtailed girls sitting behind a rickety folding table. We drain our glasses, and the girls' mouths pop open when Nick leaves another dollar on the table.

"For good service," he tells them.

We climb back into the car, licking the sticky wetness from our lips, and Nick continues to drive us through the picture postcard landscape that is western New Jersey.

"Look Jenny, there's a stand," Nick says, pointing to an awning-covered wooden cart heaped with a cornucopia of yellow, red, and green. He signals right and pulls off the road. "You can't get vegetables like these in the supermarket," he says, jumping out of the car and opening my door just as I reach for the handle.

Plucking a tomato from one of the bins, he holds it in his palm, pressing his thumb into its top. He brings it to his nose and inhales. "This is good. It's got that earthy smell, and it's just firm enough." He slides a brown paper bag from the pile, snapping it open with a crisp pop, and fills it with tomatoes. Grabbing another bag, he reaches for a cucumber, its skin a flat shade of green. "These don't even look like the ones you get in the supermarket, do they?"

"You're right. They're not shiny," I say. "Why is that?"

"Wax is added to preserve them. No need for that when you get them straight from the farm." He smiles and fills another bag.

Selecting two heads of lettuce and six green peppers, he hands me one of the bags and pays the straw-hatted man standing under the awning. "Nice produce you have here," he says.

"Glad you think so." The man nods. "Enjoy it."

Back in the car, Nick tunes the radio to an oldies station. And as the Beatles sing about wanting 'to hold your hand', he takes his off the steering wheel and reaches for mine. A gentle squeeze, and then his hand is back on the wheel.

I still don't know where we're headed, but I no longer care.

We continue along our westerly route, passing through rich farmland sprinkled with rambling farmhouses and large barns. White letters printed across a bright green sign signals our approach to the Pennsylvania border.

"I got it! I know where we're going!" I yelp, slapping my palm against my head. "It's New Hope, right?" I turn toward Nick.

"Mm hmm, New Hope it is. Can't fool a Jersey girl, can I?" He grins.

"I haven't been there in years," I say. "Not since my dad was stationed at Fort Dix the second time back when I was in high school."

"Fort Dix can't be too far from here," Nick says as he drives across the narrow bridge spanning the Delaware River. "You must have been to New Hope dozens of times."

"Not really," I mumble.

I feel Nick glance at me as I stare at the road ahead.

"My mother took me once."

"And your father? He didn't go with you?"

"No." I swallow. "It wasn't his thing," I add softly.

That artsy-fartsy, hippie-dippy town was my father's name for New Hope. "Don't buy any knick-knacks for the house, Donna," he warned my mother. "If you want to visit the galleries, go ahead. But don't come home with any dust collectors." Then he pointed at me. "And you too, Jenny. I mean it."

Intending to follow my father's orders, as we always did, we toured New Hope's art studios and galleries. Trailing my mother, I watched as she leaned in closely and peered at each of the exhibited works. She squinted, her forehead wrinkled in concentration, as she studied the paintings. Her eyes sparkled, and her voice was breathy with excitement as she pointed out one artist's mastery of brushstroke technique and another's creative use of perspective.

"Mom, why don't you paint anymore?" I asked, thinking about the blue-gray seascape, a project she had created for a college painting class, that now hung in our den.

She shook her head. "Imagine it, Jenny. Half-finished canvases, jars of paints, different kinds of brushes lying around the house," she said. "And what would we do with all of it when Dad gets orders?" She raised her shoulders in a helpless shrug.

I had no answer.

Exploring the town, we popped in and out of galleries, antique stores, and craft shops. We stopped for ice cream, vanilla for me and Rocky Road for my mother, and headed toward the car. As we rounded the corner, my mother's blue Toyota in view, I spotted a crowded store window packed with brightly colored purses, hand-painted boxes, and vintage signs for Coca-Cola and Texaco gas.

"Can we go in there, Mom?"

She looked down at her watch. "Just for a minute, Jenny. We need to get home in time for me to make dinner."

A bell tinkled as I pushed the door open and stepped into the store. My mother followed me as I fingered lacy doilies, beaded necklaces, and ceramic figurines. It was a hodgepodge of stuff and a world away from all the organized, tidy houses across the country that I'd lived in. The walls were decorated with old movie posters, and a dark wood coat rack topped with a black cowboy hat stood in the corner. A wooden circle trimmed with feathers and suede, its interior webbed with string, dangled from one of its hooks. Moving into the corner of the store, I stood in front of the rack and reached for the circle.

"That's a dreamcatcher." A deep, but feminine, voice came from behind me.

I turned, and looked into the gold-flecked green eyes of a smiling white-haired woman. "It's an old Indian talisman. They used it to catch bad dreams. The good ones slide through the hole in the web and glide down to the person sleeping below it," she said, slipping the hoop off the hook and handing it to me. "The bad ones die when the sun hits them in the morning."

I ran a finger along the edge of the circle and stroked one of the smooth feathers hanging from it. "Mom?" I looked at my mother who had moved behind the woman.

"Jenny, do you really—"

"Yes, I really want this," I said. "Please."

She paid for it, tucking the bag into her purse. "Don't tell your—"

"I know."

That blue, brown, and white dreamcatcher hung over my bed for the next two years until I graduated from high school and for the nine years I lived in New York. But somehow as I made my way from New York to New Jersey, the dreamcatcher had gotten lost.

"It must be..." I stop mid-sentence, closing my eyes and calculating the passage of time, "twelve years since I've been here. But not much has changed," I say, smiling at Nick as we walk past New Hope's train station, a beige wooden building topped with a witch hat-looking structure that had originally been used as a telegraph office. We stroll along time-faded red brick sidewalks and paved footpaths, passing historic eighteenth-century homes built of stone, former grist mills, the Delaware Canal, and a bed-and-breakfast complete with a wraparound verandah and porch swing.

"There's something so special about this place. The old…" Nick says, pointing to the Civil War cannon positioned in the center of a grassy square. Then, his arm grazing my shoulder, as he turns toward the street, "and the new."

I follow his gaze, taking in the row of motorcycles parked diagonally along the street. "And yet, somehow—"

"It all works," he says, finishing my thought.

I nod slowly, not quite sure why I feel so happy. Maybe I'm just in the right place. With the right person.

We wander down Main Street, passing flower-filled planters, restaurants equipped with outdoor umbrella-shaded tables, and a motley conglomeration of shops and galleries decorated with flags and awnings. Racks of merchandise spill out onto the sidewalk, and Nick and I pore through an array of handcrafted pottery, sculptures carved from metal and wood, ethnic clothing, and jewelry.

Leaning over a cloth-lined display case, he picks up a smooth translucent pendant dangling from a thin silver chain. "This is sea glass. It was probably a piece of an old bottle worn smooth by the ocean. It's a product of both nature and man. Not as easy to find as it used to be."

"Why is that?"

"Nowadays more bottles are made of plastic than glass. Also, we recycle."

"Makes sense." I nod.

He looks from the necklace to me. "I think it would look good on you," he says, the necklace stretched between his hands. "Let's see." He leans toward me. "Okay?"

"Okay," I say, feeling suddenly shy.

He drapes the chain around my neck, his fingers grazing my collarbone. Moving behind me, he lifts my hair and fastens the necklace's clasp, lightly touching my shoulders before he reaches for the mirror standing on the vendor's table.

The oval-shaped piece of glass, colored like an early frost, hangs below my collarbone, pleasantly cool against my summer-warm skin. I close my fingers around the ocean-polished pendant and hold it to my chest for a moment. "It's beautiful," I say as I open my hand and reach behind my neck to undo the clasp.

"No, Jenny. Leave it on," Nick says. "Please."

"B-but—"

"I want you to have it." He touches his hand to my lips.

I smile, still feeling the warmth of his fingers against my mouth as he pays the young woman standing behind the display case. "Thank you, Nick," I say slowly. "Thank you."

"You're welcome." He nods, smiling. "But I'm getting hungry," he says, patting his stomach. "What do you think about dinner?"

"Sounds good to me."

"Let's go then," he says, pulling my hand into his and lacing his fingers through mine. "I know just the place."

It's early evening, and the sky has turned an orange-streaked indigo. We walk along Main Street, stepping aside to allow a group of loud-talking teenagers to pass us. Just before we reach the next corner, Nick stops in front of what looks like a tan stone house. A curved sign hangs above its arched wooden door. Its white letters leap from a black background decorated with silvery stars and a sliver of moon. *The Dream Cafe.*

"Interesting name for a restaurant," I say.

"Mm hmm." Nick nods, cupping my elbow and guiding me along the gravelly path leading to the entrance. The door is open, and a set of brass wind chimes tinkles above us as we step inside the restaurant.

A smiling woman, her dark hair twisted into a braid that falls over her shoulder, stands behind a tall polished wood desk. "Hello," she says. "Can I help you?"

"Yes. I have a seven o'clock reservation under the name of 'Nick'. Table for two."

She runs her finger down a long white sheet of paper. "Yes, Nick," she says, looking up at us. "Come with me." She takes two menus from the pile on the desk, and we follow her through the restaurant.

We pass through a large room, filled with tables of families, couples, and groups of friends. Paintings and photos of night skies, carved wooden letters spelling out *Dream* and *Believe*, and a vintage poster promoting the Eurythmics' *Sweet Dreams* tour decorate the brick walls. Tiffany-style lamps hang from the exposed beam ceiling. We move to the back of the restaurant and settle into a corner table where the hostess lights a trio of ivory candles.

"It's nice in here. I feel like I'm inside some kind of cocoon," I say. "A dream cocoon maybe."

"That's an interesting way of putting it, and I know what you mean." Nick waves his arm through the air. "The lighting, the candles, the wall art..." he says. "And the food's good too."

A waiter takes our drink order, and we open our menus. I scan the list of salads. Poached pear, fried tomato, spinach and avocado, couscous, kale and feta, roasted beet. Moving to the selection of entrees, I try to imagine what a spicy yogurt marinade would taste like.

"I think I need some help," I say, looking up at Nick.

"Lots of choices here. Anything you don't like?"

"Not really. I don't think so." I shake my head. "Would you like to order for me?"

"Well, I don't know. That's a big responsibility." Nick puts on a mock serious face.

"I trust you," I say. And I think I do...trust him.

The waiter returns with our drinks. "Are you ready to order?" he asks.

"I think so," Nick says, glancing at me.

I nod.

"The lady will start with the couscous salad, and I'll have the kale and feta. Then she'll have the coconut mango chicken, and I'd like the crabmeat ravioli."

"Thank you," the waiter says and takes the menus.

"This way you can taste it all and choose what you want, or we can share everything," Nick says.

"Like Chinese food."

"Like Chinese food," Nick repeats my words and grins.

His smile makes me feel like a schoolgirl with a crush on the older boy next door.

"Food wasn't important to your family when you were growing up, was it?" he asks.

"No, I guess it wasn't. I mean we ate. My mother cooked. We always had a protein, a starch, and a vegetable at dinner. But she didn't make anything creative. My father was a meat-and-potatoes kind of guy." I shrug. "And what about you? What did you Russos eat?" I ask, realizing that I actually want to know. Funny, I've never been interested in food before.

Nick leans back in his chair, his arms resting on his thighs. "In my family, food was…" He draws the *s* out into a long note as he thinks about my question. "Everything. It was central to who we were and everything we did."

"I guess that makes sense though because your family's in the restaurant business."

Nick shakes his head. "It's more than that. Both my parents cooked, although they each had their specialties, and the kitchen was the center of our home. It was where we came together as a family—sharing stories, interrupting each other, and of course, eating. Cooking and serving food was a way of showing love. It's cultural. Part of being an Italian-American, I guess."

"Sounds nice," I say, trying to imagine a family dinner where people were allowed to interrupt each other.

"It was. It is." Nick nods. "And Sundays were the best. When I was a kid living at home, I'd wake up to the smell of my mom's cooking."

"Me too. I love that smell. Coffee, eggs, pancakes."

"I love that smell too, but it's not what I'm talking about." Nick laughs. "In my house, it was the gravy."

"The gravy?"

"That's what we called our version of tomato sauce. *Gravy.* It's made with braised meat, tomatoes, wine, crushed pepper, and fresh basil. It has to cook for three to six hours. So, my mom always started it in the morning."

"Three to six *hours?*"

"Yup. And while it cooked, she made the meatballs. My sister and I helped with those, running our fingers under warm water after we finished rolling the cold meat into balls."

"And you did this every Sunday?"

"Every Sunday." Nick says. "And my mother also made pasta. Usually cavatelli. My father did the salad and vegetables."

"It sounds like a lot of work, but you're smiling when you talk about it. Even your eyes are smiling."

"Great memories for me. Even now, I try to visit my parents for Sunday dinner when I can. And I make a *mean-a* meatball. Mmm." He kisses his fingertips and flips his hand into the air.

We both laugh, open-mouthed and loud. Nick stops first, his face turning serious. "But that's enough about me," he says. "Tell me about your family."

My family. I close my mouth mid-laugh and swallow. "Well…"

The waiter appears with our salads. Good timing.

"This looks great," I say, admiring the colorful mix of corn, red pepper, and black beans dotting my dish.

"Try it. I want to know what you think."

I dig my fork into the salad and bring it to my mouth. A little nutty, a little sweet, the flavors merge into a delicious mix. I chew and swallow. "This is excellent. A lot different from the salads I throw together."

"Now taste mine," Nick says, handing me his own fork topped with kale and feta.

"Not sure if I'm going to like this," I say, wrinkling my nose. "I've had kale before. It's a little bitter for me."

"Just try it." Nick reaches across the table and takes my hand, curling my fingers around his fork.

"Okay. For you, I'll taste it." I clamp my lips together, fighting off a smile. Closing my eyes, I slide his fork into my mouth. I chew slowly. Earthy, but not bitter, and spiked with feta, the kale really isn't bad.

"Well?"

"I'm not sure. It's not what I expected. Not bitter at all. Maybe the cheese cuts the bitterness?"

"I'll make a foodie out of you yet, Jenny." Nick laughs. "You're right that kale and feta combine well. But the stems are actually the only bitter parts of kale. You just have to make sure to get rid of them. Also, there's garlic and lemon in this salad. Those add to the flavor." He drums his fingers on the table. "So, what's your final verdict?"

"Hmmm...I think I'll stick with the couscous for now," I say, handing Nick his fork.

Looking up, I spot a tall man with a short blonde beard heading toward our table. He steps behind Nick and lays a large hand on his shoulder.

"Nick! It's been a long time, my friend."

Swiveling in his chair, Nick looks up and smiles. "Tim!" He extends a hand toward me. "I'd like you to meet Jenny."

Tim looks at me, appraisingly. "Pleasure to meet you, Jenny." Turning back toward Nick, he pushes his lips together, stifling a grin, and nods. "You sure know how to pick 'em, Nick."

For a microsecond, Nick's face turns serious. Then he laughs and shrugs.

Tim pulls a chair away from an empty table, slides it next to Nick, and sits down. "So, what brings you down to my neck of the woods?"

"Your food," Nick says. "Of course!"

"But why didn't you tell me you were coming? I would have done something special for you."

"C'mon, Tim. Everything here is special."

"But I would have—"

Nick lifts his hand, his wrist still on the table. "No 'would have'. Everything is perfect. Just the way it is."

I turn toward Tim. "Are you the cook?" I ask. "I mean, the chef?"

"I guess you could say that." Tim chuckles. "One of them, anyway."

Nick shakes his head at Tim, squinting his eyes and clicking his tongue. His gaze moves from Tim's face to mine. "Actually, Tim owns The Dream Cafe," he says.

"But I wouldn't if not for—"

"Yes, you would," Nick says.

"Not true, Nick, and you know it. If not for you and your parents—"

"Tim, please…" Nick holds up his hand.

My head ricochets as my eyes dart from Nick's face to Tim's, then back to Nick's. Their expressions are neutral. Unreadable.

"So, how are your salads?" Tim asks.

"Excellent!" Nick and I chorus, look at each other, and smile.

"Good. Enjoy!" Tim says, rising. "And I better get back to the kitchen. I'll see you both later." He returns his chair to the other table and heads toward the back of the restaurant. Stopping, he pivots, turning back to us and aiming a finger at Nick. "Next time let me know you're coming." And with an exaggerated shake of his head, he walks back toward the kitchen.

Nick leans over his plate, suddenly intent upon evenly distributing crumbly bits of feta throughout the leafy kale of his salad.

"Nick?"

He pushes a forkful of salad into his mouth and raises his head.

"What did Tim mean by 'if not for you and your parents'?" I ask.

Nick chews slowly, his eyes fixed on mine. He swallows and puts his hands flat on the table. "I met Tim when I was in grad school at Rutgers. We lived in the same apartment building. He'd started there as an undergrad, but college just wasn't for him. So, he dropped out after his freshman year. He was a couple of years older than I was. When I met him, he was a cook for one of the fraternities on campus."

"That must have been great for the guys who lived there," I say.

"It was. Tim revamped the house's entire menu. Instead of greasy hamburgers, macaroni and cheese, or dried out turkey breast, he cooked everything from chicken satay to jambalaya to lasagna as good as my mother's. He did Middle Eastern nights with baba ganoush and tabbouleh, and he came up with his own recipe for a vegan breakfast hash. Everything was fresh, and most of it was locally sourced. Tim was incredibly creative and had such a sense of flavor, a real feeling for food. He was a natural."

"But how did you know all this?" I ask. "You were in grad school. You weren't in the frat."

"Tim worked part-time for a caterer. I had seen him in my building and recognized him at a professor's holiday party. We started talking and later became friends."

"So, how did he go from frat cook to restaurateur?"

"Tim's dream was to open his own restaurant, and he wanted to do it in New Hope. He grew up in Lambertville,

New Jersey just across the river from here. He knew and loved this area, and he thought it would be the perfect spot for the restaurant he dreamed of opening."

I nod. "That's why he called it The Dream Cafe."

"Exactly."

"But you still didn't answer my question, Nick. Why did he say 'if not for you and your parents'?" The words tumble out of my mouth.

Nick lays his fork across his empty salad plate. A reddish flush creeps into his olive-toned skin. "I...well—"

"I'm sorry," I interrupt him, closing my eyes and shaking my head. "I didn't mean to pry. It's not important."

"What's not important, Jenny?" Nick asks, his voice soft and clear. "The actual answer to your question or the fact that I've been avoiding giving it to you?"

"Both," I say. "I didn't mean to push you, and I am sorry."

Nick flicks his hand as if swatting a fly. "No reason to be. Besides, I hope we'll have lots of time to learn each other's secrets," he says, lifting his eyebrows.

I smile and glance away, hoping he doesn't notice the beginning of a tiny quiver in my right eyelid.

Our main courses arrive, and we exchange bites of chicken and crabmeat ravioli. I've never tasted food this good. And I don't remember the last time I smiled widely enough to make my mouth hurt. After the waiter clears our plates, Tim sets a slice of ice cream-topped apple crumb pie in front of each of us,

"I can't," I say, leaning back in my chair.

Nick sighs. "I think we have to," he says, cocking his head toward Tim.

I dip my spoon into the ice cream and pie combination. "Mmm," I murmur as it slides down my throat. With a dessert that tastes like this, my "I can't" quickly becomes a "maybe I can."

"Next time you'll have to try my red velvet cake," Tim says as he wraps Nick in a bear hug and squeezes my hand.

As we make our way out of the restaurant, I stop in front of the large wooden circle crisscrossed with webbed yarn that hangs above the door. Reaching up, I stroke one of the smooth feathers hanging from it. "A dreamcatcher. I used to have one of these," I say quietly.

"And?" Nick asks.

"I lost it," I say, turning back toward the door.

A late summer breeze floats through the car's open windows as we head back to Sea Grove. Pinpoints of light shining from faraway stars dot the velvety dark sky. I breathe in a potpourri of grass and earth as Nick drives through pastures and farms before turning onto the highway. The traffic is light, and we zip eastward. The wind whooshes into the car, and I lean back, letting it lift my hair and tickle my face. I close my eyes.

"You look comfortable," Nick says, with a sideways glance and a gentle pat on my knee. "Tired?"

My eyes snap open. "No, not at all." I reach down and adjust my seat into a more upright position. "Don't worry. I'll stay awake."

"It's okay. You don't have to," Nick says. "You can close your eyes."

Memories of childhood car trips seep into my head. *Stay awake. It's the least you can do. I'm doing all the driving,* my father would bark each time my mother's eyes closed during the long drives from state to state, base to base.

I shake my head, shutting out the memories. "No, I'm not sleepy. Just adjusting my seat."

I turn to my window and gaze at the forested silhouette lining the highway, its dark outline barely visible in the pale moonlight. Up ahead a brightly lit sign emblazoned with white letters on a green background marks the exit to Sea Grove. *Sea Grove.* The perfect name for a town a few miles from the forest and a few steps from the ocean. Moving here was a good decision—for lots of reasons. I curl my fingers around the cool smoothness of my sea glass pendant and glance at Nick, his mouth relaxed in an almost-smile, his gaze focused on the road ahead. His hands curve over the steering wheel, his grip secure without being tight. The long leanness of his body stretches out into the eased back driver's seat. He looks comfortable in his skin, and I sense that he carries his secrets lightly, willing to share and to trade. But I can't let him know about the *Jenny* who created the fiction of a living brother in a college essay or the *Jenny* who is building a thing-filled refuge in a secret second apartment. Those are *my* secrets, and I can't share them. Not with anyone. Not ever.

Nick is beginning to know the good parts of me, the healthy parts. And I want him to know more. He parks the car in a spot near the front of my building, and I realize that I don't want the night to end. I feel Nick's solid warmth behind me as he follows me up the walkway to my building. I want to lean back into his body. Instead, I keep my spine straight, my shoulders squared. I need to think.

Should I invite him in for a cup of coffee? A drink? I must have a bottle of wine somewhere. I do a mental walk through Apartment 1E, the one Nick knows about. The floors are swept, the carpets vacuumed, the furniture dusted. No stacks of mail or bookmarked novels litter the area. A vase of fresh white roses rests on the coffee table. The space is immaculate, as always. The refrigerator holds yogurt and orange juice, and the kitchen counters are clean. Moving through the apartment in my mind, I picture my bedroom. I haven't slept there in weeks, but my clothes hang in the closet, and my toothbrush is damp. Just because I like to fall asleep under a cloud-patterned comforter surrounded by relics of my childhood in a room next door doesn't mean that I don't live in my original apartment. And besides, who would bother to keep fresh flowers in an unlived-in home? Nothing to worry about, I tell myself as Nick and I walk into my building.

Greg, a white envelope in his hand, rounds the corner. "Hey, Jenny." His voice slices into the air.

"Greg, uh…hello."

"Just getting my mail," he says, holding up the envelope. His head swivels, his gaze moving from me to Nick and back to me.

"Nick, this is Greg," I say evenly. "He lives in the building."

Greg stares at Nick through squinted eyes and mumbles "Nice to meet ya." Then, he turns back to me. "So, Jenny, what's the deal with Chloe's old apartment? When is the tenant coming back? I want to talk to her." He stops, his mouth twisting into a Cheshire cat smile. "Or is it a *him*?"

My mind is on Nick while my eyes glare at Greg. "It's a *her*," I answer. Truthfully.

"And when is she coming back?"

"I don't know."

"But if you're taking care of her apartment while she's away, how can you not know when she's coming back?" Greg taps his chin. "It doesn't make sense, Jenny. I mean—"

"Greg." I say his name and stop, demanding his attention.

"Yeah?"

"It doesn't matter if it makes sense to *you*. I'm taking care of the apartment while the tenant is away, and Mrs. Thornton already told you that tenant information is confidential," I say. "But why are you so obsessed with that apartment anyway? You already have a place upstairs."

"Because Chloe's my cousin, and I have lots of good memories of visiting her. And maybe," Greg says, winking, "I just want to live next door to *you*." He glances toward Nick. "Good meeting you, buddy," he says and heads toward the stairway.

I stare after him, not ready to look at Nick.

Just as Greg reaches the elevator, he turns back toward me. "By the way Jenny, did you ever unpack those boxes of yours?"

"Yes, Greg. Everything's unpacked, and I'm all moved in."

"Then maybe you'll invite me over sometime, huh?" And without waiting for an answer, he climbs the stairs leading to his own apartment.

I shiver, suddenly cold, and force myself to turn and face Nick.

"Who is that guy?" Nick asks, looking like he just bit into a lemon.

"That's Greg," I say, closing my eyes and shaking my head, trying to dislodge his image. "His cousin Chloe lived in the apartment next door to mine. She moved out a few months ago, and someone else rented it. The new tenant gave me her key so I could water her plants while she's away. But now Greg wants to rent Chloe's old apartment, and he can't because someone else is living there." My words come out in a gush.

"He seems like a guy who won't take *no* for an answer."

I nod, throwing up my hands, and walk the few steps to my door. Nick follows. The mood is broken, and our evening is over. Nick lifts my hand to his lips and kisses it. Then he kisses my forehead.

"Good night, Jenny. I had a great day with you," he says, turning to leave.

"Me too," I call after him. "Thank you."

"No, thank *you*," he says, looking over his shoulder as he leaves my building.

I fit the key into the lock, open the door, and step into my apartment. "This is my home. I live here. Apartment 1E, Sea Grove Gardens." I say the words out loud, slowly surveying the space. Leather sofa, glass coffee table, floor lamps, wall unit filled with books. I remember choosing this furniture, these accessories. The care I put into making this apartment my own. My home. I walk down the hallway and step into my bedroom. The bed is neatly made with a cream-colored comforter and a pair of diagonally positioned throw pillows. I live in this apartment, and I need to start sleeping here again. The other apartment is just for storage.

I wash my face, brush my teeth, pull on an old t-shirt and a pair of boxer shorts, and slide into bed. This is my apartment. This is where I live.

And this is where I sleep.

13

"*M*y things...they're mine...no, don't take them... not again...wait!"

I wake to the sound of my own mumbling, my shoulders jerking back in a quick spasm, ending my dream. But it's *not* a dream. It's a nightmare. The sight of my collection of things strewn across the lobby of my building, Greg scooping my books, games, and dolls into a large green trash bag, bending to pick up one of my Barbies, his face twisted into an ugly leer. I shudder. My eyes fly open, but only my alarm clock's ghostly glow pierces the silent darkness. It's three in the morning. Slowly, my eyes adjust, and I make out the familiar shape of my dresser across the room.

All my things are just next door, I tell myself. I live here. This is my room. This is my bed. I need to go back to sleep. Tightening my grip around my crumpled pillow, I push the side of my face more deeply into it and squeeze my eyes shut. But my mind shifts into full wakefulness as a new set of worries clatters inside my head like a dropped bag of marbles.

Why is Greg so fixated on the apartment next door? *My* apartment. Does he somehow know that I'm the one renting it? How could he have found that out? Why did he mention my boxes? Does Nick suspect anything? And why didn't I invite him back to my apartment? Did I make a mistake?

And why can't I sleep?

So many unanswered questions. Except for the last. I know exactly why I can't sleep. Not here. Not in this apartment. Swinging my legs over the edge of the bed, I force my body into a sitting position. My mouth opens in a wide yawn. I'm so tired. Exhausted. But still, I make my bed. I smooth the sheets, straighten the comforter, and fluff the pillows. I pull a pair of jeans over my boxer shorts and reach for my keys. Locking the door behind me, I tiptoe into the apartment next door.

I need to get a good night's sleep.

Late morning sunlight streams through the blinds behind my bed, gently prodding me awake. Games and stuffed animals, toys and books, drugstore nail polishes and lip glosses. The room feels safe and familiar. It feels like home.

I turn toward the clock on the night table. Ten a.m. I sleep better, longer, and deeper in this apartment. That's a fact, and there is absolutely no reason why I can't keep doing it, even if it is every night. But I do need to start setting the alarm clock. It's already ten. That's crazy. I shake my head and tiptoe through the apartment to the front door. Cracking it open, I peek into the hallway. Good, it's empty. Locking the door behind me, I dart into 1E.

Settling onto my sofa and balancing my laptop on my thighs, I scroll through my files. My college lists are done, and I've got meetings scheduled with each of my clients over the next two weeks. Ashley is a varsity tennis player who volunteers at a homeless shelter, and Jason is an animal rights activist who performs magic tricks at children's birthday parties on the weekends. Then there is Derek who will probably graduate as the valedictorian of his class and is the son of a waitress and a construction worker. I've marked the top of his file *N/C. No Charge.* Interesting clients with supportive parents. I click on the file labeled *Megan Campbell.* Another interesting client, but with a less than supportive parent. I tap a finger against my upper lip. I need to think about this one. Shaking my head, I slip into a bathing suit and cover-up and head to the beach.

It's late summer. Still hot, but the slant of the sun is different. I walk along the edge of the ocean, the water rushing in to tickle my feet before racing back toward the horizon. No longer bringing the icy shock of its early summer temperature, the foamy water feels pleasantly cool against my toes. I pluck a smooth purply-white shell from the wet sand and make my way back to my striped chair. My feet sink into the soft pale sand.

The college students who have made the Jersey shore their summer home have returned to their campuses, and younger students and their parents have begun to prowl the malls in search of sneakers, backpacks, and notebooks. Putting on my sunglasses, I lean back in my chair and listen to the music of the crashing ocean and squawking seagulls interrupted only by the occasional sound of a human voice. When the sun moves over my shoulder, my stomach begins to rumble. I slip the shell into my bag, tuck my chair under my arm, and trudge back through the sand toward Ocean Avenue.

Stopping at the bank of silver boxes in the entrance hall of my building, I slide my tiny key into the box marked *1E* and pull out a folded supermarket circular made bulky by the stack of rectangular window envelopes nestled inside. *Bills.* My mouth tightens into a straight line as I walk to my apartment, the mail heavy in my hand.

I lean over the kitchen table and open the thinner envelopes quickly. Bills for utilities, rent, food, toiletries, and occasional clothing purchases. Nothing unexpected and all expenses that I've budgeted for. I leave my American Express statement for last, balancing the envelope across my outstretched palm. It's heavier than last month's. That means more pages and more charges. I drop my tote bag on the floor, pull out a chair, and sit down. Sliding a finger under the envelope's flap, I pull out my statement and flip through pages of charges to Amazon, Toys "R" Us, Target, Walmart, and to PayPal for my eBay purchases. And these don't even include the trio of Beanie Babies I found online last week.

Smoothing out the folded pages of my bills and aligning their edges, I gather them into a neat pile and open the tall, narrow kitchen cabinet that serves as my filing system. I pull out the thick black folder marked *Unpaid Bills*, slide the new statements in with the others, and close the door. Stashing my tote bag in the closet, I move slowly through the apartment, admiring the clean, the open space, the tasteful furnishings. Hard to believe that less than five months ago every wall and even the hallway leading to my bedroom was lined with rows and rows of unopened cardboard boxes. But I did it. I saved, I planned, and I made it happen. Two apartments, one to share with the world and one just for me. But my plan had a flaw. I realize that now.

Wrapping my arms across my chest, I breathe in and then slowly out, letting a thin stream of air escape from my nose. I thought I'd already collected everything I needed, and that it was all packed into meticulously labeled cardboard boxes. But what I didn't know was that once I had the space to open those boxes, I would remember all the other things I had lost. I would want them, and I would buy them.

"I can't deal with this now," I say aloud as I open the refrigerator and set a package of turkey, a head of lettuce, and a jar of pickles on the counter. "Lunch, shower, teach my class." I tick the day's to do-list off on my fingers.

I pull two slices of whole wheat from the bread drawer and carry them to the counter. The kitchen cabinet, holding its bulging black folder, looms above.

Time creeps by slowly as I explain the structure of the five paragraph essay to my SAT prep class. Luckily, the format is lodged within my brain from my own high school days, so my prepared remarks tumble out of my mouth while my mind drifts to the file of unpaid bills stashed in my kitchen. When the class ends, I assign the students an essay topic to prepare for homework and head to my car. I check my phone. I have a single voice message.

"Hello, Jenny. This is Mrs. Thornton. A package was left for you. Please stop by to pick it up. Thank you."

That's odd. Usually I just get a delivery notice in my mailbox. I glance down at my watch. It's after five. The management office is closed for the day.

Mrs. Thornton, telephone pressed to her ear, holds up a red-nailed finger, signaling me to wait. "I'm sorry, Mrs. Walling," she says into the phone, her voice calm while her left hand, clenched into a white-knuckled fist, rests on her desk. "But as I already explained to you, Sea Grove Gardens does not provide reserved parking spaces."

Mrs. Thornton moves the phone away from her ear, and I hear the high-pitched squawk of an irate voice.

"I understand that you usually park there, Mrs. Walling. But our tenants can park wherever they wish. We don't assign specific spots. You know that," Mrs. Thornton says. "Isn't there another open parking space in front of your building?"

The voice on the other end of the phone barks.

Mrs. Thornton moves the mouthpiece away from her face and lets her breath out in a deep exhale. "One row over?"

I swallow a giggle as Mrs. Walling's voice hisses through the phone.

"Once again, I'm sorry for your inconvenience, Mrs. Walling. Unfortunately, there's nothing I can do. But thank you for your call. Have a good day." Mrs. Thornton pulls the phone from her ear and slams it into its base.

She closes her eyes, shaking her head, and then looks up at me, her lips pressed together. Probably not a good time to ask her for my package.

"I'm sorry to bother you Mrs. Thornton," I say softly, "but I got your message yesterday."

"My message?"

"That you had a package for me?"

"Oh, yes," Mrs. Thornton says, raising from her chair. "I'll get it for you."

Did she just smile? I watch her hips sway as she walks toward the back office.

She returns with a flat white box balanced across her outstretched arms. And yes, she is smiling. "This was *delivered* for you yesterday." She hands me the box. "By a young man."

"A young man?" I repeat her words. The box feels light in my hands. From one of my clients? Printed out applications or essays for me to edit? I usually do them through email, but...

"He said his name was Nick."

I feel my face grow warm. Mrs. Thornton stares at me, her eyebrows curved into twin arches, her head tilted.

"Thank you," I say, although I can see she wants more. She wants to *know*. "Thank you," I say again and start to turn toward the door.

She peers at me over her glasses. "We don't usually get packages personally delivered. I told Nick that, but he was quite charming. He thanked me quite profusely." The soft pink on her blush-powdered cheeks deepens to red. "And he came back twenty minutes later with a box of chocolates." She giggles, her sixty-something-year-old face turning girlish. "For *me*. Not that I need candy." She pats her stomach.

"I don't think you have to worry, Mrs. Thornton," I say sincerely, feeling my mouth burst into a smile. "And thank you again."

"You're welcome, Jenny," she says with a slow nod.

Cradling the box to my chest, I hurry across the parking lot to my building.

Nick was here yesterday? With something for me? My heart thumps, and an excited tingle races up my arms. I dig the key out of my pocket and dart into my apartment. Setting the flat white box on the kitchen table, I slide my fingers under its taped lid. Gently, I lift if off, uncovering a square envelope resting on top of layers of white tissue paper rounded by the object resting beneath them. I open the envelope and pull out a plain blue card.

"*Sweet dreams, dear Jenny*," I whisper the handwritten words.

Peeling back the tissue paper, I stare down at the string-webbed wooden circle trimmed with feathers and beaded suede. A dreamcatcher. I run a finger along the smooth wood and catch one of the soft feathers in my palm, closing my eyes.

Nick. I need to call him. Now.

I reach for my phone and scroll through my contacts. Lifting my finger from the screen, I let it hover over his name. *Nick Russo*. I hesitate, suddenly nervous. I've never actually called him before, and I'm not sure what to say. *Thank you? I love it? What a great gift?* That's not what you say to someone who you might...Don't overthink it. Just make the call. Clearing my throat and swallowing, I touch Nick's name and then his number.

The phone rings twice, and I hear his voice. "Jenny? Hello."

"Nick, hi. I...uh...I don't even know what to say to you. The dreamcatcher is...uh...I love it! And I can't believe you—"

"I'm glad you like it," he says.

"But you don't understand...what you did...it was so thoughtful. I don't even know how to thank you."

"You just did," he says quietly.

"No...what you did...just saying 'thank you' isn't enough—"

"Yes, it is, Jenny. 'Thank you' is always enough."

"No, I—"

"Okay, okay. I give up. You win. I'll tell you how you can thank me. Meet me for dinner," he says. "after your SAT class Thursday. Okay?"

"Thursday is good." I say. "It's a date." Oops! A *date*! Why did I say that? My stomach lurches.

"Yes, it is a date." He laughs the kind of laugh that makes me feel wrapped in a soft blanket. "I'll be waiting for you after your class."

"But Nick, I do need to thank you, to tell you how much—"

"Jenny, I'll see you Thursday."

The day after tomorrow. Yes!

Carefully draping the dreamcatcher over my arm, I poke my head into the hallway. Coast is clear. I scoot into the apartment next door and make a beeline for the night table next to my bed. I loop the dreamcatcher's corded hanger over the lamp and step back, studying the pale wooden circle hung with white feathers and ivory beads floating just beyond my pillow. Its shimmery moon colors glow against my cloud-patterned wall. It's perfect, and I can't wait for Nick to see his gift hanging next to my bed.

Suddenly, a tiny shiver tickles the back of my neck, and I remember. Nick can never know that this bed or this apartment even exists.

My cell phone rings, lighting the screen. *Mom.*

Airline tickets won in a raffle. A mother-daughter weekend. Fun, don't you think?

I press the phone to my ear and close my eyes, trying to make sense of my mother's torrent of words.

Excited to see what your apartment looks like without all those boxes. So glad you got rid of them.

I open my mouth, then quickly close it.

"Jenny? Are you there?"

I fake a sneeze followed by a cough.

"Are you sick?" She doesn't wait for my answer. "I'm sorry. Maybe this is a bad time. It's probably not even a good idea. I know you're busy with your clients, and now your class—"

"Mom, stop. Of course, it's a good idea. It's a great idea. When are you thinking of coming?" I push the string of sentences out in what I hope sounds like a rush of enthusiasm. "And how long can you stay?" I ask, my gaze moving from my new dreamcatcher across the cloud-painted walls to the bed where I sleep each night.

"When is up to you," she says. "Later this month? Or should we wait until October? I'd only stay for a long weekend. I'm taking that painting class at the community center. It only runs for eight weeks, so I don't want to miss any."

A long weekend. Thursday, Friday, and Saturday? Or Friday, Saturday, and Sunday? Either way, she probably means three nights. Three nights of sleeping in my original apartment, *trying* to sleep anyway.

"Jenny, are you there?"

"I'm here, Mom. Sorry about that. And no, you definitely shouldn't miss a class. It's great that you're getting back into painting. Good for you."

"Well, we'll see how it goes. It's been a long time, you know."

I do know. Jars of paint and stacks of canvases? Not when my father was alive. But I keep those thoughts to myself.

"I know it has," I say. "But I'm glad you're doing it. I'm proud of you. I really am."

"Thank you, Jenny. Thank you. Mwah."

The smack of her kiss into the phone makes me smile. "So, why don't you check your calendar and decide when you want to visit? I can free up a long weekend."

"I'll do that. And Jenny?"

"Yeah?"

"Maybe I can even meet your new boyfriend."

I swallow. "Yeah, maybe you can," I say slowly.

We say our good-byes, and I click off my phone. Suddenly, the prospect of three nights of tossing and turning in my original apartment becomes only a minor inconvenience. My mother wants to meet Nick.

Nick, the man who believes the fabricated essay which I presented as truth, the man who thinks my stillborn brother is a college student at Duke, the man who doesn't know about my ever-growing collection of things, the man whom I'm beginning to...No, my mother *cannot* meet Nick.

I'll figure it out. There's got to be a way of handling this without hurting anyone's feelings and without giving up my secrets.

I circle the apartment. Clenching and unclenching my fists, I move past the bed, the dresser, the shelves, the stacks of plastic crates, and stop in front of my desk. My gaze settles on my Rubik's Cube, that infuriating colored block that became my go-to companion each time I boarded a familiar-but-not yellow bus that would take me to yet another school in another state. My original had been lost or left behind years ago, but a replacement had been easy to find. I snatch up the cube and stretch out on my bed. For now, I'm just going to work on solving *this* puzzle.

14

When the last of the students in my Thursday class leaves, I slide my instructor's manual into my bag, close the classroom door behind me, and hurry to the staircase. The rush of students has passed, so I can move quickly. I reach the bottom step and walk straight into the building's reception area. Nestled into the corner of a striped couch, Nick is already here waiting for me. His eyes lock with mine, and we both grin.

He jumps up and walks toward me. "Hey you."

"Hey *you*."

"Hungry?"

I nod.

"Do you like pizza?"

"Who doesn't like pizza?" I laugh.

"Then, let's go." Cupping my elbow, he leads me to the door.

We step onto the sidewalk, our shadows long and thin against the pale gray concrete. A ribbon of mauvey-pink streaks across the deepening blue sky. It's just after six, the time of day that in early September still feels like late afternoon. A swarm of backpack-laden students scurrying along the New Brunswick street are the only sign of summer's end.

"Have you ever been to Vinnie's?" Nick asks.

"No. I've never heard of it."

"It's just a block up. Best thin crust pizza in the county." He chuckles. "I think so anyway."

"That's a big claim. We'll see," I say, raising my eyebrows and holding back a grin.

We stroll past a bakery, a bank, a drugstore, and a nail salon. Nick points across the street to a low building shaded by a red awning inscribed with white letters. *Vinnie's*. We cross at the light and step inside. The walls glow golden yellow, and a smattering of dark wood tables dots the pizzeria's small interior.

A short gray-haired man, wearing an apron over his t-shirt, looks up from behind the counter. His mouth widens into a smile. "Nicholas, my boy!" he bellows, wiping his hands on a towel. He hurries toward us and wraps his thick arms around Nick.

Nick returns his hug and steps back. "Vinnie, it's good to see you," he says. "Always."

In exaggerated slow motion, Vinnie turns his gaze from Nick to me and then back to Nick. "So Nicholas, tell me, who is this beautiful young lady?" he asks, his eyes twinkling.

"Vinnie, this beautiful young lady is Jenny. And I've told her that you make the best thin crust pizza in the county."

I can feel my face turning red. "Nice to meet you," I say, extending my hand.

Vinnie clasps my hand between both of his, nods, and smiles. "The pleasure is mine. Please, sit down," he says, leading us to a table and pulling out a chair for me. Nick sits across from me, and Vinnie disappears into the kitchen.

"What would you like to drink?" Nick asks me.

"A diet soda? But, don't—?"

Nick walks toward the counter, steps behind it, and returns with a glass of ice water for himself and a soda for me.

"Don't we have to order?" I ask.

"No. Leave it to Vinnie. He knows what to do. You'll see." Nick says, grinning. "So, how was your class?"

"It was okay," I say.

"Okay?"

I click my tongue against the roof of my mouth, thinking. "I guess teaching techniques and strategies to a group of students who are only interested in scoring high on a test…" I shrug. "But they've asked me to teach the next session. So, I'm going to stay on."

"Why would you do that?"

I need the money. I close my mouth around the words. Instead, I say, "I went through the training, and they need someone." I lift my hands, palms up.

"Can't they train someone else? This is a college town. It's full of students and teachers. And if you don't enjoy it—"

"No, it's not that I don't enjoy it," I say carefully. "Maybe it's just that…" I look up at the ceiling for a moment, buying time. Feeling Nick's eyes on my face, I meet his gaze. "Actually, I really don't mind it. I just don't *love* it. Not the way I love being a college counselor." I smirk. "Guess I'm just spoiled."

"Spoiled? You?" Nick laughs. "I don't think so." He shakes his head. "But tell me what you do as a college counselor. What do you love about it?" he asks, leaning toward me across the table.

"That's a tough question. Well," I say. "I work with each client individually, usually for almost two years. We go through the whole process from developing a list of target schools to completing the applications to actually committing to a particular college." I pause for a sip of soda. "And I really get to know my clients. That's the best part. They're at such a great age. Beginning to feel their independence, excited but afraid. They tell me their hopes, their dreams, their frustrations, their secrets. I'm a combination advisor, best friend, teacher, even therapist sometimes."

Nick nods slowly, his eyes smiling along with his mouth. "I bet you're very good at what you do."

"I try to be. Anyway, I know I'm good at the organization and record keeping parts of it." I laugh. "That comes with growing up military."

"Not a bad skill to have." Nick taps his lower lip.

"Now you tell me, how are your classes going?"

"Very well. I'm teaching a couple of upper level courses this semester, not the intro class. That means smaller class size, no big lecture halls, more student engagement. And I'm advising the senior English honor students. It's the kind of dream schedule that drew me to college teaching in the first place." He grins. "I'm having fun."

"I can see that in your face," I say, the ripple of his happiness echoing deep within my chest.

The wood floor vibrates with the slap of leather-soled shoes, and we both look up.

"I hope you're hungry," Vinnie says as he leans over our table and sets an individual pizza in front of each of us.

Islands of mozzarella dot a sea of red sauce framed by a bubbled thin crust. The hot-from-the-oven smell of tomato and cheese wafts up into my nostrils.

"I am now," I say.

"Enjoy," Vinnie says, bending at the waist and dipping his head before turning back toward the kitchen.

I look down at my uncut pizza, much larger than a personal size pie, and I'm not quite sure how to eat it. Piece by

piece with a knife and fork? Cut in quarters? Folded? I look
up at Nick. "So…?"

"Not what you expected?" He grins.

"Well, not exactly."

"This is Pizza Margherita," Nick says, rolling his *r*.
"Traditional Italian. Napoletana." He lifts his knife and fork.
"It's always served uncut."

"Even when it's this big?"

"Yes, always. And you have a choice. You can cut it
into quarters and fold your slices, or you can cut each piece
individually and eat it like a steak."

"And what method do you recommend, Signor
Nicholas?"

"Well, since I don't want to risk dripping or spilling in
front of the lovely *signorina*, in this case I plan to cut it into
bite-size pieces. And I like to start from the center," he says,
cutting into the middle of his pizza.

"The center?"

"You'll see."

Mimicking Nick, I dig my fork into the middle of my
pie and cut a small piece. Tomato, mozzarella cheese, olive
oil, and basil. The flavors meld together into the perfect balance. "This is incredible."

The corners of Nick's pizza-filled mouth turn up and
his eyes widen. "Mmm."

We eat the middles of our pizzas, chewing, swallowing, and looking at each other.

"No mas," I say, leaning back, leaving a small section of pizza and the crust on my plate.

"You're a lightweight, Jenny," Nick says. "But you've got to eat the crust. It's the best part."

"The crust?"

"Absolutely." He cuts off a section of crust and picks it up in his hands. Sweeping it across his plate, mopping up sauce and olive oil, he pops it into his mouth.

Cutting into the crust on my plate, I copy his technique and bite. This is nothing like any pizza crust I've ever tasted. Crisp, but still chewy without that bready taste, and flavored with tomato, oil, and basil. I nod, chewing with my eyes closed. I swallow and open my eyes. "Wow," is all I can say.

"Glad you like it," Nick says.

"Like it? I think I've just found my new favorite food."

"Mission accomplished then. Now what do you think about paying our compliments to the chef and walking off this meal?"

"Good idea."

Before we leave, I make my way down the narrow hallway at the back of the restaurant and step into the ladies' room. I wash my hands and look up into the mirror, catching a glimpse of the knickknack-filled shelf positioned above the toilet. I turn around and lean in to get a closer look.

A postcard picture of a bridge in Venice, a miniature version of the tri-colored flag of Italy, a collection of scented candles, and a small glass bowl filled with potpourri.

The bowl...I reach for it, fingering its scalloped edge. It's the kind of greenish-tinged thick glass dish that used to be sold in dollar stores. But I haven't seen anything exactly like it in years, not since I used one to stash paper clips when I was twelve. I *need* it. Quickly, I dump the potpourri into the toilet and flush. I tuck the bowl into my bag and meet Nick by our table.

We say good-bye to Vinnie, and I tell him that Nick lied. He doesn't make the best pizza in the county. He makes the best pizza in the state.

"I like this girl, Nicholas," Vinnie says, squeezing Nick's shoulder.

"I do too, Vinnie." Nick says. "I do too."

I slip my hand into my bag, pushing the bowl deeper inside.

We leave Vinnie's and step out onto the street. The evening sky is a velvety indigo, and the storefronts are brightly lit. The sidewalk thrums with energy as people head to restaurants, stores, and cars. There's something special about walking in a small city during the early evening. But maybe that's just because Nick is holding my hand.

"So? Dessert?" he asks.

"You're kidding, aren't you?"

"I knew I was right about you." His lips turn up in an impish grin.

I stop and turn to face him, hands on my hips. "What?"

"You *are* a lightweight."

"Nick, if you're hungry, we can—"

"No, I really was kidding," he says. "For now." He laughs. "Anyway, let's walk. My place is only a block away." Still not moving, he looks at me, his gaze steady. "Would you like to see it?"

"I would," I say quietly.

"Good. Let's go then," he says, touching his hand to my back. "But I do have to warn you that I'm not quite as neat as you are."

"Most people aren't." I laugh. "And that's probably a good thing."

"We'll see." He sighs, his shoulders bouncing up and down in a quick shrug.

We turn into a side street, and the concrete of the city sidewalk gives way to smooth cobblestone. A stucco-faced restaurant lined with outdoor tables is the only commercial spot in the suddenly residential neighborhood. We cross the street, walking through a tree-dotted island to get to the other side. Nick stops in front of a two-story red brick townhouse sporting large bay windows, and I follow him up the three stairs leading to the door.

"Welcome to Casa Russo," he says, motioning me inside.

A narrow table stacked with mail, magazines, and piles of paper greets us as we step into the foyer. Following my gaze, Nick winces. "Guess I should have gone through those before you came."

I push my lips together and shake my head, holding back a smile.

The foyer opens into a spacious living room. A wall-to-wall set of shelves, overflowing with a mass of books arranged into a haphazard-looking assortment of rows and piles, dominates the room.

"I need to organize that," Nick says.

I move closer to the shelves, stepping side to side and moving my eyes up and down as I scan his collection. Fiction, history, art, philosophy, music, cooking. A tangled jumble of books, cluttered and chaotic. Yet, somehow wonderful.

"Actually, I kind of like it the way it is."

Nick cocks his head, looking at me through squinted eyes. "Well then, if this work-in-progress," he says, his arm sweeping through the air, "doesn't scare you, I'll show you the rest."

We walk through the kitchen past gleaming stainless steel appliances, a wide, deep sink, and a lighted hanging pot rack hovering over a large center island. It's a place for serious cooking. Alien to me, but kind of interesting.

I follow Nick down the hallway, and he stops in front of an open door. "This is my bedroom."

Dark wood furniture, a night table piled with books, and a chair decorated with a striped shirt draped over a pair of jeans. A navy comforter, its edges slightly uneven, covers the large bed.

A tingle crawls up my back. "Nice."

"Thanks. Now come, and I'll show you the upstairs."

He leads me up a narrow circular staircase and into a large single room. "This is my office, study, whatever-you-want-to-call-it," he says, stepping back against the wall, watching me. Tapping his hands against his thighs, he rocks back and forth, heel to toe.

A carved wood executive desk, the kind that makes me think of a pinstripe-suited lawyer, fills the center of the room. Stacks of papers topped with makeshift paperweights checker its surface. I turn my head slowly, moving my eyes across the desk, focusing on each of the paperweights. A miniature globe, a purplish-white seashell, a ball made of colored rubber bands, a scuffed baseball.

"You've got an interesting filing system," I say, looking up at Nick.

Moving away from the wall, he joins me at the desk. Our shoulders touch. "I know it doesn't look like it, but I really do know where everything is." He points, his finger moving from pile to pile. "Exams to grade separated by class, student essays also separated by class, thesis outlines from my advisees. All at my fingertips."

"As long as it works," I say. "And I like your paper-weight collection." I reach for the baseball and trace its faded red stitching.

Nick squeezes my hand and takes the ball. "My father caught a foul ball at a Yankee game. I was sitting next to him." He looks up at the ceiling, then at me. "Imagine seeing that as a little kid!" He tosses the ball from his right hand to his left before setting it back on the desk.

"I can't," I say, feeling a tickle in my nose. I inhale sharply and swallow.

Nick looks at me, his lips pressed together, a question in his eyes.

"I wasn't a baseball fan," I say quickly, leaning over the desk, avoiding his eyes. "But tell me about the rest of your collection."

"Don't laugh," he says, smiling as he wags a finger at me.

I follow his gaze from object to object.

"I won the globe in a high school history bowl, the shell is from a family trip to Florida, and the rubber band ball...We all made them." He shakes his head. "So, you can see I have a hard time getting rid of things."

"Not such a bad problem," I say, moving through the rest of the room, taking it all in. A computer table holding a laptop and a red Rutgers mug stuffed with pens and pencils, a set of wall mounted shelves, each bowing under the weight of a hodgepodge conglomeration of books, a standing brass rack spilling out a jumble of magazines, a worn leather armchair draped with a blue and gold UC Berkeley throw. Nick's office is a mix of dark wood traditional and IKEA contemporary accessorized with the mementoes of his life. A warm and welcoming space.

Turning back to him, I touch his arm. "I love this place."

"Really?" He smiles, his eyes wide as a little boy's on Christmas morning.

"You sound surprised."

"I wasn't sure how you'd react to all of this mess. I was hoping you'd come over today, so I tried to straighten up a little. But I didn't get very far. I really need to get rid of some of this stuff."

"But why would you want to get rid of anything?"

"All this clutter. Sometimes it's just too much. I feel overtaken by all these things." He pauses. "Does that make sense?"

No, it doesn't, is what I think. "I'm not sure," is what I say.

"It's a lot different from your apartment. I know that."

"I guess," I say, feeling a tiny pulse above my right eye. I keep my expression neutral and wait for him to say more.

"I remember walking in," he says, his gaze focusing somewhere beyond me. "There was so much space, light, air. It was calming. Nice. Peaceful." He looks at me, the corners of his mouth turned up. "Like you."

Calm? Peaceful? *Me?* Visions of the recreated childhood home that is my secret second apartment, the file of unpaid bills lurking behind a cabinet door in my immaculate kitchen, and the stolen glass bowl tucked deep inside my bag stampede across my brain. I blink, shutting out those images, replacing them with Nick's face.

"Let's go downstairs," Nick says, grabbing my hand. "I just thought of something. Something I want you to hear."

I follow him down to the living room.

"Just stand here," he says, leading me into the center of the room and heading for the iPod system wedged into a corner of his overstuffed bookshelf. "This is an old one, but it makes me think of you."

I recognize the opening chords, and as the Eagles begin to sing 'Peaceful Easy Feeling', Nick walks toward me and wraps me in his arms.

He kisses me, and I kiss him back, and we are kissing.

"Stay with me tonight," he says.

And I do.

I wake only once in the unfamiliar bedroom, opening my eyes in the dark to shadows of things not my own, Nick's arm around my waist, his breath in my hair.

My things. I can't sleep without my things. The thought jumps into my head, but I shoo it away. Pulling Nick's arm tighter around my body, I close my eyes and listen to the steady rhythm of his breathing.

"Morning, sleepyhead." Nick's gentle whisper eases me into wakefulness. His lips graze my cheek.

I yawn, stretch my arms over my head, and open my eyes to his face. Standing over the bed, he kisses me softly.

"How long have you been up?" I take in his long, lean body dressed in a t-shirt and gym shorts. "What time is it?'

"It's a little after ten." He smiles.

"Oh no, I'm sorry I slept so long," I say, spotting my clothes on the chair across the room. I pull the comforter up to my chin, suddenly self-conscious.

"Don't be sorry. I'm glad you were comfortable. Would you like a t-shirt? A shower?"

"No. I mean no, thank you. I should go. I…I—"

"Stop, Jenny," he says quietly, running a finger down my cheek. "You don't teach today, and you told me you don't have any appointments. My class isn't 'til two, so we can have brunch together." He moves away from the bed and pulls a pile of t-shirts out of a drawer. "What's your preference? Camp Hiawatha? Rutgers? Berkeley? Vinnie's Pizza?" he reads, dropping each shirt in a row across the foot of the bed.

"That's a no-brainer." I laugh and hold the comforter to my chest as I reach for the red shirt screen printed with white letters. *Vinnie's.*

"Good choice," he says, tossing me the shirt. "I left you a towel in the bathroom." He points. "And please use whatever you like." He heads toward the bedroom door, turning around just before he leaves, and shoots me a wide, happy smile.

After a quick shower and a finger toothbrushing, I pull Nick's t-shirt over my head and step into the pants I wore yesterday. The buttery cinnamon and coffee smell of a *real* breakfast drifts into the bedroom, making me suddenly hungry. Following my nose, I make my way into the kitchen.

From the doorway, I spot Nick peering down at the stove, adjusting the flame. I tiptoe into the room, and he turns toward me, his mouth bursting into a grin. "That shirt looks better on you than it does on me," he says. Returning his gaze to the griddle on the stove, he flips over a row of pancakes. "Just about done. Have a seat." He points to the table already set with white dishes and blue checked napkins.

"What can I do to help?"

"Absolutely nothing. It's all done," he says, setting a platter of pancakes on the table and motioning me to sit, settling himself into the chair across from me.

Pancakes, an egg and cheese soufflé, blueberry muffins, orange juice, coffee. The food is delicious. It tastes like home. My *idea* of home.

I feel pampered, special, and maybe even loved. But I can't say all that. Not yet. I settle for, "I feel like I'm a guest in a bed-and-breakfast, but with even better food! Do you do this every day?"

"Let me think about how to answer that. Hmmm…" he says, pressing his lips together and squinting his eyes. "Would you like me better if I said I did this all the time, or if I said I did it just for you?"

I laugh so hard that I snort orange juice out of my nose. I swallow and touch my napkin to my face. "I don't think you have to worry about me liking you," I say, feeling my face grow warm. "So, you can just tell me the truth."

"Whew," he says, running his hand across his brow and grinning. "That's good to hear. I do like to cook when I get the chance. And cooking for *you*?" He sips his coffee and puts down his cup. "I like that even more."

I nod slowly. "I like it too."

We clear the table and wrap the leftovers, both of us reaching, bending, and moving so that our bodies collide accidentally on purpose.

"Where should I put the orange juice and butter?" I ask, standing in front of the open refrigerator.

"Anywhere you like. It doesn't matter. As long as it's in the refrigerator." He shrugs and smiles.

I slide the pitcher of orange juice, handle facing out, onto the top shelf, spacing it evenly between a carton of milk and a bottle of water. I wedge the butter into the only open spot in the crowded refrigerator door.

Nick loads the dishwasher, and I wipe the table.

"I've never had so much fun cleaning the kitchen," Nick says.

"Me either," I say, realizing that it's true. "But you have a class to teach, and I need to get going. I'll just be a minute." I turn toward the bedroom. "I have to change into my own shirt."

"Don't," Nick says, reaching for my arm. "Keep that one."

So, still wearing Nick's shirt, I drape my own top over my arm, and we walk together to my car. A kiss, a good-bye, and plans to see each other over the weekend.

Nick watches as I back my car up and then inch forward, maneuvering out of my parking spot and onto the street.

New Brunswick to Sea Grove. Traffic is light this time of day, and the road is familiar. Route 18 South for twenty minutes and two turns will bring me home. My car seems to drive itself with minimal guidance from me. I'm not one to chat on the phone or text while driving. But thinking? There's no law against that.

Nick…Nick…Nick…

I turn into the parking lot for Sea Grove Gardens and pull my car into a spot. With my bag slung over my shoulder and the shirt I wore yesterday folded over my arm, I stroll up the walkway leading to my building. The air is cooler here at the shore, and an ocean-scented breeze cuts through my light jacket. I look up at the sky and watch as a v-shaped formation of birds moves across the cloudless blue. Fall is here. A new season, and a new beginning.

"Jenny, hey." A voice, irritatingly familiar, calls out from behind me. "Wait up."

I stop and turn around slowly. "Oh, hello Greg."

He swaggers up the walkway, stopping by my side. "Haven't seen you in a while. How've you been?"

"Fine," I say. "And you?" I force myself to ask, turning back toward our building.

"Never better," he says, timing his gait with mine. "The real estate business is booming, and I'm really enjoying life in Sea Grove."

"Good." I nod and keep walking, lengthening my stride.

But Greg's legs are longer than mine, and he matches my pace. Then, with a quick step forward, he positions his body in front of me, blocking my path. His eyes move from my face to my chest.

I shiver and cross my arms, pulling my jacket closer.

"What does your shirt say?" he asks, leaning toward me.

"It says *Vinnie's*. It's from a restaurant," I say slowly, enunciating each word with exaggerated patience.

"Never heard of it. Is it around here?"

"No, it's not," I say, meeting his eyes.

He cocks his head and squints. "I was just curious because it looks big on you."

"Gee, I'm sorry, Greg. Guess I didn't check the size when I got it."

"Actually, it looks like a guy's." He snickers and points to the shirt hanging over my arm. "*That* looks more like what you usually wear."

"I didn't realize you were such an expert on my wardrobe," I say, stepping around him. "Now if you'll excuse me…"

Just a few more feet to the door of my building. *Our* building.

"I'm not an expert," he says, falling into step with me. "I just notice things."

Maybe you should stop noticing things and mind your own business, I tighten my jaw and press my lips together, swallowing the unspoken words.

We reach the door, and Greg holds it open for me.

"Thank you. See you later," I say, turning toward my apartment.

"Remember, Jenny, I notice things," he calls after me.

I shrug without looking back and keep walking. The elevator dings, and its door opens and closes with a heavy whoosh. Greg must have gone up to his apartment. I reach my door, turn the key in the lock, and step inside. Everything is as it should be. Sofa, floor lamps, wall unit, coffee table, vase of white roses. Nick is right. It's a calm and peaceful place awash with space, light, and air. As far as he knows, the woman he just spent the night with lives here.

But there is a loose cannon upstairs, a loose cannon who 'notices things' and asks way too many questions. A loose cannon who could very easily blow my fairy tale world apart.

I hang up my jacket and drop yesterday's shirt into the laundry basket. I slide my hand into my bag and pull out the small greenish glass bowl. Snatching up my keys, I peer out the door and into the hallway. It's empty and quiet. Rising onto my tiptoes, I scurry next door.

I open my top desk drawer and pull out a tiny cardboard box filled with paper clips. Turning it over, I spill its silvery contents into my new glass dish. I slide the dish next to my pencil cup and step back. It's just as I remember. Perfect!

Kicking off my shoes, I plop onto the bed and stretch out on top of the cloud-patterned comforter. This place is really shaping up nicely. Books, games, toys, even desk accessories. If I had spent my childhood in one home, my bedroom would have looked a lot like this. Maybe I would have decided to part with some of my things, but the choice would have been mine. Now as an adult, I spend most of my free time searching flea markets and eBay for tangible pieces of my past.

I tilt my head back and look up at the toy hammock, sagging beneath the weight of a rainbow-colored menagerie of stuffed animals, that stretches over my bed. My collection of huggable bears, giraffes. elephants, puppies, kittens, and rabbits lives up there in a home of nylon netting.

I'm still missing Teddy Ruxpin though. I remember the day my mother came home with that talking bear, a cassette buried in his back. His mouth and eyes moved while he told stories. My mother had waited on a line that snaked around the perimeter of a Toys "R" Us to get him for me. It was soon after my father was transferred to Fort Leonard Wood in Missouri which meant a new school, a new address, and a new phone number. Again.

The bear got left behind somewhere between Missouri and New York, or maybe it was between New York and Colorado. No matter. I've got a bid in on eBay.

I feel a vibration through the pocket of my jeans, and my cell phone rings. I check the display before answering. *Clayton Professional.* My office building?

"Hello?"

"Hello. May I speak to Jennifer Gilbert, please?" The woman's voice is curt, businesslike.

"This is Jennifer," I say slowly.

"Yes, Jennifer, my name is Anne Brady. I'm with the Clayton Professional Group." She pauses. "You rent an office in our Sea Grove location."

"Yes," I say, trying to keep my voice steady as I envision the thick black folder stuffed with unpaid bills that resides within a kitchen cabinet in my apartment next door.

"We haven't received a check from you for this month's rent."

"Oh, I'm sorry. I thought I mailed it out," I say, deciding that honesty is not *always* the best policy.

"I can assure you, Ms. Gilbert, that we did not receive it. As you know, rent is due on the first of the month. We sent you a notice last week, but we didn't hear from you." Her loud sigh blasts through the phone. "It is well past our grace period."

"I really am sorry," I say quickly, "and I do apologize. I'll drop a check in the mail today."

"Unfortunately, Ms. Gilbert, I noticed that your check for last month's rent was late also. So, I think it might be better if you left a credit card on file with us."

"H-how would that work?"

"It's very simple. On the first of each month, we would charge your rent payment directly to your card."

"Uh…that might be an option," I say, weighing her words 'the first of each month'. The arrangement would mean no more grace periods. No more late payments. On the other hand, the rent would just be another charge added to one of my credit card bills. I'm late on those anyway. "May I think about it?"

"Okay. Just remember that October's rent is due in less than two weeks. At this point, if your payment is late again, we'll be forced to add a service charge of fifty dollars." She pauses. "But for right now, would you like to give me your credit card for September's rent?"

"Yes…um…I can do that. I just need to get my card. Can I call you back in a few minutes?"

"I prefer to hold if you don't mind," she says, her voice icy.

"No, I don't mind," I lie, feeling like a scolded child. "It'll just be a moment." With my cell phone in one hand, I lock the door behind me with the other, hurry back to my original apartment and pull my wallet out of my bag. "I have the number when you're ready," I say, looking down at my card.

She takes the information and reminds me that my next payment is due October first. "Check or credit card. October first," she repeats. "Have a good day." *Click.*

"Have a good day," I say out loud, tossing my phone onto the sofa and plopping myself down next to it.

A surge of heat climbs up my body, and my scalp starts to burn. I look down at my phone, and I want to throw it and watch it break. Instead, I dig my nails into my palms.

Anger? It's not a familiar emotion to me, and it doesn't feel good. But then again, humiliation feels worse. I lean over the vase of white roses on my coffee table and force myself to breathe in deeply, slowly. Exhaling, I uncurl my hands and shake them out. I force myself off the sofa, move into the kitchen, and slide my black file out of the cabinet. It's time.

Reaching inside, I pull out each statement, one by one, and lay them in straight rows across the table. Bills for credit cards, utilities, rent, eBay, and stores. A checkerboard of debt. I open my laptop and scan through my bank accounts.

The numbers won't work. I plant my elbows on the table, resting my chin against my clasped hands. No more putting this off. I need to figure it out—now.

I start with the credit card statements, scrolling my finger down the lists of charges for board games, toys, books, stuffed animals. All necessary. No expenses I can cut until...*Macy's*. The store name jumps out at me, and my finger stops at the charge. Last month's pre-season sale. The new leather boots I'd put away for the winter. I feel my jaw tighten as I stand up, push my chair in, and head down the hallway to my bedroom.

I pull the white box down from the top shelf of my closet and carry it to my bed, feeling its heft. I lift the lid and look down at the chocolate brown boots I planned to wear come November. Reaching out to touch the smooth leather, I jerk my hand back.

"I don't need these," I say out loud, shaking my head and closing the box, receipt inside. I return to my closet and flip through the hangers, but I don't find anything else new, anything that can be returned. I move to my dresser and open each drawer, sifting through its contents. Nothing.

My mountain of bills didn't arise from overspending on clothing or feeding an addiction to fashion. My credit card purchases don't hang in a closet or lay folded in a drawer. Bit by bit, piece by piece, almost every single thing I buy is a building block essential to the home I've finally been able to create next door. I don't even have to check. There is nothing in there that I can possibly return. And doing without one pair of boots, although I'll return them tomorrow, won't solve my problem. Somehow, I need to get out from under the avalanche of debt waiting for me on the kitchen table. And there is only one expense that I can eliminate.

I need to give up my office.

15

With my hands clasped in my lap below my desk, it is an effort to keep my face neutral as I watch the drama play out between Megan and her mother.

"I'm going to ask you one more time, Megan. In front of Ms. Gil...I mean Jenny. Will you reconsider applying early decision to Columbia..." Mrs. Campbell glares at her daughter, "as your father and I have requested?" she adds, tapping her foot in a slow measured beat.

That would constitute a binding commitment to enroll if accepted. I close my mouth around the words, deciding not to repeat what Megan and her mother already know.

"Then I'll have to go there if I get in," Megan says flatly.

Good girl, Megan. I don't say that either.

"Yes, that's what early decision means," Mrs. Campbell says, her foot tapping louder and faster.

Megan glances at me and then turns to her mother. "I-I'm sorry," she says, a quaver in her voice. "But I don't want to close myself off to other possibilities."

"Cornell? Is that what this is about?"

Megan nods, looking down.

"You saw the campus. It's in the middle of nowhere. And Columbia is ranked higher according to the—"

Megan looks up and faces her mother. She speaks slowly, clearly. "Mom, I like Cornell. I like the location. I like the campus. I like the Fiber Science and Apparel Design program. And I'd apply *there* early decision." She pauses. "If it were up to me."

Mrs. Campbell breathes in, her shoulders rising, and exhales. "Well Megan, it's not up to you, not completely anyway. It's a family decision." She leans closer to her daughter. "Your father and I can't, or rather we *won't*, force you to apply to Columbia early."

"Okay." Megan nods.

"But we don't think it would be wise for you to commit to Cornell at this point either. Therefore, you may apply to both Columbia and Cornell, as well as some of the other schools on your list. Regular decision." She smooths her skirt over her knees. "That is our compromise."

Megan swallows. "Thank you," she says quietly.

"You're welcome," Mrs. Campbell says.

Their conversation over, mother and daughter turn to face me.

I don't need to remind either of them that an early decision application offers a competitive advantage. They already know that. But Mrs. Campbell has alluded to her family's financial generosity to Columbia, and with both parents as alumni, Megan is a double legacy there. My guess is that Mrs. Campbell isn't too concerned about jeopardizing her daughter's chances for admission to her and her husband's alma mater. My job is to make sure that Megan's applications, *all* of them, are presented as effectively as possible.

"Well, now that all of your applications will be regular decision, the deadline for most of them is January first. Still, I'd like you to have everything done by early December, if possible. That way, you can focus on studying for your finals and then, relax and enjoy the holidays." I look at Megan. "Does that seem realistic to you?"

"I don't see a problem with that time frame," Mrs. Campbell answers. "Megan's already started on some of her essays."

Forcing myself to be polite, I nod at Mrs. Campbell. Then I turn toward Megan and wait for *her* answer.

"It's realistic," she says.

"Good," I say, directing my words to Megan. "We're in good shape then. We have your final list of schools, so you can start completing the online portion of those applications. I'd like to read through all of them when you're done just to make sure your activities and awards are presented in the best way possible and also to check for typos." I smile. "I want to make sure everything is perfect."

"Me too." Megan returns my smile.

"You also need to start asking a couple of teachers for recommendation letters. And is there anyone else, other than an academic instructor, who can add another dimension to your application? Someone who knows you in a different capacity?"

"The lieutenant governor and one of our congressmen are family friends. They've known Megan since she was a baby. I'm sure they wouldn't mind writing letters for her," Mrs. Campbell says.

Friends in high places. It figures. "Actually, I'm thinking more in terms of someone who can tell us something about Megan that doesn't come through on her paper application," I say.

"Well, as I've said, they've known her since—" Mrs. Campbell says, her jaw tightening.

"I've been thinking about asking Miranda Nelson," Megan interrupts her mother, directing her gaze at me. "I did a series of sewing workshops at her store this summer. I came up with all the lesson plans and project ideas myself, and Miranda told me that business increased substantially in the last couple of months. She said they're going to keep running the workshops all year long." A pink flush spreads across Megan's cheeks. "And I got to train the new instructors."

"Miranda Nelson?" Mrs. Campbell, her eyebrows arching over her narrowed eyes, asks her daughter. "What kind of letter would she write? Did she even graduate from college?"

I press my lips together, remaining silent. Mother and daughter need to play this out.

"Yes, Mom. Miranda graduated from college. She was an investment banker, but left her career to stay home with her kids," Megan says. "She always loved sewing and needlecraft, so she opened her store five years ago."

Mrs. Campbell looks at her daughter, opens her mouth, and then closes it. She turns to me.

I nod at Mrs. Campbell and then look at Megan. "I think Miranda Nelson might be able to provide just that bit of uniqueness that could really make your application stand out from the pack."

Megan smiles, and Mrs. Campbell fixes her eyes on me. "You're the college counselor, *Jenny*. I'll defer to your judgment."

"Okay then." I look at Megan. "I'd like you to email me some notes or rough drafts of your essays in the next week or so. Then we'll set up another time to meet."

"Okay," Megan agrees.

Mother and daughter stand, and so do I. "Before you leave, I just want to let you know that as of November first, I'll be meeting clients in my apartment instead of this office. I live in Sea Grove Gardens. It's just a few miles away from here."

"You're giving up your office?" Mrs. Campbell asks, her question sounding like a challenge.

"Well, for the time being, I—"

"That's very unusual, Ms. Gilbert. Everyone I know meets their college advisors in their offices." She sniffs. "Not in their *apartments*. May I ask you why the sudden change in venue?"

Because I can't pay my bills, I don't say the words that catch in my throat. Instead, I offer my prepared excuse. "The office is being renovated."

Her eyes scan the space, moving from the walls to the floor and finally up to the ceiling. "What are they doing?"

Why are you the only one of my clients to ask that? I don't say those words either. I choose to go with, "I'm not sure exactly. I just know they plan to renovate and need me to relocate, at least temporarily."

"Is the whole building being renovated?" Mrs. Campbell crosses her legs and stares at me, her head tilted. "Do all the tenants need to relocate?"

"It's being done in sections," I say quickly. "I'm not sure of the exact timetable."

"Okay, then." Mrs. Campbell lets out an exaggerated sigh. "We'll meet in your apartment after November first."

We say good-bye, and I walk them to the door. Leaning against it, I survey my office. Three upholstered client chairs face a large polished wood desk with a cushioned swivel chair positioned behind it. My mother's seascape painting hangs over a long credenza on the perpendicular wall, and a set of shelves filled with college catalogues and reference books dominates the opposite side. It's the space of a successful professional, a space that was important for me to have.

Was important.

I remember the day I signed the rental agreement for this office. It was just over a year and a half ago. I had already found my first apartment in Sea Grove Gardens, filling it with my as-of-then unpacked boxes. But there was no way I could meet clients there, not in an apartment decorated with columns of cardboard. I juggled the figures and crunched the numbers, and even now, I can still smile when I recall the Eureka moment when I realized that yes, I could afford to do this. And I *could* afford it. *Could.* Past tense. But that was *before.* Before I rented my second apartment, before I unpacked my boxes, and before I realized how much more I still need to buy.

And those, the things I still need, *are* important. Much more important than an office that exists only to showcase my professional success.

Anyway, I do have this space until November first. I gather up my laptop and my bag, turn off the light, lock the door, and head for home.

16

"Can you come for Sunday dinner at my parents' house?" Nick's invitation had sounded casual.

"I'd love to," I'd told him, not sure if it was true.

Why am I so nervous? I'm almost twenty-nine years old. I've met boyfriends' parents before, and I'm not even sure that Nick is my boyfriend. We haven't put a name on each other. Are we exclusive? I certainly don't want to see anyone else. But does he? *Is* he?

"Stop!" I command myself. Out loud. I'm being ridiculous. He's a *man*, not a boy, and I'm a woman. I should be past the point of needing labels. We are...something. And that's enough. But his parents? Their house? *Sunday dinner?*

I stare at my reflection in the full-length mirror in my bedroom. White shirt tucked into my best jeans, black not blue, the right degree of casual for a Sunday dinner at home, I hope.

No, the shirt won't work. What if I spill tomato sauce on myself? I move to my closet. My black shirt? No, too much black. Olive? No, that color makes me look sallow. Purple? That's the one. I change my shirt and step back to the mirror. It works.

Turning around and letting my eyes roam, I survey the room. My bed is made, my pillows are fluffed, and my books are neatly stacked across my headboard. Everything is in its place. No one would know that I haven't slept here in weeks. But suddenly, I remember that there's one thing missing.

I grab my keys, peek out the door, and scamper into my apartment next door. My eyes go straight to Nick's gift, the ivory dreamcatcher trimmed with feathers and beads, dangling from my bedside lamp. Snatching it up, I dart back into my original apartment and hang it over the edge of the slatted blind covering my bedroom window. Just in case...

I curl my hand around the smooth sea glass pendant hanging from my neck, my first gift from Nick. I always wear it.

The doorbell rings.

"Coming," I call out and hurry to the door.

In Nick's car, we leave Sea Grove. The trees pass by in a blur as we zip along the Parkway heading north. I look down at the bottle of Chianti nestled in my lap. It was recommended by the manager of the liquor store in town. *The perfect complement to an Italian dinner at home,* he told me. Should I have brought a dessert instead? Should I have brought the wine *and* a dessert?

I glance over at Nick. He's quieter than usual, his eyes trained on the road ahead. His hands, curved over the steering wheel, aren't clenched, but they're not relaxed either.

Maybe he knows his parents won't like me. Maybe I shouldn't have brought wine. Maybe...

He clears his throat. "Listen, Jenny," he says, not looking away from the road. "I know I haven't told you a lot about my family."

I touch his thigh, a 'go on, I'm listening' gesture.

"It wasn't my idea for you to meet them yet. I do need to tell you that." He takes his right hand off the wheel and squeezes mine.

For me to meet them or for them to meet me? I swallow, not quite sure how to respond.

"No, that didn't come out right. For an English professor..." He laughs, his eyes crinkling at the corners. "I told my sister about you. A lot about you, actually. But I hadn't told my parents." He shakes his head. "I'm not sure how many Italian-Americans you know with a thirty-three-year-old unmarried son, but my sister mentioned to my mother that...Anyway, you get the picture." Again, that crinkly-eyed laugh. "No pressure though."

I feel my body relax, and I laugh too. "No pressure."

Nick exits the Parkway and drives a couple of miles along the highway before turning onto a two-lane road. We pass a development. Big houses and manicured lawns. Then suddenly, the road curves, and the sidewalks and mown grass disappear, replaced with a thick canopy of trees dressed in their fall colors of orange, yellow, and a deepening green. A light breeze, earthy and cool, floats into the car through our open windows. This part of New Jersey doesn't sell TV shows, but it's the best part of the Garden State. This and the shore. I lean back, inhaling and letting the wind tickle my face.

Nick drives for another five minutes into what looks like a gravelly cul-de-sac. He circles three-quarters of the way around and turns into a narrow paved road marked only by a pair of stone pillars half-hidden by two matching clumps of leafy bushes. The road seems to be cut into the forest.

Where are we going? I don't ask.

"This is my parents' street," Nick says, reading my mind.

The road opens into a wide vista sprinkled with five or six houses, each served by a single lane branching off the main thoroughfare.

"This is…" I begin.

"Different?" Nick laughs.

"That wasn't the word I had in mind. I was thinking more along the lines of 'beautiful' or maybe 'lovely'. But yes, it is…" I hesitate. "Different."

Nick pulls over onto the side of the road, stops the car, and turns to me. "I guess I should explain. These houses," he says, pointing his finger and sweeping his arm from one side of the car to the other, "belong to my family. My aunts, uncles, and cousins live in them. It was my parents' idea, a way for us all to remain close, physically as well as emotionally. It's kind of like a neighborhood of family." He studies my face. "I know this must seem odd to you."

"Wait a minute. I'm not sure I understand." Slowly turning my head, I scan the surrounding landscape. It looks like a small development carved into the woods. It looks like something out of a fairytale. "This is all your family?"

"Well, not *all*." He chuckles. "I have some cousins in Pennsylvania, Florida, Italy." He ticks the locations off on his fingers.

"But how did—?"

"My parents found the property, and they arranged everything."

"And everyone made the move at the same time? Built their houses together?"

"No, it didn't happen all at once. It was a process. People moved as they were ready." He points through the windshield. "You can see there's still room for more homes." He laughs. "As my parents keep reminding me."

"But what if somebody else wants to build here?" I ask.

"Well, that would be up to my parents. They own the property."

I keep my face neutral, not allowing myself to ask the questions racing through my head. *They own the property? Is that what he said? All of it?* Instead, I tilt my head and nod.

The road ends in front of a single house perched on a small hill. The home's ivory stucco exterior showcases an arrangement of terracotta roofs and a series of large arched windows underlined with chrysanthemum-filled planter boxes. It's big, *very* big. Nick parks his Jeep Wrangler on the curve of its circular driveway. I give up trying to make sense of this picture. Instead, I tell myself to go with the flow and ignore the tiny flutter tickling my right eyelid.

Nick jumps out of the car and circles around to open my door just as I reach for the handle. With my left hand gripping the bottle of Chianti and my right hand in Nick's, we walk up to the house. Nick opens the door, and I follow him inside. Even in the foyer, the air is warm and rich with the smell of food. Tomato, garlic, and I-don't-know-what-else. It smells like home, my *idea* of home. It smells like family.

"Nicky, is that you?' a woman's voice calls.

"Rose, they're here," a man's voice answers.

The clattering sound of an approaching avalanche of footsteps grows louder.

"I think they're coming." Nick says with a grin.

I feel my body loosen, and I can't help but smile.

A short woman, her dark hair exploding into a riot of curls framing her face, bounds into the foyer. "Nicky!" She stands on her toes, reaching up to kiss her son.

Nick bends and wraps his mother in his arms. She breaks free and smiles at me, the corners of her makeup-free eyes just a little more crinkly than her son's. "Jenny, welcome!" She grabs my hand and squeezes it, looking into my eyes. "I'm so happy to meet you!"

"And I'm happy to meet you, Mrs. Russo," I say, gripping her hand.

A broad-shouldered man, his thick hair more salt than pepper, comes up behind her. "Never mind this 'Mrs. Russo' business. This is Rose, and I'm Tony." He leans forward and sandwiches his wife's hand and mine into his own.

Nick laughs. "Oh hi, Dad. Nice to see you too."

Mr. Russo/Tony claps a hand on Nick's shoulder. "Nicholas, my boy, it's ladies first. You know that. Ladies first." He winks, catching my eye.

"Why's everyone standing in the hallway? Come in. Come in." Rose shoos us inside.

Still holding the Chianti, I hand it to her. "This is for you."

"That's so thoughtful, Jenny. Thank you. Now go into the living room, all of you," she says, heading into what I assume is the kitchen.

Nick and I follow Tony. A large fireplace set into a stone-covered wall dominates the room. The other walls are painted a warm golden color, and a tapestry rug partially covers the marbled tile floor. Tony stops in front of a large lacquer coffee table and an L-shaped leather couch, motioning us to sit.

"We're sitting here?" Nick asks. "Not in the kitchen?"

Tony whispers, "Your mother says it's nicer to start in here and then move to the kitchen." He rolls his eyes. "She even wanted us to eat in the dining room."

"But there's only six of us, counting Lena and Tom," Nick says. "They're coming, right?"

"They're coming. But you know how your sister is about time." Tony shrugs. "They'll be here. Anyway, I talked your mother out of the dining room. I told her the kitchen was more comfortable. *Nicer.*" He laughs.

Nick turns to me. "This is the 'decorator room'. We never use it." He shakes his head.

Rose comes in and sets a tray laden with a set of glasses, my Chianti, and an antipasto platter onto the coffee table. "I heard that, Nicky." She ruffles his hair. "Don't listen to him, Jenny." She smiles at me.

"Mom, you never let anyone eat in here," Nick says.

"Shh!" She waves a hand at him. "You're not making a very good impression, Nicky."

"I'm afraid it's already too late for that. Right, Jenny?" His mouth curves into a little boy grin as he lightly kicks my foot.

Shaking his head, Tony reaches for the wine and pours. "Please," he says pointing to the filled glasses and raising his own. "I'd like to make a toast to our guest, Jenny, and to her wine and to—" His eyes move to Nick.

"To Sunday dinner!" Nick finishes.

"Yes, to Sunday dinner." Tony nods. "Salud!"

We drink, and Rose points to the antipasto. "Eat, eat."

We feast on bruschetta topped with peppers and olives, skewers of mozzarella and tomatoes, and prosciutto roll-ups. We eat, we talk, we laugh. I watch Nick with his parents, drinking in the casual ease and comfort of it all. A warmth spreads through my body, and it's not because of the food. It's not because of the wine.

"Hel-lo!" the cheery voice of a young woman calls out from the foyer.

A tiny dynamo of energy, preceded by her belly, zooms into the living room. "Hi!" She swoops toward us, bending to hug her mother, father, and then Nick. "I'm Lena," she says to me. I reach out my hand. She takes it and leaning over me, wraps me in a quick hug. "And you're Jenny," she says, her face breaking into a smile. She plops onto the couch next to me.

"I'm Jenny." I laugh, meeting her happy eyes. This girl is seriously beautiful. A pregnant version of Eva Longoria.

I turn at the sound of another set of approaching footsteps. A broad-shouldered man with sandy blonde hair and matching eyebrows steps into the room. "I can't keep up with her even when she's pregnant." He throws up his hands and grins. He kisses Rose's cheek and shakes Tony's hand. He pats Nick's shoulder and stops in front of me. "I'm Tom. Glad to meet you, Jenny." He smiles. "Finally."

"Finally? What are you guys trying to do?" Nick looks at Tom. "You're as bad as they are!" He chuckles.

"Sorry, man. You're right." Tom looks at me. "It's just the Russo way. I'm used to it." He shrugs and smiles.

I smile back, liking the 'Russo way'.

Rose asks about my family. My answer is quick and practiced. My mother in Florida and my brother at Duke, both far away. She nods, her lips pressed together. Lena asks about my career, how I got started, how I find clients. The Russos' own shop talk is limited, but I gather they all work in the family's restaurant. Lena and Tom's first child is due at the end of November. If it's a boy, he'll be named *Thomas* after his father and grandfather.

"That's what I get for marrying an *O'Reilly*," Lena says, patting her husband's arm. "But if it's a girl—"

"Then you choose it." Tom smiles.

Names are tossed into the air like confetti. *Kate, Emma, Samantha, Ashley, Claire…*

"And I guess we have to eliminate *Jennifer* now." Lena laughs.

Nick shakes his head at his sister, then turns to me. "Please excuse my family, Jenny." He rolls his eyes.

I smile, returning his head shake. This is a family that doesn't need excuses.

Tony stands and claps his hands together. "Come, let's go into the kitchen."

Carrying the dishes and glasses from the coffee table, we follow Tony and Rose into the kitchen. The tomato and garlic smell is even stronger in here. It draws me in. Beckoning, inviting, welcoming.

The kitchen is large, huge really, outfitted with stainless steel appliances, granite counters, dark wood cabinets, a long rectangular table, and a center island equipped with both a cooktop and a sink. It's a place for serious cooking and serious eating. I *see* where Nick comes from.

The meal is served in courses. I jump up to help Lena clear the table after each, catching Nick's smile as he watches me. Rose and Tony move toward the cooking area and bring out the next round of food. Nick and Tom serve. An Italian bean soup to start, spaghetti with the cooked-all-day sauce they call 'gravy', chicken parmigiana and roasted vegetables followed by an arugula and gorgonzola salad and then, a fruit and cheese platter.

Delicious, Perfect, Mmm. You're the best! The compliments rain down, and Rose beams, basking in her family's appreciation.

Everyone gets up, carrying dishes to the sink, wrapping leftovers, and loading the dishwasher. The whole family works together, a happy well-oiled machine of six, and I'm a part of it. So different from the way my family operated with my mother cooking and both of us cleaning, waiting for my father's approval. Guess we were a well-oiled machine too. But working together? I shake the memories of my own family dinners out of my head.

Tony pulls a stack of dessert plates from the cabinet and hands it to Tom. Lena grabs the silverware, and I help her set the table. Nick arranges a group of small cups on the counter, and Tony pours water into the espresso machine.

Dessert? After all this food?

Nick opens the refrigerator.

"No," Rose says. "You sit, Nicky." She points to the table and looks at the rest of us. "All of you, sit."

Tony shrugs. "Listen to your mother. She's the boss."

"Never mind, 'the boss'." Rose laughs.

We take our places at the table. Rose opens the refrigerator and pulls out a large covered cake dish, setting it in front of us. "Tony?" She looks at her husband.

Tony lifts the cover. "Voila!"

The cake, wrapped in some sort of glazed shell decorated with a series of graceful swirls and squiggles, is topped with what looks like a flower made of candied fruit, its petals created with cherries, figs, and orange slices. I've never seen anything like it. It's beautiful. For a moment, there is silence. Then the *oohs* and *aahs* begin.

Nick leans forward, stares at the cake, and then looks up at his mother. "Mom? What is this?"

"It's called cassata siciliana." Rose pauses, her face bathed in a happy glow. "It's made with sponge cake, ricotta, candied fruit, marzipan, cannoli filling, and some other things too. But those are the basics."

She cuts into the cake, following the petal outlines, and Tony serves it.

It tastes like cheesecake, but not. The combination of tastes and textures…Even I know this cake is the work of a master.

You've outdone yourself. Fantastic. Incredible. We shower Rose with compliments and praise, and Tony hugs his wife. Love and pride. The kitchen thrums with good feeling.

"We're thinking about including this on the dessert menu," Tony says, gesturing with his fork in midair. "But it takes a lot of time and skill to make it." He pauses and smiles at Rose. "I'm not sure if it would be cost effective."

Tom strokes his chin. "We'd need to consider the price of the ingredients too," he says.

"Marzipan? Candied fruit? They're expensive," Lena chimes in.

"Yes, the ingredients are expensive, but I'm thinking about offering it in only one of the locations." Tony raises his eyebrows. "Maybe Manhattan?"

One of the locations. This house, the property…It's all beginning to make sense to me now.

"That seems like a good idea. The New York customers might be more receptive to a higher priced dessert," Tom says.

Tony looks at Nick, who has been silent, concentrating on his cake. "And you, Nicholas, what do you think?"

Nick glances up at his father. "Mm hmm. Sounds good," he mumbles and digs his fork into the cake.

"Of course, the tiramisu would probably still be the most popular Buon Gusto dessert," Tony says. "The cassata siciliana would just be another option."

Buon Gusto? *The* Buon Gusto? Even *I* know of Buon Gusto. It's supposed to be one of the best places for authentic Italian food in the city. It was too pricey for me as a student, and I never made it there later. I didn't even know they had more than one location.

Buon Gusto…

I glance at Nick, but he's staring down at his plate.

"You have a great family, Nick," I say the moment he settles into the driver seat of the car. "Really. They're so down-to-earth, so casual, so welcoming. They made me feel..." *like one of them*. The words pop into my head, but I stop myself before saying them. I close my eyes and pause, carefully choosing the words I do say. "They made me feel so included."

Smiling, Nick puts the car into gear and heads down the driveway. "My family really liked you, too. My mother already told me that you have the 'Russo seal of approval'."

"You're making that up." I swat at his thigh. "You didn't talk to her privately. I was there the whole time."

"Clearly, you don't know my mother, Jenny." Nick chuckles. "Remember when you were clearing the table? When she asked me to help her pack up the food for all of us to take home?"

I nod, giggling. "She's a sneaky one." I turn my head and peek into the backseat, glimpsing two plastic bags, each holding a stack of food-filled plastic containers. "Does she always send you home with food?"

"Always." He nods. "She sent food home with Lena and Tom too, and there's a bag for each of us. One for you and one for me."

"For *me*?"

"Of course, for you. Why not?"

"That's exactly what I mean about feeling included," I say softly, hugging my arms across my chest.

"My family likes you, Jenny. And they've gotten pretty good at reading people." He pauses. "By necessity," he adds in an almost whisper.

"By necessity?"

"My parents...well, now you know they own Buon Gusto," he says, his eyes on the road. "But most people they meet—most people *I* meet—already know that. Ahead of time."

"So?" I say, thinking that he's right. I don't understand.

"So, people usually have...*expectations*." His knuckles whiten as he tightens his grip on the steering wheel. "They want something."

"You mean a job? In one of the restaurants?"

"No, it's not usually just a job." He snickers. "Most of the time it's a loan or an investment, sometimes even an outright gift. 'You can afford it,' they say."

I look through the windshield at the road ahead. So, Nick comes from a wealthy family, and people tend to ask them for favors. It's a common story. It happened time and time again on the army bases. With a career in military financial management, my own father was a frequent target. Additional paid leave time, increased housing allowances, or reimbursement for dubious expenses…there were always people looking for favors and special treatment. My father adhered to the rules. But, I guess the Russos' situation is different. They *make* the rules.

"We've been burned before." Nick presses his lips together. His shoulders lift and lower in a quick inhale-exhale. "*I've* been burned before."

"Okay…" I say. An open-ended response. I respect privacy. I respect secrets.

He swallows, his Adam's apple moving up and then down. "Her name was Dana." Taking his eyes from the road, he shoots me a quick sidelong glance, gauging my reaction.

"Okay…" I repeat the word, forcing my facial muscles to relax, keeping my expression neutral.

"She was a junior accountant at the firm my parents used. Years ago, before Tom took it on, I helped out with the restaurants' quarterly reports, taxes, things like that. Quite a few times I met with the accountants on my parents' behalf. Dana worked on our account." He shrugs. "It didn't seem like a bad idea at the time," he says, sneaking another look at me.

"Okay…" I say again when what I really mean is *tell me the rest*.

"We were engaged. I broke it off soon after, but I never should have let it get that far. There were so many signs. After she moved in with me…" He shakes his head.

Engaged? Moved in with him? I inhale slowly, quietly. Nodding, I wait for him to go on.

He pushes a long stream of air out of his mouth. "Her spending habits began to change. A new car, more expensive clothing. Just about every day she'd come home with something new. For herself, for the apartment, for...I don't even know what for. She was paying a small portion of the rent, but eventually, she stopped even doing that. We had been talking about getting married, and she was very clear about the type of ring she wanted. The size of the stone, the setting, everything. And I bought it. I tried to please her. There was only one thing I wouldn't do." His mouth closes into a thin line, and he shakes his head. "I wouldn't leave the English department and go into the restaurant business. It took many sleepless nights, a lot of arguments, and a great deal of soul-searching for me to finally realize—"

"How long ago was this?" I ask.

"We broke up about five years ago. I haven't seen her since, and my parents use another accounting firm."

"I'm glad you told me, Nick." I put my hand on his knee. "Thank you."

He smiles and squeezes my hand. "So, Jenny dear, now that you know me a little better, maybe you can understand certain things."

"I do," I say softly.

"Ultimately, it was about honesty," he says. "I didn't know the real Dana. She only showed me what she wanted me to see."

I run a finger along his arm, and my eyelid begins to twitch.

17

Nick's in my apartment. Nick's in my bed. My body, my body together with Nick's, shuts off my brain. No lies, no secrets, nothing comes between us. It's just Nick and me, and the world falls away.

He stays the night, his body curved around mine. The steady rhythm of his heartbeat against my back lulls me to sleep. I wake once, twice, three times, searching for the shadows of my things in the darkness. My body stiffens, and my hands ball into fists. Nick mumbles something in his sleep and moves closer to me. Everything's just next door, I remind myself. Just next door. I lean back, glimpsing the outline of Nick's dreamcatcher hanging from the window blind. The warmth of his body flows into mine, and I close my eyes.

Nick leaves early, rushing back to New Brunswick to teach a morning class. I pull on a pair of sweatpants and a t-shirt, check the hallway, and dart into my apartment next door. I scan the room. My books, my toys, my games, my miscellaneous odds and ends are all here. My body relaxes and I hop onto the bed, sprawling across my cloud-patterned comforter.

Something happened yesterday between Nick and me. A kind of turning point, a moving forward. His family, so warm and kind, so welcoming. I felt...embraced. Yes, that's the word. *Embraced.* But he hadn't wanted me to meet them yet. And now, I understand why. Nick has secrets, too. *Had* secrets. He shared himself with me yesterday. I felt his relief, his sense of unburdening. It was palpable. But my own secrets hang between us.

First, there's Ryan—the brother I wish I had, the lie behind my made-up essay, and the reason Nick remembered me in Starbucks. Then, there's *this* apartment, my secret home. And last, and based on Nick's own revelations, a more important secret than I would have thought, there are my bills and my debt. Nick could make them go away. But I would never allow that. Never. Not now and not before either. That's just not who I am.

I feel a tightening deep within my chest as I remember Nick's words in the car. *Ultimately, it was about honesty. I didn't know the real Dana. She only showed me what she wanted me to see.*

I *want* to be honest with Nick. I *need* to be honest with him. I've been digging myself into a hole, burying myself deeper and deeper. I just don't know how to climb out. And I'm afraid, but there's no solution. I just need to keep being careful.

I look around the room. So many important things here. Pieces of myself. The apartment is still, silent. I get off the bed and stand in front of my black CD tower. Melissa Etheridge, that's who I'm in the mood to hear. I run a finger down the column of discs. No Melissa. I settle for Mariah Carey. Loading the CD into my boombox, I switch it on, adjusting the volume to low, and bring it into bed with me. I let the music wash over me, and I close my eyes. After the final track, the room is quiet. I return my boombox to its shelf and snap the CD into its case, sliding it alphabetically into its place in the tower. Moving to my desk, I open my Trapper Keeper and in neat printing, add one more item to my long list. *Melissa Etheridge CD.*

I head back to my original apartment and take a long, hot shower. I towel dry my hair and pull on a pair of jeans and a long-sleeved shirt. Seeing a missed call on my cell phone, I tap the voicemail icon.

"Hi Jen, it's Mom. But I guess you know that." She laughs. "Anyway, I know it's only a few days away, but I was wondering if you have plans for the weekend. *This* weekend. I just remembered that I signed up for part two of my painting class and also a drawing class that starts a week from Monday. So, I was thinking if you're free, I can use the tickets I won in the raffle to come visit before then. Maybe this Friday to Monday?" There's a pause. "And I'd love to meet Nick. Don't change your plans though. Love you." The message ends with a kiss blown into the phone.

She'd love to meet Nick. I sit down on the edge of my bed, crossing one leg over the other and squeezing my hands together in my lap. I breathe in deeply and slowly breathe out. I could warn her not to mention the boxes. I could tell her I've outgrown that phase, that I've cleaned house. And actually, I'd like her to meet Nick. I can even picture it…my mother, nervous and a little shy, and Nick, drawing her out, asking her about her art. Then my mother would ask him about his family, the classes he teaches, and maybe even what he reads. Eventually the conversation would turn to food. My mother would be charmed. They would both be. Until Nick asked about Ryan. And I *cannot* tell my mother that Nick remembered me, and our relationship began, because of a fantasy I passed off years ago as truth. A fantasy woven from the greatest tragedy of her life, of *our* lives. A fantasy Nick still believes in and a truth I'm afraid to tell him.

I blink, snapping a curtain down on the vision. I can't tell my mother not to come, but I can't let her meet Nick. Not now. Not yet. There's only one way. I dial her number.

"You have reached…" her recorded voice begins.

"Hi Mom, just got your message, and I'd love for you to come this weekend. Friday to Monday would be great. Can't wait to see you! Love you," I say into the phone. "Oh, and Mom, book the flights now so you don't lose them."

I'll let her get the tickets before I happen to remember that Nick will be at an out-of-town conference from Friday to Monday. My next call will be to Nick. I'll tell him that I'll be away for the weekend. Another lie. I press my palm against my throbbing forehead. It's the only way, I tell myself. The only way.

I stare down at my cell phone, my finger hovering above Nick's name. I squeeze my eyes shut and press my lips together. I don't have to do this right away. I can wait for him to call me. For now, maybe I just need to relax. I open my laptop, click on the search bar, and begin to type.

Melissa Etheridge CD.

The afternoon passes, and Melissa Etheridge's *Yes I Am* is on its way. So is Bruce Springsteen's *Greatest Hits* and a six-disc set called *Super Hits of the 90s.*

When the phone does ring, I press it to my ear, listening to Nick's voice, bubbling with the excitement of a little boy lobbying for a trip to an amusement park. "Jenny, I have an idea for the weekend. Would you want to go apple picking?"

Without waiting for me to answer, his words tumble out. "I know a place in upstate New York. They have hayrides and a corn maze too. We could stay over at a bed and breakfast. What do you think?"

What do I think? I think I have to say no. I think I have to lie. Again. I'm prepared. I know what to say. I'm getting good at this. Too good.

"Oh Nick, I'm sorry. That's a great idea, and I would love to go. Especially with you." All true. "But I'll be visiting colleges this weekend." I spit out the lie, keeping my voice even.

"Visiting colleges?"

"Yeah, I do a trip or two a year. I check out the campuses, go on the tours, and talk to admissions officers in order to keep myself current. I go to different schools each time."

"Hmmm, that sounds like a good idea. Maybe even fun," he says. "Where are you going? When are you leaving?"

I'm ready for those questions, too. "This time I'm visiting Penn, Johns Hopkins, Maryland, and Georgetown. I need to leave Friday, and I'll be back either very late Sunday or early Monday."

"Are you going by car? By yourself?"

"Yeah, that's the only way I can get to all the schools in one weekend."

"That's lot of driving," he says. "What time are you leaving on Friday?"

What time am I leaving on Friday? Why does he want to know that? I feel my skin go clammy and cold. "Uh…in the morning. Early."

His disappointed sigh whooshes through the phone. "Too bad. I have classes, or I could go with you." He stops, his voice getting softer. "If you wanted me to, that is."

*If I wanted him to…*I smile just thinking about it. "I'd like nothing better. Maybe you can come next time if *you* want to, that is." The words gush out of my mouth. What am I saying? Not only am I not visiting colleges this weekend, I'm not going at all this year. Those trips are an expense I can no longer afford.

"I do want to, but don't think you're off the hook for apple picking," Nick says. "We'll just have to do it another weekend."

"It's a deal," I tell him.

18

The traffic isn't bad at all, I think as I exit the New Jersey Turnpike and head toward Newark Airport. That's my mother's doing, arranging her flights so I won't have to drive in traffic, always thinking about how to make things easier for me and for my father too when he was alive. I feel a happy flutter deep inside my chest. My mother's coming, and I can't wait.

I follow the signs for *Arriving Flights* and *Short-Term Parking*, slide my car into a space, and make my way to the gate. My mother's plane won't land for another fifteen minutes.

Spotting a vacant seat on the orange plastic bench anchored to a wall, I make a beeline for it, settling in next to a gum-chewing man wearing a New York Giants sweatshirt. I pull my phone out of my bag, bring up my email, and begin to read a client's first draft of his college essay. Lots of work to be done on this one. I catch myself groaning out loud and look up into the gum-chewer's stare. Returning to my phone, I continue to read, tapping out notes until I hear a stampede of footsteps and the hubbub of voices coming down the arrivals ramp. I drop my phone into my bag and jump up from my seat, stationing myself behind the security barrier. A melting pot of passengers spills down the ramp. Couples, singles, a group of laughing teenagers, an elderly man with a cane, and a set of parents toting two sleepy-eyed toddlers. Finally, my mother comes into view, her arm raised in an excited wave, a wide smile stretching across her beaming face. She moves quickly, but without pushing through the crowd in front of her. And then we are wrapped in each other's arms.

"Oh Jen," my mother squeezes me against her, then releases me and steps back. "Look at you," she says, cocking her head. "My beautiful girl."

"My beautiful mother." I smile. It's true. My mother, her face still youthful, her body slim, and her hair thick and shiny, is beautiful. When people say we look alike, I say thank you. So does she.

We have a friendly tug of war, which I win, over who should pull her rolling carry-on suitcase. Then, we're in the car heading down to Sea Grove, my mother and me.

The leafy trees bordering the highway are that early October combination of green splashed with patches of copper, crimson, and gold. My mother's eyes flit from window to window. "I forgot how beautiful New Jersey is in the fall. So different from Florida," she says. "Florida has its own beauty though," she adds quickly.

"Yes, it does," I agree. "Especially when it comes to the winter weather."

"That's for sure, but then, the summers there are brutal, and we're in the hurricane belt during the fall. We've been lucky though. No major storms since I've been down there."

"Well, that's another selling point for New Jersey, then." I laugh. "Direct hurricane hits are pretty rare here. Even last year, Hurricane Irene was downgraded to a tropical storm by the time it reached us."

My mother leans back in her seat, and her voice grows quiet. "You know your father had originally wanted to be a meteorologist, don't you? Before we got married and he joined the army."

"Uh huh." I nod.

"Well, I remember him telling me once that he'd read a statistic that the yearly odds for a direct hit by a hurricane to the New Jersey shore was one in two hundred."

"That's good enough for me."

"It would be for me too." She taps her lower lip. "I miss living here. Sometimes I..." She speaks so quietly I can barely hear her.

"Sometimes you what?"

"No, nothing. Never mind," she says, shaking her head.

"Mom, are you...?" I take my eyes off the road for a moment and glance at her. "Are you thinking of moving up here?" I ask.

I hear her breathe in, and then out. She swallows.

"You know, that wouldn't be a bad idea, Mom. I'd like it," I say. "I'd love it, actually."

"I have been thinking about it," she says slowly.

"And?"

"And…did you know that I was never thrilled about moving to Florida in the first place?"

"No, I thought you and Dad both wanted to go. He got a position with that accounting firm down there. I thought you were happy about going."

She sighs. "I was happy that your father could retire from the army. Twenty-five years was enough. I was happy that he'd found another opportunity, and I was happy that we could finally live in one place. I just wasn't happy that it was in Florida."

"But the weather, the beaches, the condo, the community…I thought you were excited about starting the next phase of your life down there."

"Oh Jenny," she says, shaking her head slowly, her lips pressed into a sad smile, "your father was the one who wanted to move there. I put a good face on it. Just like I always did," she says. "But remember, at the time, you were working in the admissions office at Columbia, and you'd begun to see a few clients privately. You were talking about ultimately moving back to New Jersey." She pats my thigh. "I wanted to be where you were. I wanted to make a home wherever *that* would be."

I blow a long stream of air from my mouth. "But then why didn't you—?"

"Why didn't I...?" she starts to finish my question, then stops.

I keep my eyes on the road, giving her time. I hear her fumbling in her purse. She blows her nose.

"I'm not sure. I guess I wasn't used to questioning anything. That's the way it worked in the army, especially for army wives. Anyway, that's how it was back then," she says. "We all made sacrifices. Not only you and me, but your father too."

"But that was his choice." My grip tightens on the steering wheel. "He was the one who decided to enlist, not *you*."

"Jenny, I got pregnant, and he had to support *us*. It seemed like the best option at the time."

I nod, accepting her answer. Accepting, but not understanding.

"Anyway," my mother continues, "he was diagnosed soon after we moved, and we lost him within the year. You know all that."

"But Dad died three years ago."

"Uh huh."

I need to tread lightly. I choose my words carefully. "So, did you think about moving up here? Back then?"

"Of course, I did. But we overpaid for the condo, and

by the time your father passed away, the housing market had tanked. I couldn't sell it for anywhere near what we had paid."

"I never knew any of this. Why didn't you tell me?" I steal a glance at her.

She shrugs. "There was nothing to be done about it."

"And now?"

"And now, three years have gone by. I have friends. I'm part of a community, and I'm happy down there, except…"

"Except?"

"Except for being so far from you."

"So, would you consider—?"

"We'll see, Jenny. We'll see." She runs her hand along my arm. "Right now, I'm looking forward to a nice, long mother-daughter weekend," she says. "And I can't wait to see your apartment now that you've gotten rid of all those boxes."

"Wow!" My mother says, standing just inside the door to my apartment. Open-mouthed, she follows me in and positions herself in the center of the living room. She pivots as she scans the walls, the floor, the furniture. "I'm speechless," she says, throwing her arms around me and pulling me close.

I kiss her cheek. "So, what do you think?"

Stepping back, she lays her hands on my shoulders. "I think it's wonderful. I think *you're* wonderful, and I'm so proud of you." She stops and looks into my eyes. "I know what all that stuff, all those things, mean to you. *Meant* to you. But the boxes, the stacks, the piles…Everything was getting—"

"Out of control?" I complete her thought, forcing my mouth into a half smile.

"That's a good description." She nods. "But what made you…? How did you finally decide to…?"

"I don't know." I shrug. But of course, I *do* know. The apartment next door became available, and I could afford it, that is before my buying got out of control. And yes, that's a good description. *Out of control.*

My mother's eyebrows shoot up in twin arches. "But what made you finally—?"

"I guess it was time. It became overwhelming. The apartment got so crowded I had to walk sideways down the hall to get to my bedroom. And even though I bought nice furniture, it looked unfinished. It *felt* unfinished, like I had never unpacked. But I couldn't. I knew didn't have the room to put everything away." The words spill out of my mouth. All true. "Also, I got tired of explaining the boxes to anyone who came over. So, I stopped inviting people." True too.

"And now for the big question…Where is everything?"

I swallow, not wanting to lie to my mother. "Well, I donated a lot of it, but I did keep a few things. Do you want to see?"

"Of course, I want to see."

"This way then," I say, wheeling her suitcase down the hall to my bedroom.

"Nice," my mother says as she glances around my immaculate room. Everything in its place. No boxes. "Very nice." Her gaze stops at my bed. "Sunny Bear!" she yelps as she reaches for the bright yellow bear propped up against my pillows.

"I had to keep *him*," I say.

I've prepared. Carefully picking and choosing, I spent yesterday afternoon moving some of my things over from next door *for now*. My mother knows me too well to believe that I would ever, that I *could* ever...

"Of course, you kept him. How could you not?" she says.

"I also held on to these." I open the bottom drawer in my night table and lift out a stack of books. The first five Harry Potters, three Nancy Drews, *Where the Wild Things Are*, *The Cat in the Hat*, and *Goodnight Moon*.

She spreads the books in a fan across my bed. "I remember all of these, and I do understand why you want them." She picks up *Where the Wild Things Are*. "This was one of your favorites. You must have read it a zillion times.

And then later on you fell in love with *The Velveteen Rabbit*. Remember that one?"

I nod, smiling. "How could I not?" I say, echoing her earlier question. How could I ever forget the story of the toy rabbit who becomes real through the love of a child? I have to get a copy of that one, I think, making a mental note to add it to the ever-growing list sitting on my desk next door.

"What else did you keep?" my mother asks.

"Just a couple of Barbies and an American Girl doll," I say.

She gathers the books into a neat pile, returning them to the drawer, and looks up at me. "Jenny, did you buy all of these? And the dolls too?"

"Uh huh."

"Plus everything else that was in those boxes?"

Uh oh. I see where she's going. "Well, I didn't actually *buy* everything. Some of those boxes were filled with things I already had. Papers, clothes I didn't want to get rid of, stuff like that. And the things I did buy...not everything was new. I scoured secondhand stores, flea markets, garage sales, eBay." I slide the night table drawer open again. "Look at these books," I say, pointing inside. "None of them are new."

She runs a hand through her hair. "But still, it must have been a very expensive habit." She stops. "Never mind.

I'm sorry, Jenny. It's not my business. I'm sure you knew what you were doing."

"Mom, don't worry. Please. I've got everything under control," I say evenly. "And besides, look around." I wave my hand through the air. "You can see for yourself that I've given up buying and collecting. I'm reformed." I make myself smile.

"Yes, you are." She nods. "And the apartment looks great."

"Thanks. I even cleaned out a drawer for you," I say, moving to my dresser and pulling a drawer open. "You can unpack. Make yourself at home. But I hope you don't mind sharing a bed with me."

"Mind? Are you kidding? I'm thrilled," she says, stretching out on the bed and leaning back against a pillow, her eyes drifting upward. She points to the feather-trimmed wooden circle hanging from the corner of my window blind. "I see you bought yourself another dreamcatcher. I like it." She reaches up and strokes a feather.

"I like it too, but I didn't buy it."

"That's the one we got in New Hope? Where did you find it?" Her eyes widen. "In one of the boxes?"

"Nope."

"You didn't buy it?"

"Nope," I say with a grin, enjoying her confusion.

"Okay, I give up." She lifts her arms in surrender.

"Well, it is from New Hope, but I didn't buy it," I say, tossing out a couple of clues. This is fun.

Smiling, she narrows her eyes and points a finger at me. "Is it from Nick?"

"Uh huh." I nod.

"But how did he know…?" She pats a spot on the bed beside her. "Come, tell me."

Kicking off my shoes, I plop onto the bed and scoot over next to her, letting my head sink into the pillow.

"This is like the old days. You and me in bed talking about what you did in school, the boys you liked…" she says. "It's good." She smiles, her eyes growing misty.

I reach for her hand and squeeze it. "I'm glad you're here, Mom."

"I am too, Jenny. I am too," she says, returning my squeeze. "But now, tell me."

"We went on a trip to New Hope. I told you about that."

"Yes, you did." She nods. "But go on."

"Anyway, I saw a dreamcatcher in a restaurant there, and I admired it, saying that I used to have one. Nick asked me what happened to it, and I told him I lost it. A day or two later I got a delivery notice, and…" I stop speaking and roll onto my side to face my mother.

Her mouth slowly turns up into a smile. "And?"

"And he dropped it off with Mrs. Thornton."

"He drove down here just to drop it off? To surprise you?"

"He did," I say. "And after he dropped it off, he came back with a box of chocolates for Mrs. Thornton. She told me about it. Now I think *she* has a crush on him." I giggle.

"I bet she does!" my mother blurts out, then covers her mouth.

"Me too," I whisper, touching the sea glass pendant hanging from my neck. "He got me this also."

My mother leans over to look at my necklace. "It's beautiful." She reaches out to stroke it with a finger. "Oh Jenny, I'm so happy to see you like this. You're glowing. You seem filled with...love?"

"Maybe," I say quietly.

My mother sighs. "I just wish I could meet him." She shakes her head. "I was so disappointed when you told me he wouldn't be here this weekend. And it was too late to change my flight. But Jenny, I really wanted to meet him. I *want* to meet him. You have no idea..." Her voice cracks, and so does my heart.

I say all the right things, spouting out all my practiced lines about how disappointed Nick is, how it was a last-minute conference, how he *had* to go, and how upset I am. My chest tightens, and my skin goes clammy. But, I do what I have to do.

We order in pizza, play a few rounds of gin rummy, and fall asleep watching a rerun of *You've Got Mail*. This time when I wake in the night, missing the physical presence of the things that I know are just next door, I have a plan. I slip out of bed, careful not to wake my sleeping mother, and tiptoe into the bathroom. Opening the medicine cabinet, I reach for a bottle of Tylenol PM and shake out two tablets. I don't have a headache, but I do need to sleep.

The late morning sun filters through the slatted blinds and warms my face, gently nudging me awake. Well-rested and just a little dry mouthed, I yawn and stretch, opening my eyes to the day. I'm alone in my bed. The comforter is smooth and neatly tucked in on my mother's side.

"Mom?" I call out.

The apartment is silent. I climb out of bed, peek into the bathroom, check the kitchen, and walk into the living room. No Mom. I unplug my cell phone from its charger and press her number. The front door scrapes open.

"Good morning," my mother sings out, closing the door behind her. Wearing a zippered sweatshirt and jeans, her hair tied up in a ponytail, she holds a Jodi Picoult book in one hand. My keychain dangles from the other. "I must have dropped my book in the car. You were still sleeping, and I didn't want to wake you. I borrowed your keys. Hope you don't mind," she says, dropping my keychain back into the small dish I keep on a ledge by the door.

"Of course not," I say. "I usually don't sleep this late. I must have been really tired. Guess I just can't keep up with you." I laugh.

"Guess not." She shrugs. "Anyway, I got a chance to meet one of your neighbors."

"Really? I barely know them myself except to say a quick 'hello' or 'good-bye'. Which one did you meet?"

"Greg, the one upstairs."

"Greg? You met Greg?" The words come out more sharply than I intend. I quickly change my tone to sound more casual. "How'd you meet him?'

"I was just leaving your apartment. He was getting his mail, and he stopped me when I walked past. He asked me if I was your sister," she says with a girlish giggle. "Can you imagine?"

Oh yes, I can imagine. I can imagine it perfectly. Greg, spotting my pretty and young-looking mother coming out of my apartment, his nosy antenna perking up at the sight of her, then moving in on her like a vulture. My skin prickles at the thought. I shudder.

"Jen?" My mother leans toward me, staring at my face.

"Oh, I'm sorry. I'm just surprised. That's all." I shake my head. "Not surprised that he'd think you were my sister,"

I add quickly. "No, definitely not that. Just surprised that he was here. Out. This early, I mean," I say, my tongue tripping over the words.

"Well, it's not really that early. It's already after nine."

"No, you're right. Guess I was just a little disoriented when you weren't here."

"I'm sorry," she says. "I didn't want to wake you."

"Mom, please. Nothing to be sorry for. I'm the one who's the lazybones," I say, turning toward the kitchen. Time to change the subject. "So, are you hungry?"

"Kind of. Can I take you out to breakfast?"

"Well, I thought we could eat here, then head out to the boardwalk. It's beautiful outside," I say. "Unless...I didn't even ask you...What do *you* want to do while you're here?"

"Nothing special. I don't have an agenda, other than spending time with you."

"Sounds good to me. Then let's eat, shower, and head outside."

I switch the coffeemaker on and arrange boxes of cereal, cartons of milk and orange juice, a basket of bagels, and packages of butter and cream cheese in a neat line on the kitchen counter. My mother sets the table.

"Sorry I'm not much of a domestic goddess," I say.

"Are you kidding? This is perfect for me." She reaches for a bagel. "I miss New Jersey bagels. Somehow, they don't make them quite the same in Florida. I think it has something to do with the water."

"Good. Glad you like them," I say, looking down as I pour the orange juice, "So, tell me about your conversation with my neighbor."

"Oh yes, Greg. He seems like a very nice guy. Good looking too. And he seems to be very interested in you, not that you're available." She smiles.

"What makes you think he's interested in me?" I ask. Casually, I hope.

"Hmmm...I don't know exactly. Just a feeling. He told me he met you when his cousin lived in the apartment next door, and that you're taking care of it now while the new tenant is away. He said he had wanted to move in there. 'Next to Jenny'." She raises her hands, bending her fingers into quotation marks. "He seemed...I don't know...like he wanted to get to know you better."

"He's a salesman. I think that's just his way." I shrug.

"Well, he seemed nice," she says.

"Yeah, he's nice," I force the words out and bite into my bagel.

Finishing breakfast, we clean the kitchen, shower, and grab our jackets from the hall closet. As we pass through the living room, my mother leans over the vase of white roses centered on the coffee table and breathes in. "You've really made this your home, Jenny," she says, squeezing my shoulder as we head to the door.

My mother and I climb the three shallow steps leading up to the boardwalk. As if pulled by an invisible magnet, we walk straight ahead to the metal railing separating the weathered gray planks from the sand and drape our arms over its ancient crossbar. The beach vista opens up into a layered trio of colors. The cloudless sky a shade of blue that doesn't look quite real, the deeper turquoise glint of the ocean, and the golden tan of New Jersey beach sand. A salty breeze blows across our faces and lifts our hair.

"I think this might be my favorite time of year at the Jersey shore," my mother says. "It's not too hot, not too cold. The summer crowds are gone, but people are still around. And everything's open, at least on the weekends." She leans back against the railing and turns to face the boardwalk.

"And there's no traffic. No line for the bathrooms." I laugh. "People down here call this time of year, from Labor Day 'til Halloween, 'local summer'."

"Local summer," she repeats, nodding slowly. "I like that."

"C'mon then, it's all waiting for us. We've both got our walking shoes on," I say, pointing down at our sneakered feet. "Let's go." I link my arm through hers, and we set off.

Sharing the boardwalk with strolling couples, laughing teenagers, and the occasional runner, we wander into a small shop selling souvenirs and sundries at postseason slashed prices.

"I could use a new visor," my mother says, sifting through a hodgepodge of hats, scarves, and visors spread across one of the crowded store's many display tables.

I meander through the shop and drift past beach balls, sand shovels, sunglasses, towels, and screen printed t-shirts. Summer's leftover merchandise. Not much of interest.

My mother plucks a pair of black canvas visors from the table and waves me over.

"What do you think?" She slips one onto her head and hands me the other. "One for you and one for me?"

"It looks good on you, Mom, but I don't need one."

"Never mind. Put it on, and let me see," she says. "Please."

I position the visor on my head and stick out my tongue. "Okay?" I giggle.

Her shoulders shake with laughter. "Okay," she says, snatching the visor from my head and carrying them both to the register.

I pull out my wallet, but she catches hold of my hand. "Put that away, silly." She hands the smiling cashier four singles. "Two dollars each. I can't leave them for someone else, can I?" she says, holding back a grin.

As we leave the store, sporting our matching visors, I spot a dusty collection of tiny seashell dolls lined up along the sill of the front window. The kitschy figurines with painted faces and bouffant skirts are made entirely of glued together seashells. I bend down to get a closer look. I had one of these once, a small souvenir from a childhood trip to the beach.

My mother peers over my shoulder at the row of dolls. "Does anybody still buy those?" she whispers.

"Guess not. They have a lot of them." I shrug, and we walk out into the sunshine. I turn back to the store and glance at the sign hanging in its window. *Beach Treasures.*

We spend the afternoon walking the boards punctuated with a few well-earned rest stops at strategically placed ocean view benches. After playing a round of mini-golf, we duck into a noisy arcade for a quick game of Skee-Ball. Then we gorge ourselves on hot dogs and frozen custard. When the sun sinks, turning the sky a fiery orange and gold, we head back to my apartment, tired and happy.

"What a day, Jenny," my mother says, untying her sneakers and collapsing onto my couch. "I haven't had this much fun since...I can't remember when."

"It was a great day for me too, Mom." I plop down next to her. "But don't you do anything for fun in Florida?"

"I didn't mean it that way, Jenny. I do have fun in Florida. I work part-time in the gift shop, and I take art classes. I paint, draw, exercise, swim. I have a nice group of friends too."

"What kind of friends? Women? Men?"

"Both," she says.

"So, does that mean you're…uh…dating?"

She shakes her head. "I'm not really interested in dating right now. I've got enough to keep me busy."

"You know Mom, Dad's been gone three years. Maybe it's time to—"

"This is going to be hard to explain, Jenny," she says, placing her hand over mine. "Dad and I got married young. We started a family right away, and then with military life, there were always so many rules to follow. I never really had the chance to be on my own before." She pauses and looks into my eyes. "And I kinda like it."

"Mom…" I swallow and run my tongue across my bottom lip. "I know I wasn't a planned baby."

She holds up her hand. A stop sign. "Jenny, you came earlier than we had expected. That's true. But your father and I loved you with all our hearts. Maybe you weren't planned, but you were very much wanted."

"I know that, Mom. And I've always felt loved by you *and* by Dad. It's just that our lives were so rigid, so controlled. And Dad didn't seem to have a problem with any of it. It's like he was born for the army."

She shakes her head. "No, Jenny. He wasn't *born* for it. He adapted, and so did I. And you…you were born *into* it." She pauses. "When we were in high school, your father was what you'd call a 'scholar athlete'. He played baseball and football, and he graduated at the top of our class. Everybody loved him. He wanted to be either a meteorologist or a science teacher. The military wasn't on his radar back then. You know that. But when I got pregnant, we decided to get married and…" She stops speaking, and her hand flies up to her mouth. Her face pales.

A sudden chill grips my shoulders and moves down my arms. My mouth falls open, and I hold a fisted hand against my throbbing chest. "Wait…You…What…?" My tongue trips over the words.

My mother presses her hands to the sides of her face and looks into her lap. Slowly, she lifts her head, and her wet eyes meet mine. "We never told you. No reason to, your father said, and I agreed. No good would have come of it."

"So, you were pregnant with me when you got married?"

She nods.

"But what about Dad's proposal when you were on spring break? With the beer can flip top? Your barefoot wedding in Florida? Are those fairy tales?" The avalanche of questions tumbles out of my mouth.

"No, not at all. They're not fairy tales. That's exactly the way it happened." Her lips turn up in a sad little smile. "But what you didn't know was that at the time, I had just found out I was pregnant."

"But why? Why didn't you tell me?"

"I don't know." She shakes her head and closes her

eyes. "No, I'm not being fair. That's the easy answer." She moves closer to me, and we sit together, our bodies touching from hip to knee. "It just never seemed to be important for you to know. But maybe I was wrong. Maybe it would have helped you to understand your father." She reaches for my hand. "Jenny, he put his own dreams aside because that's how much he loved us," she says. "*Both* of us."

"But what about *your* dreams, Mom? What did *you* put aside?"

"Nothing. I was young. I was in college. But I'm not like you, and I'm not like your father. My dream back then, my only dream, was to spend the rest of my life with him... and with you."

I feel a hot tear make its way down my cheek. "I just have one question then, and I need you to answer it truthfully, Mom," I say.

"I will. I promise."

"If you hadn't gotten pregnant, do you think you and Dad would have eventually gotten married?"

"Yes." Her answer comes quick, and her voice is strong. "Oh, yes."

I lay my head against her chest, and she pulls me into her arms.

"I'm sorry, Jenny. I'm so sorry I didn't tell you," she whispers the words into the air. "Please forgive me."

Laying a hand on each of her shoulders, I lean back

and look into her eyes. "There's nothing to forgive, Mom. Nothing. It's okay to keep secrets to protect someone you love," I say.

Or yourself.

Sunday morning. The beginning of my last full day with my mother before she flies back tomorrow. Propped up against my pillow, I gaze down at her sleeping form. Her face is smooth and relaxed. She's free of a burden. Secrets can be so very hard to carry, especially when you're keeping them from the people you love.

As for lies…they're even worse.

Quietly, I slip out of bed so as not to wake her. On my way to the bathroom, I catch sight of my cell phone plugged into the charger on my dresser. I haven't even looked at it since we got back here last night. That's not like me. I press the center button, and the screen lights up with a text from Nick.

Missing you, Jenny. Hope your college visits are going well.

I check the time the message was sent. Seven o'clock. Last night.

It's a quarter to nine now. More than twelve hours have gone by. It's a long time for me not to answer a text. Especially from Nick. I type quickly.

Just got your message. Had phone on silent all day. Forgot to turn sound back on. So sorry! Visits going well. Miss you!

I add two more words and three exclamation points.

A lot!!!

I hit *Send*, then walk into the bathroom and turn on the shower. The warm water rains down on my head and over my body. I massage my neck and shoulders, willing their tense achiness to disappear down the drain. I need to relax and enjoy the day. Everything will be fine. I've got it all under control. Wrapping myself in a warm fleecy robe and gathering my hair into a wet ponytail, I open the door to the bedroom.

My mother is sitting up in bed, flipping through a magazine.

"Morning!" she says, looking up with a smile. "Looks like today I was the sleepyhead." She pats the space next to her. "This is a very comfortable bed."

It is comfortable, or anyway, it *was*, that is before I got the bed next door. Just one more night 'til I can sleep there again.

"Glad you like it," I say. "So, what do you want to do today?" I peek through the blind behind her. Another clear and sunny day. "I ordered good weather for your visit," I say, kissing the top of her head.

"Definitely something outside then. Any ideas?"

Ideas? Of course I have ideas. A garage sale junket, a

trek through the Englishtown Flea Market, or maybe even a trip into New York City for a tour of the secondhand and vintage shops. But, never mind. Those are ideas for another day—without my mother, without anyone.

Instead, I say, "What do you think about going to Deerwood Park? We can make sandwiches and have a picnic. Hike the trails?"

She claps her hands together and bounces on her toes "I love that idea!"

A quick stopover in the kitchen, and we've got two tuna sandwiches, a couple of bananas, water bottles, and a bag of pretzels stuffed into a cooler. Lunch is ready, and so are we.

We drive fifteen minutes west, away from the shore, and the land is different. Homes built on sandy soil decorated with hedges and vegetable gardens give way to leafier landscapes and greener lawns. The air is different too. The salty tang of the ocean breeze is gone, replaced with a fresh cut grass scent sparked with the earthy smell of clean dirt. A few more miles and I spot a weathered wooden sign mounted on a wide stone base announcing that we've arrived.

As we pass under a canopy of trees, each a collage of green, red, and gold, I drive slowly along the narrow road leading us into the park. The lot is dotted with cars, but there are still plenty of spots. This time of year, the lure of pumpkin picking has probably drawn a lot of regular visitors away from the parks. Apple picking too.

Would you want to go...? I know a place in upstate New York.

The memory of Nick's voice, his excitement, jolts me. Tomorrow. I'll talk to him tomorrow.

I slide my car into a spot and point across the parking lot to a tree-shaded meadow sprinkled with a scattered array of picnic tables. "Lunch time, Mom." I say, grabbing the cooler from the back seat.

We claim a table and unpack our food. The crinkly rustle of a light breeze floating through leafy trees, a chorus of bird chatter, and the whooping laughter of a group of children playing freeze tag in the grass merges into a Sunday-in-the-park kind of soundtrack.

"Did you ever notice that food always tastes better when you eat it outside?" my mother asks, biting into her sandwich.

My mouth full, I answer with a crooked smile and a nod.

We finish eating and head back to the car to drop off the cooler, now holding only the bag of pretzels neither of us could finish. Water bottles in hand, we follow the signs to the hiking trail. As we step onto the dirt path and move into the wooded area, the fallen leaves snap-crackle-pop under our feet.

"I miss this," my mother says, her cheeks rosy in the slight chill of early autumn.

"Hiking?"

"Not only that. The whole thing. The fall, the woods, the shore, the seasons. And you." She stops and turns to face me. "I miss *you*."

"I know." I nod, biting down on the corner of my lip. "I miss you too."

"And I wanted to meet Nick, Jenny. I really, really wanted to meet him."

"I know. I wanted that too, and so did Nick," I say. "But you will," I add, knowing that it's true. "Next time." I just need to figure everything out. Somehow.

We meander along the trail, passing old fence posts, a large pile of logs, and a few fallen trees. A family of white-tailed deer runs deeper into the woods, and my mother snaps a picture. After we traipse through a muddy intersection, the path gently inclines and then descends until it opens onto a grassy, flatter area with lots of trees. Following a series of white arrows, we continue on past what looks like a tool shed and a fenced-in nursery flanked by twin birdhouses. The trail bears right, and the terrain becomes slightly hillier as we complete the loop and catch sight of the parking lot. We head downhill to the car, and tired-in-a-good-way, we climb inside.

"Jenny?" my mother says my name, her voice a question mark.

"Yeah?"

"Is it too early to think about dinner?" she asks sheepishly.

"Not for me," I say, suddenly conscious of the dull emptiness in my stomach. "What are you in the mood for?"

"Well, now that I'm back in New Jersey, let's hit a—"

"Diner!" I yell out, finishing her sentence.

"Great minds…"

"Uh huh," I say, driving out of the park. "And I know just the place."

When I make a right turn into the Silver Bell Diner, my mother says one word, "Yes!" With its shiny chrome exterior and brightly lit sign, the Silver Bell is an updated version of the quintessential New Jersey diner.

At the entrance, we are greeted by a bored-looking hostess wearing a too-tight shirt. "Table or booth?" she asks.

"Booth," my mother and I answer in unison.

We follow our unsmiling leader past a long counter and a refrigerated glass case stocked with the biggest cakes and pies I've ever seen. Stopping beside a red upholstered booth, she drops two menus onto the table. "Someone will be right here to take your order."

We flip through the laminated pages of the gigantic menus even though we both already know what we want. Turkey and bacon club sandwiches, the kind that are cut into quarters and held together with frilly toothpicks, along with a pile of golden brown French fries to share. We devour our dinners, which also come with small plates of coleslaw and sides of pickles.

"Can I get you ladies dessert?" the waitress asks.

My mother leans back in the booth and groans. "Not for me."

With my own stomach the kind of full that is bordering on discomfort, I shake my head no. My mother snatches up the check, and we lumber back to the car. It was worth it.

Monday morning. The time for my mother's flight back to Florida has come too quickly. I walk with her as far as the security gate.

"Mom…" Her name catches in my throat.

She wraps her arms around me, pulling me tightly to her chest. "No long good-byes," she whispers into my ear. "I don't want to cry."

Too late for that.

Blinking back my own tears, I step back and squeeze her hands. "I love you, Mom. So much."

"And I love you, my darling daughter." She kisses my cheek and walks through the gate.

19

"How was your trip?" Nick asks.

Even over the phone, the sound of his voice sends an electric tingle down my arm. What's wrong with me? I'm a grown woman, and I feel like a lovesick teenager. I need to get control of myself because his question is dangerous. *How was your trip?* But like the high school debater I was and the good student I've always been, I'm prepared.

"The trip was good. Very productive. Everything ran smoothly," I say.

"So, tell me."

I'm ready for this too. Penn, Johns Hopkins, Maryland, and Georgetown. I did that trip last year. Four college visits in three days with two nights in hotels and a lot of driving. Walking tours, group information sessions, and individual meetings with admissions officers and alumni. I share the details of my trip, just not the fact that I did it a year ago rather than over the past weekend.

"Too bad you couldn't extend it a little and make it down to Duke."

My brother at Duke. Another lie that Nick believes.

I cough to hide the tremor in my voice. "Yeah, it is too bad," I say, glad he can't see my face which I'm sure has gone pale.

"That way you could have combined a college trip with a visit to Ryan. Probably even expensed it." He chuckles.

"Actually, I did make the trip down there with him when he was accepted," I say. A small fib in the scheme of things. "But I wouldn't mind doing it again. Maybe in the spring."

"I'd like to go with you," he says. "If you want me to."

"Of course I want you to," I say. I'll figure out a way to deal with it later. Spring is a long way off.

"But more importantly, when can I see you?" he asks.

My mother's gone, the bed is made, and my things are back in my second apartment. My answer is a no-brainer. "Now."

His warm chuckle is my reward for an instinctive response. "How about an early dinner at the shore then? Casual. Wanna bundle up and brave the boardwalk? I can get down there around five, if that's good."

"Yes, that's good," I say. "It's very good."

Five minutes to five. I do a quick walk through my apartment. I know everything's in its place. Nothing from next door lying around. But I want to double check.

Living room, kitchen, bathroom, bedroom. I don't see anything that doesn't belong. But something's missing. Something...The dreamcatcher! It's back in my other apartment. I need to get it *now*.

Dashing into the hallway, I race next door and fit the key into the lock. As I push the door open and step inside, I hear a voice call my name. Nick's voice. Spinning around, I trip on the doormat, knocking my knee against the wall.

"Are you okay?" Nick runs toward me and reaches out for my shoulders, steadying me as I step backward into the apartment, regaining my balance.

"I'm fine," I say as he follows me inside.

"What were you doing?" he asks.

"I-I'm sorry. I'm ready. I just needed to... I forgot to...I...uh...I thought I heard...a noise. In the apartment." I look around, my head bobbing like a nervous pigeon's. The place is just as I left it. One large space furnished with a bedroom set, a desk and chair, an assortment of plastic storage boxes, toys, games, books, dolls, and things. Lots of things.

"Who lives here?" Nick scans the room, his mouth open, his eyes wide. "And what is all this stuff?"

"Oh, her name is...uh...Ashley. She's away, and I'm checking on her apartment. You know... watering the plants and that kind of thing." I shrug. "She's a little unusual, I guess."

"I'll say." Nick walks the perimeter of the apartment, scanning the bookcase filled with children's and young adult books, stacks of games, and accumulations of toys and dolls. "How old is she?"

"Late twenties, early thirties. I'm not sure exactly."

Nick tilts his head back, looking up at the toy hammock stretched over my bed and sagging beneath the weight of dozens of stuffed animals, and lets out a long, low whistle. "Why does she have all this?"

"I-I think she buys and sells this stuff at flea markets, maybe on eBay too. I don't know a lot about it."

"And why doesn't this apartment have walls? Rooms?"

"Oh that? Chloe, the girl who used to live here, was an artist. She took down the walls, and Ashley liked it that way." I move toward the window, lift the blind, and check the lock. "Anyway, looks like everything is fine here. I probably didn't hear anything. Must have been my imagination. So, we can leave," I say heading toward the door.

"Jenny…?" Nick stares at me.

"Yeah?"

"I don't see any plants here," he says.

"Oh…uh…they died."

"They died?"

"Uh…yeah. I used to water them though."

"Okay…"

I'm at the door, but Nick hasn't moved. He stands rooted to the center of the room, his eyes on the night table next to my bed. He turns to me. "Jenny…?"

I follow his gaze, and my body goes weak. The room begins to tilt, and I feel nauseous. Seasick.

He walks to the night table and lifts the dreamcatcher, his gift to me, from the bedside lamp, letting it dangle from his hand. "What's going on here?"

Nick's face is a mask of confusion, his brows lowered over his squinted eyes, his mouth partway open. I've never seen him look like this before, and I'm afraid. Afraid to watch as his expression turns from confusion to hurt, which I know it will. I can't do this anymore. I can't. My right eyelid twitches in a series of vicious spasms, and a wave of dizziness whooshes through me, making it hard for me to keep my balance. I stumble to the bed and gripping the corner of the mattress, I turn and sit. My head falls into my hands, and I cry. Great heaving sobs rock my body. I cry and cry and cry.

The bed creaks, and Nick's solid warmth is beside me, his arm around my shoulder. "It's okay, it's okay, it's okay," he whispers into my hair.

My breath comes in ragged bursts, and I bury my face in my sleeve. Nick reaches for the box of tissues on my night table and hands it to me. I blot my eyes and blow my nose.

Holding my face in his hands, he kisses my forehead. "Tell me, Jenny. Tell me."

I swallow and lean back, meeting his gaze. I open my mouth, but my words are trapped inside.

"Who lives here, Jenny?" Nick's voice is soft, gentle.

The answer to his question floats in the air just out of my reach. "No one," I say.

"Then who does all of this stuff," he asks, his head turning, his gaze taking in the room and everything in it, "belong to?"

"M-me," I mumble, staring down at the floor. "It belongs to me."

"Jenny, please." Nick lays a hand on each of my shoulders. "Tell me what's going on. Explain it to me because I don't understand." He lowers his head and presses his forehead to mine. "And I want to."

My throat is raw. My voice is hoarse, raspy. "It's hard… hard to explain. I-I don't even know where to—"

"It's okay. Take your time," he says, reaching for my hand.

I breathe in. And out. My shoulders rise and fall. I run my tongue over my lips and open my mouth. "When I was a child, we moved. And we moved. Then we moved again. That's how it was for all military families. My father got orders, and we left. My friends, my school, everything. It was the way things were. The way we lived. I had to make new friends, try to fit in, learn my way around a new base or a new neighborhood. Again and again and again. It's hard to explain…" I stop, pulling my lower lip into my mouth.

"I'm listening," he says quietly.

"I know. It's just that…you see…" I press a crumpled tissue to my nose. "Every time we moved, I didn't only lose people and places, but I also lost *things*. *My* things. Or the things I *thought* were mine. Dolls, books, games, toys. I had to leave behind or give away so many things. Over and over and over."

Nick nods, his eyes on mine, his forehead wrinkled. He's listening, and I know he's trying to understand.

I click my tongue against the roof of my mouth, trying to come up with a way to explain it to him. "Nick, when you took me to your apartment, it was filled with so many things that were important to you. The baseball your father caught at a game, a globe you won in high school, even a rubber band ball."

"You remember all of that?"

"I do," I say, "because those things have meaning. They have value. They're part of who you are. And no one made you get rid of them. No one ever said…" My voice grows hard. "*There isn't enough room* or *You're too old for that.*"

"But how did you get all of this?" he asks, his head

turning slowly, taking in the room and everything in it. "Where did it come from?"

"I've been searching and collecting and buying for years. It started in college when I saw a Pound Puppy in a secondhand shop. It looked just like the one I used to have. I wanted it. I *needed* it. So, I bought it. From then on, I found more and more things, and I started to buy them."

"But why the second apartment? Couldn't you just keep everything next door where you live?"

"I did for a long time. I kept everything packed in cardboard boxes, hidden away. I couldn't let anyone see. No one would understand." I feel my eyes begin to water again. "But a few months ago this apartment became available, and I could afford it." *Could.* I wrap my arms around my shoulders, enfolding myself in my own cocoon.

"Jenny...?" Nick leans toward me, his arms crossed in his lap, our thighs touching. "Where do you live?"

"Next door. I live next door," I answer quickly. "But I do spend time here."

"Doing what?"

"Nothing." The answer pops out of my mouth, but it's not really true. And I do want to tell Nick the truth. Finally. At least about this. "No, not exactly *nothing*. I think. I relax. I dream. It comforts me to be around all these things, the physical pieces of my childhood. Nick, lots of people can go back to a home, a childhood bedroom, a place from their past." I swallow. "For me, this is that place."

"And the dreamcatcher?" he asks, pointing to the feathery circle that he'd dropped onto the bed.

"I sleep here sometimes," I say quietly.

Nodding and reaching for the dreamcatcher, Nick carries it to the night table and carefully drapes it over the lamp. He returns to the bed and positions himself in front of me, bending to take my hands in his. Gently, he pulls me up. "Show me, Jenny. Show me your things."

We tour the apartment, Nick's hand on my back, supporting me. My books, my dolls, my stuffed animals, my games, my toys. He wants to know everything—what I remember about the originals, where I found the replacements, how it's all organized.

I talk and talk, answering his questions as best I can. I smile. I laugh. My embarrassment, my shame, my self-consciousness all begin to fall away, peeling off of me like layers of an onion. Hours pass, and we collapse onto the bed, facing each other.

"So, now that you know," I say, turning serious, "do you think I'm crazy? Deranged? Ridiculous?"

"No, that's not how I would describe you, Jenny." Nick rubs his chin, his eyes focused on a spot somewhere above my head. A thinking posture. He lowers his eyes to meet mine before he speaks again. "I like the word you used to describe the fictitious Ashley."

My mind is hazy with words, lies, stories. "What word was that?" I ask.

"Un-us-u-al," he says slowly.

"Unusual," I repeat the word. "I'll settle for that."

"But I do think you are also a neat freak and a...collector," he says. "And maybe a bit of a hoarder."

My head drops, and my jaw goes slack.

He brings a finger to my lips. "Let me rephrase. You are an *unusual* neat freak and collector with hoarding tendencies," he says. "But that doesn't disturb me."

"No?" A hopeful flutter flickers deep inside my chest.

"No." He inhales and lets his breath out slowly. "What disturbs me is that the woman I seem to be falling in love with has kept such a big secret from me."

On top of my cloud-patterned comforter, surrounded by the things of my childhood, Nick pulls me closer. Something inside of me loosens, comes undone. We open our mouths, ourselves, to each other. And we are together.

I wake in Nick's arms, his hand in my hair. The room is an early evening kind of dark. I yawn and stretch my legs, pointing my toes. Nick reaches back and turns on the lamp, bathing the feathery dreamcatcher in its soft glow.

"Looks like we both fell asleep," he says, glancing down at his watch. "Eight o'clock, and I still owe you dinner. Hungry?"

"Actually, I think I am." I say, suddenly conscious of my empty stomach.

"What are you in the mood for?" Nick props himself up on an elbow and turns toward me.

I tap a finger against my lips. "I have an idea," I say. "What do you think about staying in and ordering Chinese food?"

He nods. "I like it."

Forty minutes later we are in my original apartment slurping wonton soup and picking up pieces of kung pao chicken with wooden chopsticks.

"Do you ever eat next door?" Nick asks, wiping his mouth with a napkin.

"No, I really don't. I don't even have a kitchen table in there. You saw it. It's set up more like one big room than an apartment."

"That's true. It is. But then why didn't you just rent one two-bedroom apartment instead of two one-bedrooms? It probably would have been less expensive."

"You're right. It would have been, but...the truth?"

"The truth," he says, laying his chopsticks down. "From now on, Jenny. 'The truth, the whole truth, and nothing but the truth'." His mouth smiles, but his eyes are serious.

"I was embarrassed. I didn't think anyone would understand. And how would I explain an apartment with a room that was always kept locked?" I shake my head. "It was easier this way."

"So, does anyone else know about the second apartment?"

"No."

"Not even your mother? Not even Ryan?" Nick asks, his eyebrows lifting.

Ryan. I flinch at the sound of the name, and my body goes rigid. "No," I answer quickly. "No one else knows. Only you."

Nick reaches across the table and takes my hand.

"So, what do you think?" I ask. "Are you okay with this? Is it weird? Am *I* weird? Do you understand it? Even a little?"

He smiles. "Those are a lot of questions." He shakes his head. "Weird? Maybe. Does that matter? Not to me," he says, answering his own question. "Do I understand it? I don't know. I need to think about it. But again, it doesn't matter. You know Jenny, if at some point you lived in a house with someone who..." Not finishing his sentence, he stands up and moves behind me. His warm hands grip my shoulders. "You could have a room. All to yourself. And it wouldn't matter." His lips brush the top of my head. "But please, no more secrets, and no lies. Ever." He wraps his arms around my chest.

I lean back, melting into his embrace, breathing deeply and hoping he doesn't feel the hammering of my racing heart thudding against his arms.

20

*M*egan sits across from me, my desk between us. She seems taller, somehow older without her mother next to her. Mrs. Campbell was ill and couldn't make the meeting. She'd wanted to reschedule, but Megan had insisted on keeping our appointment. *Go Megan!* I had silently cheered her on.

This will be our last meeting here. November is only three weeks away, and then I'll be leaving. Leaving the Clayton Professional Building, leaving this office. *My office*, the space I've rented for almost two years. But I don't *live* here. It's not my home. Still, I need to get my head around the idea. It'll be fine. I know that. Everything will be just fine.

The space was fully furnished when I rented it. So, it's only a matter of packing up my files, some desk accessories, and my mother's seascape. I brought a box so I can take them with me when I leave today. Starting next month, I'll meet clients in my apartment, and I'll save all that money in rent. I really don't need an office, and with the extra cash, I can get more of the things I'm missing in my second apartment. Those are the things I do *need*, not an office.

"Can I send you my essays by the first week in November? Would that be okay?" Megan's voice summons me back to the present.

I blink and quickly return my focus to her. "That would be fine, Megan. You're applying regular decision everywhere. So, your earliest deadline is January first. Your rough drafts are excellent which means it's only a matter of doing the revisions we discussed. I'll do the final edits, and then you'll be good to go." I drum my fingers on the desk and lean toward her. "Hopefully, we can get everything finalized before Christmas break."

Megan grins and nods. "That's my plan."

"Okay then." I push my chair back, ready to end our meeting.

"I-I just have one more question," Megan says.

"Sure. Ask away."

"I'm thinking of re-doing my essay on the person who's been the greatest influence on me. The one about my sewing teacher?"

"Really? That's a great essay. A creative choice and beautifully written," I say.

A pink flush spreads across Megan's face, and her chest rises and falls as she slowly breathes in and then out. "I want to write about you."

"Me?" I feel my own face grow warm and picture it reddening to match Megan's.

"You probably think it's strange, and I realize I haven't known you for that long, but..." She looks down at her hands, tightly folded in her lap, and then returns her gaze to me. "You've influenced me," she says. "Probably more than you realize."

"I'm flattered, Megan. But I'm a little confused."

"I thought you would be. It's just that...I mean I was thinking about..." She swallows, closes her eyes, and shakes her head, as if clearing it. Opening her eyes and looking into mine, she begins again. "Since we started meeting, I've been watching how you deal with my mother. She can be difficult at times."

I press my lips together, holding back a smile. "Your mother has strong opinions on some things," I say. "But she does want what's best for you," I add quickly.

"I know that. But she's not always right. And somehow, you've gotten her to bend a little, to see that maybe Columbia might not be the best school for me."

"Megan, I don't think she's very happy with me about that."

"But that's the point." Megan puts her hands on my desk, fingers splayed, and leans toward me. "You got her to see something from another point of view. *Mine*. You were polite, and you were logical. And you didn't back down. My

mother respects you. I think she even kind of likes you."
She giggles.

My eyebrows jump up, and I bring my hand to the back
of my neck.

"So, in terms of an essay, I learned from you. And
it's not only about dealing with my mother, although that's
major, it's also about standing up for myself. Making myself
heard and earning respect, but doing it in a way that doesn't
stop people from liking me. And I could also tie this in with
some of things you've told me about your own background.
All that moving around and how you learned to adapt to
new situations, places, and people." She rubs her chin. "I
think it's all about *your* basic honesty about who you are.
That's what my mother responded to, and I did, too."

Honesty. That word again. 'Honesty is the best policy'.
Isn't it? The air around me grows cold, and I feel my arms
prickle with goosebumps. But the young woman sitting
across from me, her face hopeful and trusting, deserves an
honest response, and I give it to her.

"I'm not quite sure what to say, Megan. I'm truly flattered, and the fact that you'd consider writing about me…it
means a lot. Really."

Her eyes sparkle and widen. "So, you think it's a good
idea?"

"Well…" I begin, feeling my own eyes narrow into a
squint. "My biggest concern is with our relationship and the

way you know me." I shake my head. "I don't think it's a good idea to mention on the applications that you have a private college counselor advising you."

"I thought about that too," she says. "So, I was thinking about saying you're my cousin or maybe a friend of the family."

I press my lips together and bite back the words I want to shout. *No! Don't do that!* A small white lie on a college application. It's done all the time. But small fibs can grow, spreading their roots far beyond the initial white lie. I loosen my grip from the arms of my chair and unclench my jaw, knowing I need to tread carefully.

"Megan, I want to tell you again how deeply touched I am that you'd even consider writing about me. I mean that. But I need to take my own personal feelings out of this and put my college advising hat back on," I say, giving my head a quick double tap and clicking my tongue against the roof of my mouth. "Quite honestly, I'm afraid you'd be opening yourself up to some potential problems by using me as your subject. First off, you'd have to come up with a story about how you know me. Then, you'd have to mention my occupation, fictionalizing it, of course. After that, you'd need to create some sort of scenario for my interaction with your mother." I tick the points off on my fingers. One, two, three. "So, although your end result would have a core of truth, the details would turn the actual essay into a piece of fiction."

"But why would that matter in an essay that's only going to be read by college admissions people?"

"It only matters because the essay is an opportunity. It's *your* opportunity, not only to strengthen your application, but also for you to get to know yourself better, to clarify your own thoughts and feelings, and to express yourself. And although there are many other reasons too, those alone are enough for the essay to be…" I pause, struggling with the next word. *Honest?* No, too hurtful. *Truthful?* Same problem. Opting for diplomacy, I finish my sentence with "… completely factual."

I don't tell her that once a story is told—or even worse, *written*—it can live on for a very long time. Nor do I tell her that sometimes writing fiction, especially about something that *might* have been, can be an even more powerful way of knowing yourself, laying bare the empty places in your life. A picture of my eighteen-year-old self spinning a wishful fantasy about a brother named Ryan dances in front of my eyes. I blink and block it out.

"So, you think I should stick with the essay about my sewing teacher?" Megan asks, her voice a soft whisper.

"I love that essay, Megan, and in my opinion, it's the way to go. But ultimately, it's your decision."

Megan's forehead wrinkles, and she rubs a knuckle across her bottom lip. "I understand what you said, and I think I agree," she says slowly. "I'm going to use my original essay." Then her mouth widens into a grin. "But you're right, it is my decision." Her head bobs up and down in a happy nod.

And just like that, it is resolved.

For her.

21

I slide a chair away from my kitchen table and settle into it. Three seats remain, enough for a client and a set of parents. The padded chairs are comfortable, and the table is large enough to accommodate laptops, papers, brochures, notebooks, and anything else we'll need. By the end of the month, this space will have to function as both my kitchen and my office.

"It's only temporary, just until I finish buying what I need for my second apartment. Then I'll be able to rent an office again. It'll be okay," I say out loud. "It has to be," I add, my voice dropping to a whisper.

My cell phone rings. A welcome distraction. Nick's name lights up my caller ID. Even better.

"I know we got a little sidetracked the other night, but are you still up for that walk on the boardwalk and dinner at the shore?" he asks. "I checked the weather. It'll be clear tomorrow night. Not too cold. What do you think?"

"Does that mean you didn't get scared off by my... *hobby*?"

"Guess I don't scare that easily." He laughs. "Not in this case anyway."

"I'm glad you're a brave guy, Nick. And yes, the board-walk and dinner sound great."

"Six-ish?"

"Six is good," I say, "and -ish is fine too," I add, chuckling.

He really is okay with it, I think, clicking off my phone. The second apartment, the buying, the collecting. He knows all about it, he's even seen it, and he still wants to be with me. For such a long time, I've been hiding my things, making up stories, renting a secret apartment, telling everyone that I'd gotten rid of the boxes, that I was done. I never thought anyone, not even my mother, could ever understand it, could ever accept it. But Nick Russo is not just *anyone*. A tingly warmth rises up from deep inside of me. My body feels light and full all at once.

I skip across the floor to the hall closet and snatch up my bag, slinging it over my shoulder. There's a little store on the boardwalk that has just the seashell doll I need. I reach for the doorknob, but turning on my heel, I look back into my apartment. My mother's seascape hangs to the right of my wall unit. It looks good there. Smiling, I head to the boardwalk.

I'm not exactly sure what 'six-*ish*' means, but it's ten minutes of, and I'm ready. I vacuumed and dusted both apartments and changed the sheets on both beds. I'm not quite sure where Nick and I will end up tonight, but I hope it'll be together. I haven't moved the dreamcatcher from its spot next to the bed in my second apartment. It watches over me each night while I sleep. But this time, I don't need to race next door to sneak it back here. Nick already knows.

"And he still wants to see me," I say the words softly, gratefully.

I lean over the vase of white roses centered on my coffee table and breathe in. This is what home smells like, I think, closing my eyes. I live in this clean, bright, minimally decorated space that is my original apartment, and I live next door in my world of things too. Both spaces belong to me, and I belong to them. *In* them.

I think about Nick's words. *A room all to myself in a house with someone who...*

I settle into the sofa, sinking into its cushioned seat, and I stretch my legs out under the coffee table. For the first time, I know I'm home. Here, next door, and in my own skin. *Thank you, Nick.*

The bell rings, and I open the door. Nick, in jeans and a worn leather jacket, his longish hair combed back except for the piece that flops onto his forehead, is a beautiful man.

Inside and out. And somehow, he doesn't even seem to know it.

"I wasn't sure where I'd find you." he says, leaning in to kiss me, "here or next door." He pulls me to his chest, laughing into my hair.

I step back, slipping out of his arms, and look at his face. "Are you making fun of me?"

He moves toward me, erasing the distance between us, and presses his palms to my cheeks. "Not at all. I was teasing you," he says, fixing me with his eyes. "I'm sorry."

"Don't be. I'm just oversensitive. This is all so new for me. I've never told anyone, never shown anyone...No one knows. Not a single person. No one," I say, shaking my head.

Nick reaches for my hand, curling his fingers around mine. "Then I guess you just didn't find the right *one*," he says, "until now."

"Until now," I repeat his words, knowing they're true.

"You need to trust me, Jenny."

"I will." I swallow. "I do."

"Good," Nick says, a slow smile spreading across his face, lifting his eyes at the corners. "And now that that's settled, are you ready to hit the boardwalk? First, we walk, then we eat."

"Sounds like a plan." I nod. "Let me just grab a jacket." I pull a thickly knitted sweater coat from my closet and wrap a scarf around my neck. "I'm ready."

"Then let's do it," he says, giving my scarf a playful tug.

I lock my apartment, Nick's hand lightly touching the small of my back, and we step out of the building and into the October evening. The sky is striped with shades of pink, orange, and purple shot through with thin strands of high wispy clouds.

"Look at the sky," I say, waving my hand through the air.

Nick's head swivels, and his gaze travels up and around. "It really is spectacular tonight," he says, his lips pushing out a thin whistle.

"It is. I think there's something especially beautiful about fall and winter sunsets. It has to do with the lower angle of the sun and the longer path of light through the atmosphere." I point up at the sky. "Those are cirrus clouds. They usually mean good weather, but not always."

"Wow! I'm impressed," Nick says, turning to face me. "You remember a lot more high school science than I do."

"Not really. My father loved weather. I mean, as much as it's possible to love *weather*." I laugh. "He wanted to be a meteorologist when he was younger."

"Did he ever pursue it?" Nick asks.

"No, he couldn't. He needed to support his family. Meaning *me*. So, he got a job in the Army," I say, "which meant he had to settle for watching the Weather Channel and explaining cloud formations to anyone who would listen."

"You know, you and I are both lucky to have careers doing work we love. For most people, that's not a reality," Nick says, reaching for my hand as we follow the walkway leading from my building.

"You're right." I nod slowly. "And that's not something I usually think about or appreciate."

"On most days I don't either, but sometimes—"

"Jenny?" A familiar masculine voice calls out from behind us.

I glance at Nick and roll my eyes. He smirks, recognizing the voice, and we both stop walking and turn to see Greg loping down the walkway, hurtling toward us.

"I thought that was you, girl," he says, directing his words only at me. "I know you even from the back." He winks, showing off his large white teeth in a wolfish smile. Then, quickly glancing at Nick, he mumbles a "hey buddy."

"Hello Greg," Nick says, extending his hand.

Greg shakes Nick's hand, his eyes darting from Nick's face to mine. "Hello, uh..."

"Nick," Nick says evenly.

"Oh, that's right. Nick. Now I remember. Sorry about that." Greg nods and shifts his gaze to me, raising his eyebrows. "So where are you guys off to?"

"Just the boardwalk," I say and turn to Nick. "We should probably get going though."

"Don't let me keep you then," Greg says, his voice overly bright. "I'm just going to my car." He points toward the parking lot. "So, I'll turn off here. Nice seeing you both."

"Have a good evening, Greg," Nick says.

"You too," Greg says and turns toward the lot.

Nick smiles and shakes his head. I shrug, and we continue along the walkway.

"Hey Jenny?" Greg's voice calls out. Again.

Nick lets out a groaning chuckle, or maybe it's a chuckling groan, and we both stop, turn, and look at Greg. I glower, telegraphing my annoyance through my clenched jaw and the tight line of my mouth. What now?

"I forgot to ask you," Greg says, taking a step toward us. "Did your mom tell you I met her last weekend?"

My body goes rigid. My knees lock, and my legs grow leaden. A cold sweat prickles the back of my neck, and my right eyelid begins to twitch.

"W-what?" I shake my head, trying to dislodge the right answer. The answer that will make this moment go away.

"I saw her by the mailboxes." Greg's eyebrows dip down over his eyes. "She didn't tell you?"

"Uh…"

"Nice lady. You guys look alike, and that's a compliment." Greg winks. "To you both. Anyway, I gotta get going." His hand flips up in a quick wave.

I stare at his back as he strides across the grass toward the parking lot. My feet are rooted to the ground, and I stand still. Frozen.

"What was that about?" Nick asks slowly.

My heart thumps wildly, and a wave of dizziness sweeps over me. I swallow and wet my lips, but the words don't come.

Nick steps in front of me and turns, his eyes drilling into mine. "Jenny, was your mother here last weekend?"

"Well...she...I mean..." My throat closes, and my eyes begin to water.

Nick looks at me. He doesn't move. He doesn't touch me. "It's a simple question, Jenny. Was your mother here last weekend? Yes or no?"

He stands, and he waits. The air grows cold, and an icy chasm opens between us.

I sniff and nod, biting down on my lower lip.

Nick's face goes pale. "And where were you?" he asks.

"Here," I whisper.

"But, what about your college trip? Weren't you...? Didn't you...?"

I shake my head.

"You didn't go?"

"No." My answer comes out in a croak.

"So, everything you told me...the driving, the meetings, the tours?"

I push my lips together and shake my head again.

"You made that all up?" he asks, the large vein in his neck pulsing. "You were here the whole time?"

I swallow and nod.

Nick's mouth falls open, and his eyes go small, turning into hard pebbles. He crosses his arms over his chest and steps to the side, planting his feet wide apart. "Why? You didn't want me to meet your mother? She didn't want to meet *me*? She doesn't know about me?" His questions explode in a fierce outburst of hurt and anger.

"I do want you to meet her, Nick, and she wants to meet you too." I stop, closing my mouth.

"So…?"

"I told her you were away for the weekend."

Nick leans toward me, then steps back. "Let me get this straight," he says, his brown eyes turning darker, colder. "You told *me* that you were on a college trip, and you told *her* that *I* was away?"

"It's not that simple, Nick. I can explain. Please…" I reach for his hand. "Come back inside. We'll talk there."

He pulls his hand away and shoves it into his jacket pocket. "I don't want to go back inside. We're alone here. There's no one else around." He moves his head in an exaggerated swivel. "I'm listening," he says.

I ball my hands into fists, digging my nails into my palms, and hold my trembling arms against my body. I close my eyes and breathe in. Then, opening them, I exhale. "I couldn't let you meet my mother because then you'd find out…" I stop and close my mouth, swallowing the rest of my words.

"Find out what?" Nick asks.

My eyes go watery. I blink. "About Ryan," I say quietly.

"Your brother? Was he here too?"

"No. No, it's not that." I shake my head and squeeze my eyes shut.

"Then what is it?" Nick asks, not waiting for me to answer. "He's in prison? He's a serial killer? What, for Chrissakes, Jenny? What?" He stretches his hands out in a palms-up plea for the truth.

I open my eyes and clear my throat. Then I force out the next words. "He's not real. I made him up."

"What?"

"I don't have a brother, Nick."

"You don't have a brother." He repeats my words in a monotone, his right foot tapping a hard staccato on the concrete walkway.

"No, I don't have a brother." I repeat his words in a whisper.

"Okay," Nick says, stepping back and clamping his hands across his chest. Waiting.

"I know the essay I wrote for your class was supposed to be non-fiction, but mine wasn't true. It was a fantasy.

Ryan was a fantasy. He was the brother I wish I had, the brother I was supposed to have. He was the baby my mother lost." I tell Nick my story in a gush, the words tumbling out. The truth.

"You told me he was at Duke, that you visited him there. You told me lots of things about him. I don't even remember them all."

"I know," I say, looking down at my feet.

"But why, Jenny? Just tell me why."

I lift my head, my chin trembling, and meet Nick's eyes. "Back when we met, in Starbucks, you approached me because of that essay. That's why you remembered me, and that's why you wanted to see me again." My mouth tastes of metal, like I'm chewing pennies.

"So, after all this time, after everything we've become to each other, you still didn't tell me the truth." He shakes his head slowly. "And not only that, you came up with even more stories." He rubs his forehead. "Jenny, you turned your original writing assignment," he spits out the words, "into a full-blown fairy tale."

"I only told you what I had to in order to answer your questions."

"Why didn't you just tell me the truth? That's all. Just the truth." Nick's voice is flat. His body slumps, his shoulders hunching forward.

A flood of nausea surges through me. "The timing never seemed right. And then, after I told you about my second apartment, I couldn't tell you this too. Not yet."

"Jenny, you didn't *tell* me about your second apartment. I discovered it. By accident."

"But I would have told you," I say, "eventually."

"E-ven-tually," he repeats the word slowly, shaking his head. "This is a different situation, Jenny. Your second apartment was a secret. This is a lie. More than *one* lie. It's a..." He stops, searching for the right words. "It's a web of lies. Layers of lies upon lies upon lies."

I shift my gaze away from him, fixing it on a spot above his head, and stare at the boardwalk and the ocean beyond it. "I just wanted to be *that girl*. The girl who wrote the essay, the girl who had Ryan as a brother, the girl you seemed to be—"

"Do you honestly think our relationship is based on an essay? That's it? An essay you wrote ten years ago?"

"No, I don't. But I was afraid. I didn't know if you'd—"

Nick moves toward me and lifts my chin with his finger. "No, Jenny. You don't know. That's the problem. You don't know me, and I don't know you." He presses his palm to my cheek and turns away.

I stare at his back and watch as he leaves me.

"Nick?" I call out, his name scratching against my throat.

He stops and turns, his face a mask of sadness.

"Goodnight, Jenny," he says and turns back toward the parking lot.

22

*M*y body feels heavy on the outside, hard to move. But inside, I'm completely empty, a vast blank space. I'm like a ghost trapped in a suit of armor. I force one foot in front of the other and stumble into my building. My head throbs, and my throat is dry. I lurch past the door to my original apartment and go directly to my second one, fumbling with my keys until I finally fit the right one into the lock. I push the door open and collapse onto the bed, pulling the cloud-patterned comforter around me and burying my head in the pillow.

A dull gray late morning light filters through my closed eyelids, nudging me awake. I roll onto my side and wrap my arms around myself, feeling the armhole seams of the shirt I wore last night dig into my flesh. I don't care. I just want to sink back into the peaceful oblivion of sleep. I close my eyes and start to count backwards. One hundred, ninety-nine, ninety-eight, ninety-seven, ninety-six...

I stop at thirty-five. It's no use. My mind refuses to go into sleep mode. Instead, it insists on replaying my conversation with Nick. I'm not sure what I could have done differently. Probably nothing. Last night was already too late. I wasn't prepared. I was caught off guard. *Greg.* It figures he'd be the one to ruin everything.

A white-hot flash of anger rips through me. My mother mentioned her chance meeting with him. But instead of planning ahead for a *What if?* scenario, I brushed it off as a minor annoyance. I should have had an explanation, a story, a reason prepared in advance just in case. Or maybe I just should have told Nick the truth. The sharp bite of my sudden anger turns into a dull ache. Anyway, it doesn't matter. Not anymore. I can't change what's already happened. I close my eyes, envisioning Nick's face, his expression morphing from confusion to frustration to hurt to sadness, all over the course of a twenty-minute conversation on a concrete walkway.

'Good-night, Jenny'. That's what he said. But that doesn't mean *goodbye*, does it? Did it? Was he ending the night, or was he ending…?

I jump out of bed and pounce on the bag I dropped by the door last night. I dig out my cell phone. The screen is dark. I punch in my passcode. No voicemails, no missed calls, no text messages. Nothing. I pull up my list of contacts and scroll down to Nick's name. I stare at the letters, N-I-C-K, my finger hovering above his number.

"No," I say the word out loud, jerking my finger back. I fling the phone onto my bed.

As much as I want to dial Nick's number and hear his voice, calling him now doesn't feel right. He needs time. But my own day stretches out ahead, long and empty. My SAT class is over and doesn't begin again for a few weeks, and my clients are all busy writing their essays. So, there's no editing for me to do right now, which means that for the next week or so, all I have is time. Endless hours of time.

I look down at my wrinkled shirt, my slept-in jeans. I need to get out of these clothes. Shower. Start a new day.

I grab my keys, sling my bag over my shoulder, and take a step toward the door. Then, I turn around, facing back into the apartment. The toys, the books, the stuffed animals, and the medley of trinkets from my childhood that I've put so much of myself into finding, and actually getting, are all here, in *this* apartment. I really don't want to leave. And suddenly, I know exactly how I'm going to spend the rest of the day.

Most of the afternoon and twelve trips. That's all it took, and now I'm done. Empty kitchen cabinets and a rarely used bathroom made it easy for me to put everything away. Clothes, towels, toiletries, dishes, the contents of my refrigerator and pantry, my TV, and even the vase of white roses and my mother's seascape. I did have to take some of my games and toys out of the closets in order to make room, but they're neatly piled in stacks on the floor, and I'm all moved in. Over the last few months this apartment, my second, has felt more and more like home to me. I sleep here, and I spend most of my time here. Now I can shower and eat here too. I'll just have to buy more containers and shelving to put the rest of my things away. No big deal.

I pull a package of turkey, a head of lettuce, and a jar of mayonnaise out of the refrigerator and put together a sandwich. I pop the top on a can of diet soda, and I'm ready for dinner. There's just one problem. I don't have a table. Other than the kitchen and the bathroom, this apartment consists of the one big room that I've furnished with a bedroom set, a desk and chair, shelves, and a lot of storage bins. That layout, and the fact that it was just next door, was the reason I wanted it. My plan was never to move in here. But plans change. I still need to keep my original apartment to meet clients and have a place to host the occasional friend, but that doesn't mean I have to actually *live* there.

"And if Greg finds out? So what?" The thought, as I say it out loud, is oddly freeing. A little scary too, but mostly freeing.

For now though, my biggest concern is where to eat.

I glance around the apartment. I don't have the floor space for a table, not a full-size one. I suppose I could get some sort of a small nook and wedge it into a corner. But I don't really need a piece like that. Could I eat on the bed? In the bed? Take a chance on letting a stray crumb or an accidental spill invade my sleeping space? No. Never. I'm still my father's daughter. At my desk? No. Too many things I'd have to move. There's only one option left...

Standing in front the kitchen counter, I wolf down my sandwich and then wash and dry my plate and utensils. With my soda can in hand, I move to my desk and settle into the chair. I flip open my laptop and get to work.

The first thing I need is a bean bag chair, that squishy, shape-shifting pillow that molds to your body. It's a good place to eat, soft and comfortable, and I won't need a table. I had a denim one when we lived in New York. I close my eyes, remembering the mid-winter blizzard just after I turned twelve that forced school to close for three glorious days, the snow falling too fast and too hard for me to even think about building a snowman. Each of those afternoons my mother, with a 'don't tell your father' warning, let me plop into that mushy blob of a chair in front of the TV with a dish of macaroni and cheese nestled in my lap. But somehow when we unpacked after my father's transfer to Colorado, the chair had gone missing. Another casualty of military life. I do an online search. The denim version is a bit more expensive than the nylon, but it's the chair I had, and it's the chair I want. I'll pick it up at Bed Bath & Beyond tomorrow.

Now for the TV. I've moved my flat screen from next door in here temporarily, but what I really want is a small white TV/VCR combo like the one that sat on the dresser in one of my teenage bedrooms. My father had come home with it the day he told me he had received orders for yet another *permanent* change of station, that one coming in the middle of my sophomore year of high school. I search the local retailers online and then Amazon before turning to Google. I didn't realize that a tube TV would be so difficult to find, but eBay comes to the rescue. I pay a little extra to have it in two days.

Videocassettes are next. I want the old school stuff, no DVDs. I start with *Home Alone*, *Pretty Woman*, *Edward Scissorhands*, and *Titanic*. They're easy to find, even in VHS format. Click, click, click, click. I add all four to my online cart. And then there's *Clueless*, the movie that taught me the definition of 'makeover'. I add that one too.

A bean bag chair and an old movie will have to be my new dinnertime companions *for now*, that is until Nick… I check my phone again. Still no word. I scroll down my list of contacts. Best not to overthink this. I press my finger onto his name. The phone rings, and rings, and rings again.

"You have reached…"

I touch the red circle on my phone, ending the call. Slipping a long-sleeved t-shirt over my head and stepping into a pair of flannel pajama pants, I head into the bathroom. I wash my face and brush my teeth. With the TV remote in one hand and my cell phone in the other, I climb into bed and pull the comforter up to my chin. Zipping through the channels, I stop when I see a young blonde actress somersaulting through the air, landing with her foot thrust into a bad guy's face. Buffy, that Vampire Slayer of the nineties, does her thing on the small screen while I switch off the bedside lamp, laying my phone on the pillow beside me.

"Call me, Nick," I whisper into the air. "Please call me."

"Excuse me, can you tell me where I can find bean bag chairs?" I ask the name-tagged woman folding a stack of striped towels.

She looks up, jerking her head toward the back of the store. "In that corner. Just past the candles."

"Thank—"

"No problem," she mumbles, her eyes already back on the mound of yet-to-be-folded towels towering in front of her.

I push my cart past rows of packaged sheet sets, a three-shelf display of coffeemakers, and a hanging assortment of kitchen gadgets that I have no idea how to use. I bet Nick would know. A collage of images dances through my mind as I stare past the collection of utensils.

Nick filling a bag with tomatoes and cucumbers at a roadside stand, Nick plunging his knife into the center of an uncut pizza, Nick flipping pancakes in his kitchen, Nick scooping out servings of his mother's gravy-drenched spaghetti.

My eyes begin to water as my throat closes. Stop, I tell myself, blinking quickly and digging my nails into my palms.

A bean bag chair, a denim one. That's what I need to focus on. I steer my cart past a wall of multi-sized picture frames and around a long table stocked with an array of scented candles. Behind it, I spot a jumble of bean bag chairs wedged into the corner of the store and make a beeline toward it. Letting my eyes roam over the rainbow-colored pile until I find a single patch of blue denim, I reach into the squishy heap and carefully pull the chair out. Gently, I place the oversized bean bag on the carpeted floor and lower myself into it, sinking into its cozy embrace. It's exactly what I need. I lean back and arch myself into a full-body stretch. Perfect. Lifting the chair into my cart, I head toward the cash registers.

As I approach one of the checkout lines, the aisle narrows, forcing me to maneuver my cart between a pair of large wire bins. The one on my right is stuffed with a massive collection of bed pillows. Standard, queen, and king sizes in down, feather, and polyester. The bin on my left boasts an equally large collection of backrests, those half-chair reading pillows that appear on just about every college dorm bed. I had one when I was in high school. Guess I was ahead of my time. I poke through the bin and pull out one in navy corduroy, almost a clone of the backrest I remember, and toss it into my cart. Satisfied with both of my finds, I take a spot at the end of a checkout line.

Even with a coupon, the total is more than I expected. But now I have what I need. That's the important thing. The American Express statement won't arrive for another few weeks. I'll worry about it then. I stuff my bean bag chair into the trunk of my car and slide the backrest onto the passenger seat. Slipping my hand into my bag, I pull out my cell phone. The screen is dark. No messages. No missed calls. Nothing. I pop open my never-used ashtray and stand the phone inside where I can see it. I turn on the radio, and a smooth voice drowns out the deafening silence of my phone.

"And in the news, Tropical Storm Sandy has become a category one hurricane and is predicted to move through the Bahamas and parallel Florida's east coast without making landfall."

"Yessss." I exhale the word in a sign of relief. No touch down in Florida. That means my mother is safe.

I put the car into reverse, back out of my parking spot, and head for home.

I stand just inside my apartment, leaning back against the door, my arms crossed over my chest. The place looks good, It really does. My bean bag chair sits at the foot of my bed, and my backrest squats mid-center in front of my pillows. A denim chair, a navy corduroy backrest, and a blue cloud-patterned comforter. The colors of my youth. They work well together. They did then, and they do now.

I pivot in a slow semi-circle, my eyes sweeping the apartment. Books, games, dolls, stuffed animals, an array of things. My collection surrounds me. The videocassettes I ordered will arrive in a few days, and the TV/VCR will be here tomorrow. I need to buy more, but I'm off to a good start for now. It's a work in progress.

Still, a gnawing emptiness grows inside my stomach, reaching up to my heart. I step into the kitchen and open the refrigerator. Some cheese, a few yogurts, a carton of eggs, and an opened package of turkey. Nah. I peek inside the freezer. A couple of TV dinners and half a container of vanilla ice cream. Nothing of interest there either. I open the pantry closet. A potpourri of boxes, cans, and jars. Also disappointing, not surprising though. I'm not hungry, not for food anyway.

Nick…

I move out of the kitchen and step into the large open area that is the space where I truly live. From the toy hammock filled with stuffed animals that stretches across my bed to the dresser decorated with lip glosses, candles, and bottles of discontinued cologne to the shelves stocked with the brightly colored books I remember and love, this is the place where I've finally been able to free all the things I've painstakingly collected over the years from the cardboard box prisons that held them captive until I was able to rent this apartment. So many things, now mine, as they used to be, and I can live among them. I glance at the piles of games and toys stacked on the floor. They're neatly arranged, each column ordered by size from the largest on the bottom to the smallest on top. A landscape of carefully balanced and evenly spaced pyramids. Still, they could topple. What if that happens? What if they fall? What if I come home one day and find my toys and games strewn across the floor, pieces broken or even missing? I can't take that chance.

Stepping gingerly around and through the tiny mountain range of toys and games, I reach for my bag. I need to pick up another shelving unit and a few more plastic containers. At the door, I turn and look back into the apartment.

Furniture, shelves, my new bean bag chair, and lots of piles. It's getting pretty crowded, but I'll make room. Everything will be neat and organized, the way it's always been. I lock the door and head to my car.

23

Easy to assemble, no tools required!

So the instructions said. Yeah, right. But no matter because two hours and one bruised finger after I opened the long rectangular box I carted home from Target last night, a tall set of white laminate shelves stands in the back corner of my apartment. That unit, along with the two large plastic crates I also bought, should do it. Squatting in front of the stacks of boxed games piled on the floor, I pull them out one by one, keeping them in size order, and slide them into my newly assembled set of shelves. Everything fits except for my backgammon set. I place it on my desk, centering the leatherette case on the blotter.

Toys are next. I fill the crates with my talking Furby, a trio of Polly Pocket playsets, a bag of Playmobil figures, a box of Legos, my green and yellow Super Soaker, a six-pack of Play-Doh, and a bubblegum pink Barbie convertible. I stack the crates and squeeze them into the last open spot along the wall.

Stepping backward, I move toward the door and lean against it. Overfilled shelves, bins, crates, bookcases, baskets, and a hanging toy hammock. A desk and chair, a bed, a pair of night tables, and a dresser. The space is crowded, jam-packed actually, but I have no other choice at the moment. Once I get done buying everything I need and pay off my bills, I'll look around for a bigger place. Anyway, it's all neat, and that's what matters.

My cell phone rings, and I rush to answer it, hoping... But I don't recognize the number on the screen.

"Hello?" I say.

"Good morning, Jenny. It's Mrs. Thornton."

"Hello, Mrs. Thornton," I say, keeping my voice even.

"I have someone here who has a delivery for you. Something from eBay."

"Oh, okay. Could you please send him over?"

"I can send him right now."

"That would be fine. Thank you, Mrs. Thornton."

Unplugging my flat screen, I move it from my dresser to my bed. I leave my apartment and hurry down the hallway to my building's entrance where I spot a man in a FedEx uniform, his arms clasped around a large box, coming up the walkway. I grab the door and hold it open as he steps inside.

"Thanks," he says. "You Jenny Gilbert? Apartment 1E?"

"That's me." I say. "My apartment's down this way." I point and walk briskly down the hall.

With the clonk-clonk of heavy footsteps thumping behind me, I sail past my original apartment and stop in front of 1F.

"This is it," I say, my back covering the number on the door. I do a quick pivot, turn the knob, and lead the man inside.

"Where do you want this?"

"Just over here," I say, patting the open space on my dresser.

He lowers the box and turns to me. But then, looking past my face, he squints, and his balding head does a slow spin around the room, taking it all in.

"Interesting place you got here. You some kinda collector?"

"No…I…" I fake a sneeze and then a cough, covering my mouth. I clear my throat. "Sorry, anyway, this is all vintage." I say, sweeping my arm through the air in a wide semicircle. "I'm in the vintage business."

"You mean you sell this stuff?"

"Uh huh." I nod.

He takes a step toward one of my plastic crates. "To who?"

I jump in front of him, positioning my body between him and the crate. *My* crate. "To clients. Do I need to sign something for the delivery?"

"Oh, yes, you do," he says, handing me a pen and his clipboard.

I sign the paperwork and open the door to the hallway. "Thank you."

"No problem," he says, glancing up at the toy hammock that stretches over my bed. "Interesting set-up. Never saw anything like this. Do you—"

"It's a niche business." I open the door a little wider. "Thanks again."

"You're welcome," he says, a faint snicker in his voice, and walks out.

Carefully slicing open the packing box, I lift my new TV out. It's white, VCR included. Perfect. I connect the TV to the cable box and turn it on.

"And for the best selection of cold weather gear at prices that can't be beat..." A down-jacketed family smiles on the screen.

I switch the TV off. It works. That's all I need to know for now. Too early to think about winter. It's not even Halloween yet. I wrap the power cord around the base of my flat screen and stash it in the empty box that came with my new TV. I just need to return the flat screen to my other apartment, toss the box down the trash chute, and check my mailbox. The videocassettes should be here soon.

As I reach for my keys, a loud knock shatters the quiet. I freeze, my body a statue except for a wild twitching in my right eyelid. Another knock, louder this time, and the door shudders.

"Hey Jenny, I know you're in there. C'mon, babe. Open up." Greg's honey-toned voice oozes through the door.

My breath comes shallow and fast, and my heart pounds so hard that it almost hurts. Still, I don't move.

"I just want to talk to you, Jenny."

I open my mouth, then close it. *Go away* is what I want to say. But I don't.

He knocks again, softly this time. "Guess I'm just going to have to wait here then."

I sigh, my breath coming out in a loud huff. The moment is here. Greg is going to find out that I've been renting this apartment. Does it matter? Do I care? I feel my shoulders lift and drop. No, I don't, not anymore. My body relaxes, and my breathing slows. I smack my lips together and smile. Well then, I might as well have some fun...

Lifting myself onto the balls of my feet, I tiptoe to the door. I stop, rearrange my mouth into a neutral line, and fling the door open. I catch Greg leaning against the wall, tapping on his cell phone. With a quick head jerk, he looks up and meets my glare.

"Wow, that was quick. I was prepared for a long wait." He holds up his phone and grins.

I step into the hallway. "So, what is it that you want to talk to me about?" I cross my arms over my chest.

"Well, I was walking down the hallway, and I heard—"

"You were walking down the hallway?" I tilt my head and glare at him. "Why would you walk down *this* hallway? You live upstairs. The elevator is by the mailboxes." I toss my head to the left, keeping my arms tight across my chest. "That way."

"I don't always use the elevator. It's good exercise to take the stairs sometimes. And they're *that* way." He flicks his head in an exaggerated motion to the right.

"Fine. But back to my question. What do you want to talk to me about?"

"I want to discuss the apartment. *This* one." He cranes his neck, his eyebrows knitted together, as he looks past me into the apartment. "I wanted to see if you knew when the tenant..." His voice trails off, and he turns his gaze back to me.

I meet his eyes, tightening my jaw. For once, he doesn't seem to know what to say. I wait.

"Looks like there's a lot of stuff in there."

"I guess," I say, tapping my foot on the carpeted hallway floor.

"What's going on, Jenny?" He runs a hand through his hair. "Just tell me already. Whose apartment is this?"

"You mean you don't know? You haven't guessed?" My laugh comes out high-pitched and fast, like a hummingbird on speed.

His mouth falls open, and he clamps it shut. He cocks his head, eyes fixing on mine. "You? Is it yours?"

"Uh huh." I nod.

"But all the times I asked you…?" He shakes his head. "Why did you tell me that—?"

I shrug, my face a blank.

"What does…" He imitates my shrug with a quick up-and-down bounce of his shoulders. "…mean?"

"It means…" I shrug again.

"But why? Why are you renting two apartments next door to each another?" He moves toward me and leans forward, getting a better view of the inside of my apartment. Then, with a quick turn of his head, his eyes find mine. "Does this have something to do with those boxes? The ones you used to have?"

"Why do I get the feeling that you're not going to leave me alone until you find out what you want to know?"

"Because you're very perceptive." He winks.

"You do know that it's not your business, don't you?"

"Well, this was my cousin's apartment before you moved in. I want to rent it. And if I can't, I want to know why."

"You already know why, Greg. You can't have it because it's already been rented."

"Babe, why don't you just tell me what's going on? Then I'll leave you alone." He reaches out and runs a finger across my wrist. "If you really want me to."

"I really want you to," I say, snatching my hand back.

"So, can I come in then?"

"Why not?" I step to the side of the doorway and sweep my hand backward. "Come on in."

Greg grins and strolls inside. One, two, three, four steps, and then he stops. I follow him into the apartment and position myself against the wall next to the open door. Greg stands in the small open space in the center of the apartment and turns slowly, his feet baby-stepping in a circle while his head rotates, his eyes drifting from ceiling to floor. I feel a wave of dizziness roll through my head as I try to follow his gaze. I blink and focus on my bed, picturing myself sinking into the soft clouds decorating my comforter.

Greg shakes his head and spins on his heel, stopping to face me. "Okay Jenny, I give up." He extends his hands, palms up, fingers splayed. "What is all this stuff?"

I bite my lip, swallowing a smile. Because now I'm prepared, and I know just what to say.

"I'm in the vintage business."

Greg freezes. He opens his mouth, then closes it. His eyebrows squish together, and he takes a step toward me. And then, he opens his mouth again. His questions rain down on me in a fiery onslaught.

How long have you been doing this? How did you start? Who do you sell to? Where do you find everything?

I pull the answers from the air, embellishing my original fib until I've concocted a fantasy narrative about a thriving cottage industry with me at the helm. I don't want to lie. I really don't, not even to Greg. But it's a matter of self-preservation. Maybe if he thinks I've let him in on my secret, he'll leave me alone.

I watch as he wanders through my apartment, bending down to inspect my CD collection, peering up at the stuffed animals piled into my toy hammock, and running his fingers over my boxes of games and down the spines of my books. He plucks a Koosh ball from one of my crates and strokes the back of his hand with its rubbery strands. He seems to be moving in slow motion, and I watch him as if through a haze. I stand with my feet together and my shoulders back, my hands clasped in front of my body. My mouth is dry and tastes like desert sand.

Still holding the ball, Greg plops onto my bean bag chair. "I guess this is the big secret, huh?" He tosses the ball, *my* ball, from one hand to the other.

"Yup, this is it." I nod. "So, is there anything else you need to know?"

He leans back, sinking into the chair, and stretches his legs out. "Now I realize why you didn't want to tell me the truth about this place."

"Because it's not your business?"

"Jenny, c'mon. Be nice." He pushes his lower lip out in a man-pout.

"Okay. Why do *you* think I didn't want to tell you that this is my apartment?"

"Because Sea Grove Gardens is a residential complex. You can't run a business out of an apartment here."

"I'm not *running* a business from here, Greg. This place is for storage. That's it. Just storage," I say, planting my hands on my hips.

This apartment *is* for storage. Anyway, that was my original plan. It's the one fragment of truth in my elaborate lie about a fictitious business. But Greg doesn't believe it. I can see it in the lift of his eyebrow and the tilt of his head. Maybe I should have been honest and simply told him the truth.

Secrets and lies, starting way back when I sat in Nick's classroom and dreamed up an essay about a brother who was strong, brave, and made the world an easier place for me. Then, my collecting and buying, the boxes, my secret second apartment. I've spun a web of deceits, big and little. And now I'm so entangled that I'm not even sure what the truth is anymore. But this is not the time for me to unravel the knotty tangle I've created. Not here, not now, and not with Greg. I lock eyes with him and stand my ground.

"Storage? Yeah, right." He snickers. "Then what about shipping? Customer pickups? Meeting with vendors? Where does that all happen?"

"Online mostly," I spit the words out. "And on the rare occasions when I do have to meet with someone, I have an office in the Clayton Building."

"So, this is a…" He pauses and looks up, screwing his face into a mask of concentration as if searching the air for the right word.

I wait, my foot bobbing up and down in a slow tap.

"Warehouse," he says, nodding slowly and thrusting his chin out. "It's actually a warehouse, then."

"Well—"

"It's a warehouse, Jenny. And that, my dear, is a business."

"It's not a warehouse, and it's not a business," I fire back.

"There's something else I don't understand." He stands up, turns, and points to my bed. "Why do you have a bed in here?"

"Greg, enough already. Stop quizzing me. None of this is your concern." I move to the still open door. "I think it's time for you to leave."

He crosses the room and comes toward me, moving closer until I can feel his hot breath on my face.

"Stop," he whispers, reaching behind me and closing the door. "I don't want to fight with you, Jenny." He takes a half step back. "I never have. Somehow, we got off on the wrong foot. All I ever wanted was to get to know you better, but you never gave me the chance. Even way back, when Chloe lived here, and I first met you…" He lifts his face and leans toward me. Close and coming closer.

"No." I push my body back against the door. "Greg, please."

The sound of three sharp knocks comes through the door. Then a voice.

"Jenny, it's Nick."

My breath comes in shallow gasps, and my skin prickles.

"Showdown, folks," Greg hisses with a devilish grin.

Flicking my wrist, I aim a quivering index finger at my desk chair. "Sit there!" I hiss.

With a theatrical eye roll and an exaggerated head shake, he pulls the chair away from the desk and straddles it, draping his arms over its back.

I glare at him. Then smoothing my hair, I gulp a mouthful of air and open the door.

Nick. His striped shirt is wrinkled, and his hair is disheveled. Dark shadows underline his eyes. My throat tightens as I reach for his arm and lead him inside. His gaze moves past me, and I hear the scrape of a chair. I turn and watch as Greg stands and comes toward us. The air turns frigid, and an icy shiver runs through me.

"Hello, Nick," Greg says, extending his hand.

"Greg." Nick nods, his own hands balled into white-knuckled fists clamped to his thighs.

"Guess this means I should be going. I'll see you, Jenny." Greg winks at me and then turns to Nick. "Take care, buddy." He leaves us, closing the door behind him.

"Seems like I came at a bad time," Nick says, pushing the words out through his barely opened mouth. "I didn't mean to disturb you, Jenny." He turns and in a long stride, he is at my door, his hand reaching for the knob.

"No. You didn't. Please, I can explain. Nick..."

He stands rooted to the floor, his back to me. A tree, unbending.

"It's not what you think," I say.

He whips around and stares at me, his nostrils flaring. "I don't know what I think anymore, Jenny. Everything that I thought was true was a story, and now I have a feeling I'm about to hear another one."

"No, Nick. No more stories. Only the truth from now on. I promise." I reach for his clenched hands, slowly prying them apart and forcing them into my own. "Please stay. Talk to me."

"I don't know that we have anything to talk about, Jenny."

"Please Nick, just listen. That's all I ask. Just listen." I tighten my grip on his hands. "Sit with me. Please."

He looks around the apartment, his eyes wide, as if seeing it for the first time. "Sit where?" he asks, his face expressionless.

Sit where?

I scan the room. Shelves, crates, boxes, baskets, a bed, desk, and dresser crowd the space. Seating? My desk chair, bean bag chair, and bed. That's it.

"The bed?" I whisper.

He nods, walks to the bed, and perches his long body on its edge. I take a spot next to him, leaving space between us. We turn and face each other.

"First, let me tell you why Greg was here." I swallow.

"That's a good place to start," he says, his arms crossed in his lap.

"I was here. In this apartment. Greg was walking down the hallway. He heard sounds. Maybe it was the TV. I don't know. He knocked and said he knew I was in here, and he was going to wait 'til I opened the door. So, I did."

"You invited him in?"

"I didn't *invite* him. I stood in the doorway, and he could see into the apartment. He had all these questions, and I couldn't put him off anymore. So, I *let* him in."

"And?"

"And I told him I was in the vintage business."

"The what?" Nick's eyes go wide, and his mouth tightens, his lips trembling with what I hope is a suppressed smile.

I wait, my eyes on his face.

Then finally, his body loosens, and his mouth opens into a deep, true, belly-shaking kind of laugh.

And I laugh too. My nose runs, and my eyes water. I remember what happiness feels like.

"Okay, this is a story I have to hear," Nick says, leaning back on his arms.

"Greg's been bugging me about this apartment for so long. Finally, I couldn't stand it anymore. But I didn't want to tell him the real reason I have all this stuff. So, I told him I find and sell vintage merchandise to collectors."

Nick rubs the back of his neck and shakes his head, looking up at the ceiling.

"Is that bad?" I whisper.

He leans toward me and takes my hand. "I understand why you didn't want Greg to know the truth about this apartment. I can even understand how you let him in. But Jenny..." He shakes his head again, this time more slowly.

"What?" I squeeze his hand. "Tell me."

"Lying to Greg is one thing. But lying to me? I never expected that from you." He stares at me, his face an unreadable mask. "Not from you, Jenny."

"I know. You're right. And there's no excuse, but I want you to understand." My voice comes out hoarse, scratchy.

"We've both had some time to think about this. And I've been trying to understand. I really have," he says. "But I need you to explain it to me." He gently pulls his hand away. "You had so many opportunities to tell me the truth about Ryan. So many. But instead you just compounded the original lie. Every time I asked you about him, you invented another story. And I believed you." He shakes his head. "I believed you."

"I know. But Nick, please you have to forgive me. It was just that I wanted to be *that girl*. The one you remembered from your class, the one who wrote the essay, the one who…" I look down at the wooden floor. Pale scratches crisscross the scuffed planks.

"So being 'that girl' was so important to you that you didn't let me meet your mother."

I pull my lower lip into my mouth, my eyes still on the floor and run my hands down my arms.

"Or your mother to meet me."

I close my eyes. A heaviness presses down on my chest, making it difficult to breathe.

"And you lied to me, Jenny. You lied to a lot of people. But you lied to *me*." He speaks slowly, clearly. "I need you to help me understand why."

I wet my lips and force myself to breathe. In. Out. In. Out. Clasping my trembling hands in my lap, I lift my head and face him. "I was afraid."

"You were afraid?"

I nod.

"Of what?"

"Of you. That your feelings would change. That you

wouldn't…" I stop, not wanting to say the words out loud. Afraid to.

He puts his hands on my thighs and leans toward me, sending a tingly warmth up my body. "Jenny, I love you. I'm *in* love with you. Do you honestly believe I feel that way because of an essay you wrote ten years ago?"

"No," I say softly.

"But the lying…" He shakes his head and gets up from the bed, stepping back from me. "It seems to come so easily to you." His hands dangle at his sides.

"That's not true, Nick."

"Then what is true? Tell me now because I don't know what to believe anymore. What else is a lie, Jenny? What else?"

"Nothing. I swear. I haven't lied about anything else. Just Ryan."

"And about your mother's visit," he says quietly.

"Yes." I nod. "I did lie about that," I say, looking away.

Nick moves back to the bed and sits, this time close to me, our thighs touching. He lifts my hair into a loose ponytail and gently releases it, letting it fall onto my back. "From now on, Jenny…The truth. You need to promise me. No more lies."

"I promise," I say, leaning toward him and squeezing his knee. "No more lies."

"And no more secrets."

"And no more secrets," I whisper. A soft echo.

I lay my head on his chest, and he pulls me closer, tighter. I sink into his embrace and we breathe. Together, we breathe.

24

*A*fter...Nick and I lay wrapped in each other's arms. Slivers of late afternoon sun slip through the blinds behind my bed and dapple his dark hair with glints of caramel. We are alone in the quiet.

Propping himself up on a hand, he traces my lips with a finger. "Do you trust me, Jenny?"

"Of course, I trust you," I say. My answer comes quickly without thinking. And I know it's true. I do trust him.

"Then tell me what's going on."

All of a sudden, the room tilts, and a seasick kind of wave washes over me. "What do you mean?"

"What's going on here? In this apartment?" He sits up, his head slowly turning, taking stock of the surroundings. "There're quite a few more things in here than I remember."

"I've filled in a little here and there," I say, trying to sound casual.

"A little here and there?" His face is serious.

Sitting up in bed, I do my own visual tour of the apartment. I see what he sees. More shelves, crates, and bins.

More stuff. Less floorspace. I raise my eyebrows and look at him. But I know that's not an answer.

"Well, I kind of decided that..." I stop, close my eyes for a moment, and then spit it out. "I'm living here now."

"Living *here*?" Nick says, tilting his head and rubbing his cheek with the back of his hand.

"Uh huh."

"What about the apartment next door? Are you still renting that one?"

"Yeah, I still have it."

"Maybe I'm missing something, but if you're living here, why do you need the apartment next door?"

"I'm going to start meeting clients there."

"Okay, now I'm really confused." He lifts his hands, palms up, and shakes his head. "Don't you meet clients in your office?"

"I do, but..." I stop. But what? And suddenly I know, deep in my gut, that if I tell this beautiful man, the man I'm head over heels in love with, one more story, I will lose him. This time forever. My right eyelid begins to quiver, and I press a finger against my brow bone. It doesn't help. I clear my throat and force the words out. "I'm giving up my office at the end of the month." My voice sounds like someone else's, someone I don't recognize.

"That's next week!" Nick's head jerks back.

"Yup, it's next week," I say quietly.

"Why?"

"Why am I giving up my office or why next week?"

"Both."

Tell Nick the truth. That has to be my new mantra. I have to tell him the truth or as much of the truth as he needs to know in order to answer his questions. There'll be time for the *whole* truth later.

"I realized that I don't need to rent two apartments and an office. It's been getting expensive, and since I'm on a month to month lease in the Clayton Building, it's a good time to leave."

"But since you're living in this apartment, why don't you give up the one next door instead of your office?"

"Nick, look around." I wave a finger through the air. "This place is for me. I wouldn't even invite a friend here. There'd be too many questions. No one would understand. And I don't want to share my *collection* with anyone." I reach under the comforter and pat his knee. "Except for you."

His mouth turns up in a quick smile, and then his expression turns serious. "But why now?"

"What do you mean?"

"You've been renting all three places for a while. Why, all of a sudden, do you want to give one up?"

"It's not all of a sudden. Not really. I was thinking about it before. I was wondering if it would make sense."

He sits up straighter, propping a pillow behind his head, and looks around the room. Then he turns to me.

"Jenny, I'm going to ask you something, and I want an honest answer."

Ask me what? I press my trembling hands to my thighs, trying to still them. "O-kay."

"How much more do you plan to buy for this apartment?"

Another surprise question. But I don't have an answer because honestly, I don't know. And that's exactly what I tell him.

"So, you don't have an endgame?"

My face grows hot, and my heartbeat thumps in my ears. I swallow, blink, and open my mouth. I choose my words carefully. "The endgame is for me to get back the things that were taken away from me."

"All of them?"

"'All' is a big word," I say. "Can we settle for 'most'?" I shape my mouth into a smile.

"Don't you think you already have 'most'?"

"I'm not sure. Maybe. But then, the more I b…" I stop myself from using the word 'buy'. "The more I *find*, the more I realize what's missing."

"It's an expensive habit though, isn't it?"

"I guess." I shrug. 'Buy' or 'find'. The words don't matter. He knows.

"So, you're prioritizing collecting over having an office?"

"Nick, that's not fair." My voice takes on an edge. "And it's not that simple."

"I'm sorry. You're right. I'm just trying to understand," he says quickly, reaching for my hand and squeezing it. "And I'm concerned."

"Concerned?" I feel my eyes go into a squint. Moving away from him, I slide out of bed and pull on my shirt and jeans. "About what? That I'm a collector with hoarding tendencies? That's what you said, isn't it? That I have 'hoarding tendencies'?"

Nick pulls on his own clothes and sits on the edge of the bed.

"Jenny, stop. Please. I'm not criticizing you. That's not what I'm saying. I don't have a problem with any of this." He stretches his arms out as if embracing all of the things packed into the apartment.

I stand in front of him, my arms crossed over my chest. "Then why are you concerned?"

He doesn't answer right away. Instead, he stares at the black TV screen facing us. And I realize that this time Nick is the one who doesn't know what to say. I stand, silent and still, and I wait.

"I'm concerned because I remember you telling me how proud you were when you were able to rent an office.

How successful you felt. And now…" He doesn't finish the sentence.

"And now?"

"And now, I'm wondering why you're giving it up."

Something inside of me lurches downward, and for a moment I feel untethered, like I'm in a fast-moving elevator racing up a tall building. I press a finger against the bridge of my nose, and the feeling passes.

"I think you know why," I say evenly.

He nods. "I think I do too." He stands, takes a step toward me, and grasps my elbows, locking our arms together. "Jenny, I know you're successful, and I can't even begin to imagine what it took to get to where you are. You single-handedly built a business whose brand is *you*. You alone. I admire you, and I respect you."

"Thank you," I say.

"I mean it." His mouth curves into a sweet, sad smile. "But I do need to ask you something, and I don't want you to be angry."

I know what he's going to ask me, maybe not his exact words, but I know what he's trying to find out. What he feels he *needs* to ask. It's my last secret, the one thing I thought I could keep from him.

"I won't be angry," I say. And I know that's true. In just a moment, I'll be…something. But angry? No, I won't be angry.

"Jenny..." He slides his hands down my arms and squeezes my fingers. "Are you in debt?"

A current of heat surges up my body, and my hands go clammy. I pull my fingers back and rub my palms down the sides of my jeans. "Well, I have some credit card bills to pay. And rent. Utilities. Things like that." I lift my shoulders into what I hope passes for a shrug. "It's nothing to worry about."

"Jenny," Nick whispers my name. That's it. Just my name.

I feel my body collapse in on itself, deflating like a spent balloon. My chin trembles, but I force myself to meet his gaze.

"Okay, Nick. Yes, I have some debt."

"*Some* debt?" His voice is gentle, kind. But nonetheless, he is asking me a question.

I nod, the only answer I have.

"You don't want to tell me how much, do you?"

"Nick, I want to tell you the truth. I do." I press my lips together, my eyes open wide, and I swallow. "But the truth is that I really don't know how much."

He gathers me into his arms, and something inside of me releases. My whole body, from the top of my head to my toes, goes limp. My eyes water, and I let myself cry.

"I'm wetting your shirt." I sniffle and wipe my eyes with the back of my hand.

He holds me tighter, and his chest vibrates as he laughs. "My darling Jenny, you can wet my shirt all you want."

And now I'm laughing along with him, but crying too. And we sway together, my cheek pressed against his wet shirt.

Later, when my tears and our shared laughter dissolve into a peaceful quiet, we walk next door, back to my original apartment, the first place I called home. As I step inside, with Nick close behind me, I'm struck by the openness of the space. A smooth leather sofa bracketed by twin floor lamps, a coffee table, a wall unit, and an expanse of floor. Room to sit, to stretch out, to move. I *need* this apartment. I need both of my apartments. Like a pair of mirrors facing each other, they both reflect me. This apartment is the *front* Jenny, the self I show to the outside world. And next door is the *back* Jenny, my secret side, the side I've shared only with Nick. And now, I'm about to share one more thing with him. My last secret.

"It's in here," I say, leading him into the kitchen.

I open the cabinet to the right of the sink and pull out my thick black folder. *Unpaid Bills.* The red letters jump off its white label and sting my eyes. I drop the bulging folder onto the kitchen table.

"Have a seat," I say to Nick, pointing to a chair and settling into the seat next to him.

"Jenny, listen, before you even show me this, I want you to know that I can help you. I *want* to help you. The amount doesn't matter. We can handle the details later. Just let me—"

"No, Nick. Thank you, but no. I'm willing to let you see all of this, maybe even help me prioritize or consolidate my bills or work out some sort of payment plan. But it's my responsibility. Mine, not yours. And I can't—"

"But Jenny, it doesn't make sense. The interest charges, your credit rating—"

"*I* need to pay these bills," I say. "By myself."

"No, you don't. Let me—"

I grab the folder and hug it to my chest. "This was a bad idea," I say, shaking my head. "I shouldn't have told you."

"What do you mean you shouldn't have told me? How can you say that? How can you *think* that?" His knuckles go white as he grips the edge of the table, and a blue vein appears on his forehead.

"I didn't mean for it to come out that way. It's just that…" I throw my hands up and then drop them into my lap. "I don't need you to rescue me. I don't *want* you to rescue me."

"Then what do you want?" he asks quietly.

I raise my shoulders up and then down in a not-quite-a-shrug. "I want you to love me. Now that you know everything. No secrets. No lies. I just want you to love me."

He reaches for my hand and squeezes it. "I do, Jenny. I do."

"Then I only want one more thing…" I smile and kiss his cheek. "I want you to help me come up with a plan," I say, placing the folder back on the table.

One by one, I pull out each of the statements, smooth its creases, and lay it on the table. Nick arranges them by due date. We read the fine print and consider interest charges and grace periods. We prioritize and strategize. We develop a payment plan.

"I think I can do this," I whisper.

"I think you can, too," Nick says. "But it would be easier if you let me—"

I tap his hand with a finger. "No," I say, and I smile.

"Okay, Jenny. But you know that if you—"

I start to shake my head, and my cell phone rings. Good timing. I grab the phone and check the display.

"Hi Mom," I say.

"Jenny, have you been watching the news?" My mother's voice bursts through the phone.

"Not really." I don't tell her about the old school movies and Buffy, the Vampire Slayer. "Why? What's going on?"

"The hurricane—"

"You mean Sandy? The one in Haiti?"

"Yes, Sandy." Her sharp inhale whooshes in my ear. "Jenny, there's a good chance it's headed for New Jersey." Her words come out fast and loud. I can almost see her pacing the floor in her sunny Florida kitchen.

"No, Mom. That doesn't sound right. In fact, I was worried about *you*, but then I heard it would be traveling off the coast of Florida and *not* making landfall. So, you'll just get some wind and rain. Nothing major. Then it'll eventually head out to sea. Sandy's not going to make it all the way up to New Jersey."

Nick looks up from the piles of papers spread across the kitchen table.

"Yes, it will, Jenny. It can't go out to sea because it's being hemmed in by other weather disturbances. There's nowhere for it to go but up the coast. The latest forecast model just zeroed in on New Jersey. It's breaking news. Turn on the TV. Then call Nick, and ask him to help you."

"Help me what?"

"I don't know yet. It depends."

"Depends on what, Mom?"

"How severe it's going to be and where exactly it's going to make landfall. We don't have all the information yet. But Jenny, you're going to need help."

"Mom, please," I say, catching Nick's eye and shaking my head. "I'll make sure I have milk and bread, okay?"

"Jenny, turn on the news, please. Don't brush this off. You need to take it seriously and prepare," she says. "Promise me."

"Okay, Mom," I say, rolling my eyes. Good thing we're not on FaceTime. "I promise you that I'll take it seriously."

"And call Nick."

I smile at Nick and speak into the phone. "Yes, Mom. I'll call Nick."

We say our good-byes, and I click off the phone.

"What was that about?" Nick asks, sliding his chair closer to the table and leaning on his elbows.

"Hurricane Sandy. My mother heard that it's headed for New Jersey. Weird, huh? Did you hear that?"

"No, I didn't. But quite honestly, I've had a lot on my mind these last few days." He pushes his lips together, holding back a smile. "I haven't really been following the news."

"She said the forecast targeting New Jersey just came out. My laptop and the TV from this apartment are still next door. Let's go get them, okay?"

He nods. I snatch up my keys, and we go. Then with my laptop tucked into the crook of my arm and Nick carrying the flat screen, we dash back to my original apartment.

And we learn that my mother was right.

25

"Nick, these forecasts change by the hour. A direct hit on New Jersey is just *one* possible scenario, and it's a very unlikely one. So many factors would need to come together for it to happen. We'll probably just get a lot of rain and wind, and that'll be it. I really don't think—"

Nick puts his hands on my shoulders, his face inches from mine. "Jenny, you live near the ocean, and you're on the ground floor."

"Remember Hurricane Irene last year? That was downgraded to a tropical storm. It wasn't even a real hurricane. There was damage and power outages, but nothing like they expected. You're really being an alarmist," I say, rocking back on my heels and covering his toes with mine. "You do know that, don't you?"

"I'm just being realistic."

"Okay then, *Mr. Realist*, what do you suggest I do?"

"Well, since we have a few days before it reaches here, I suggest we pack my car with some of your things. I'll take them to my place. Then, I'll come back down here, and we'll take your car and mine along with the rest of your things to New Brunswick. You'll stay with me until the storm passes."

"Absolutely not! I'm not leaving." I step back, crossing my arms over my chest and planting my feet into the floor. "Why aren't you worrying about *your* townhouse? And what about your parents?"

"My parents live far enough west to be out of danger, and I probably do too. But Jenny, you..." He shakes his head and points to the TV. "Just look."

A slim young woman with hair that doesn't move stands next to a brightly colored map of the eastern United States. "By Sunday, the New Jersey coastline will be on alert for a prolonged period of hurricane force winds and record-setting flooding. The threat will be exacerbated by the full moon that evening which will keep the tides high." She points to a broken white line trailing up the map. "We expect Sandy to make landfall in southeastern New Jersey some time on Monday. Please be aware that by that time, it will have gained energy by interacting with other storm systems as well as from its long run over open water. We will make additional details available as we receive them."

I turn toward Nick and begin to speak before he can open his mouth. "Listen, we have a few days. Things could change. They always predict worst-case scenarios. Those doom and gloom predictions sell newspapers, and they keep people glued to their TVs. You know that. How many times do they predict blizzards and three-foot snowstorms that never happen?"

"And what about the times they do happen?"

"Nick, listen," I say calmly. "You've got to get back to New Brunswick to teach your night class. Don't worry about me. We have time, and I am taking this seriously. I'm not burying my head in the sand. Let's just see what happens, and then I'll decide what to do."

He looks down at his watch. "You're right. I do need to get going. But while I'm here, let's go next door and put some of your things in my car."

I stretch my arms out, fingers spread apart, and force myself to speak evenly. "We have time, so let's not worry. Teach your class, and we'll talk tomorrow." I kiss him lightly. "Okay?"

He protests a little, but finally leaves. He has to.

I switch off the TV and walk over to the kitchen table which is still heaped with piles of statements. I grab the stack that we decided I need to pay right away and stuff the rest into the black folder. Gathering up my laptop, my keys, and *to-be-paid-now* bills, I return the folder to the cabinet and head next door. Kicking off my shoes, I plop onto the bed. I lean back, resting my shoulders against my new backrest, and let my eyes wander around the room. It is packed to capacity, overflowing with all the things that mean so much to me. There is absolutely no way that I'm going to dismantle it.

My TV's black screen stares at me. I reach for the remote and turn it on.

"Hurricane Sandy continues to…"

I slide the switch to VCR mode, hop off the bed, and make my way over to the row of videocassettes lined up on the shelf below the television. I run my fingers over the smooth plastic cases, stopping at *Pretty Woman*. I haven't seen that one in ages. Ripping off the cellophane, I slide the cassette into the VCR and settle into my bean bag chair.

I wake early, the morning sun gently lighting the room. It's a nice way to ease into the day. I stretch, roll onto my stomach, and poke a finger between the slatted blinds. The view is postcard pretty. A wide band of clear blue sky, a darker stripe of ocean, a stretch of gold sand, and the weathered planks of gray boardwalk. I feel blessed to live here.

Breakfast is a bowl of cereal and a glass of orange juice scarfed down at the kitchen counter. I need to work on that. Maybe I can squeeze a small table and chair in here, although that's an overly optimistic thought because I really don't have the room. Oh well, I can clear a spot on the desk or continue to use my bean bag as a dining chair and my lap as a table. No big deal.

After I do my dishes and wipe down the counter, I bring my laptop and stack of bills to my desk. With Nick's help, the paper jungle of debt that was buried in a folder in my kitchen cabinet next door has been reduced to this modest pile that needs immediate attention.

I sign into my online banking account, click on *Bill Pay*, and pluck a statement from the top of the stack. I pay it online, mark the paper copy, and add it to the facedown pile on my desk, repeating the steps until my collection of overdue statements is transformed into a tidy stack of paid bills. I check my account balance. The number jumps out from my computer screen. Not good. Plus, I have more bills stashed in my kitchen cabinet next door. And I do need a few more things for this apartment. But I'll work it out. I always do.

My cell phone rings. *Mom.* I let it go to voicemail.

A minute later the phone beeps with a text message alert. *Mom.* Again.

R u watching weather? What r ur plans? Call me. Worried. Love u.

Quickly, I type back. *Everything fine. Making preparations. Nick helping. Will call later. Love u. Don't worry.*

Reaching behind my bed, I pull the cord and open my blinds. Blue sky, blue-green ocean, gold sand, and gray boardwalk. Nothing's changed. All normal, all good. A quintessential fall day at the shore and too perfect to stay indoors.

Throwing on a sweatshirt and jacket, I tie a scarf around my neck, grab my sunglasses, and head outside. I switch my phone to silent mode and slide it into my pocket.

The parking lot seems a little emptier than usual, but it's the middle of the afternoon. People are probably at work or getting an early start to the weekend. I cross Ocean Avenue and climb the three steps to the boardwalk. The wind runs cool fingers through my hair, and I pull it back into a ponytail. An older couple outfitted in matching windbreakers leans over the railing separating the boardwalk from the beach. I pick a spot a few feet away from them, edge up to the rail, and stare out at the ocean. Whitecaps dot the water, and a lone kite tethered to a teenager on the sand dances in the air.

The salty ocean breeze makes my stomach rumble. I'm hungry in a way that only Jersey shore food can satisfy. A hot dog? Soft serve vanilla ice cream? Maybe both. I arch my back into a luxurious stretch, then make my way down the boardwalk. I pass souvenir shops and a beachwear boutique closed for the season, metal grates standing guard over their doors. A hand-painted sign posted in a candy shop announces, *No candy for Sandy. Closing today at 5 p.m.* I walk past the shuttered Shore Hot Dogs. So, ice cream it is. I stop at the glass-paned store and step up to the counter.

"Could I have a vanilla soft serve in a waffle cone?"

"Sure." The short, blonde woman smiles and pulls a cone from a cardboard box.

I watch as the soft rope of ice cream coils into the cone, ending in a curled peak. It's the kind of treat that always tastes better on the boardwalk. I pay her and take the cone.

"Are you open tomorrow?" I ask.

"No." She shakes her head, her silky hair falling into her face. "Some of the other places here might be open 'til noon. But that's it, I heard."

"Really?" My eyes open wide.

She tucks her hair behind her ears and nods. "They say this is gonna be a big one."

"I hope not," I say quietly.

"Me too," she says, fingering the cross hanging from her neck.

Back on the boardwalk, passing the occasional dog walker and bicycle rider, I eat my ice cream. I peer into the windows of small business after small business, each of them with their modified closing times prominently posted. On a boarded-up storefront, a spray-painted sign demands, *Go away, Sandy!*

My cell phone jiggles with the vibration of an incoming call. I pull it out of my pocket and look at the screen. *Nick.*

"Hello?" I say slowly.

Nick wants me to pack up and leave with him Saturday. In other words, tomorrow.

"That's impossible," was my initial response, but he didn't go for it. I tried "Let's keep an eye on the forecast," but that didn't work either. We settled on "I'll start to pack." I didn't say anything about actually *leaving*.

I turn on the TV, flipping from channel to channel. Men in dark suits and brightly colored ties and women in tailored dresses seem to have taken over the airwaves. Their stories are the same. People have died in floods and mudslides in Haiti. Parts of Jamaica, the Dominican Republic, the Bahamas, and Cuba have been ravaged. Hurricane Sandy, now called a 'Frankenstorm', will make landfall at the Jersey shore Monday. Governor Christie is expected to declare a state of pre-emptive emergency tomorrow. Selected areas are ordered to be evacuated by Sunday. Power companies have arranged for out-of-state help, and widespread outages lasting more than a week are expected. New Jersey residents in Sandy's path are 'strongly advised' to get out of the way.

Standing in the middle of my apartment, I bend my elbows and press my palms into my hips, making triangles of my arms. Turning my head slowly, I look—I *really look*—at my things. All of them. Toys, games, books, dolls, and so much more. There is absolutely no way I can pack up everything. And *every thing* here is special to me. But Sandy is coming. I have two apartments on the first floor, and there will be some flooding. Those are the facts. Insurance will cover the damage to the apartments and to my furniture. But my things? No. I need to protect them.

I snatch up my bag and head to my car. Destination: supermarket.

The parking lot is packed, but I snag a spot at the end of the last row. I follow a young woman, a baby strapped to her chest in a Snugli, to her car and wait for her to unload her groceries.

"Thanks," I say as she pushes her empty cart toward me.

In the store, clumps of shoppers stockpiling supplies swarm the aisles. The milk is gone, and two women are arguing over the last remaining loaf of bread. I fill my cart with cold cuts, cheese, crackers, eggs, yogurt, diet soda, and water. A lone flashlight lies half-hidden among boxes of cereal, and I grab it. I've got candles and matches at home. Spotting a harried-looking man in a blue apron heading to the back of the store, I race to catch up with him.

"Excuse me, sir. Do you have any empty boxes?"

"Follow me," he says, pointing to a pair of metal doors. He pushes the doors open and leads me into the back room. "Help yourself," he says.

One long line and forty-five minutes later, I'm back in my apartment. I put away my food. Now it's time to get to work.

I start with the pantry. Flinging open the doors, I jam boxes, jars, and bottles into the two bottom shelves, leaving the top three open. Next, I tackle the cabinets. Consolidating dishes and glassware, I empty out two tall cabinets and one wide one. Good so far.

I move my shoes from the bottom of my closet to the top shelf and position my handbags closer together, leaving half of the shelf clear. Moving to my dresser, I combine t-shirts with sweaters and free up a full drawer of usable space.

Okay, time for Phase Two. In three trips, I transfer the books from the bottom shelf of my bookcase to an empty kitchen cabinet. Three more trips, and the next shelf is done. I move the games and toys from the lower shelves of my white laminate unit to another high cabinet and carry my toy-filled plastic crates from the floor to the kitchen counter. I pack my CDs, DVDs, Barbie convertible, and oddly shaped toys into supermarket boxes meant for cans of corn and boxes of rice and stack them on my desk chair. I slide one basket of toys onto the top shelf of my closet and empty the other into a dresser drawer. Carefully, I scan the lower edges of the walls. The area is clear except for my bean bag chair and the rug which lies under my bed. I can move the bean bag to a countertop if I need to, and Nick can help me roll up the rug.

I grab a can of diet soda and take a long drink. Everything of value to me is secure. I just need to get a few things off the floor next door.

And then, Hurricane Sandy, Jenny Gilbert is ready!

26

I dream that I'm lying on the beach, the sun warming my face. I'm listening to the gentle whoosh of the incoming tide punctuated by the squawk of a hungry seagull...

My cell phone rings, jerking me awake. *Nick*.

"Hul-lo," I say, my eyes closing again.

"Good morning, sleepyhead."

I clap a hand over my mouth mid-yawn.

"I heard that." He laughs.

"What time is it?" I ask, too lazy to roll over and check the clock.

"It's nine-thirty."

"Oh jeez, I need to get up," I say, propping my pillow behind my head and pulling myself into a sitting position.

"Yes, you do. How did the packing go?"

"The packing? Uh...good. I've got everything off the floor. It's all stashed away. What about you?"

"I'm not in Sandy's direct path, and I'm a few steps off ground level. So, we'll be safe here. I stocked up on food yesterday, and I've got flashlights and candles," he says. "Actually, I'm looking forward to having you as a roommate."

I picture his warm smile. But still, I'm not leaving. "Mmm…" That's the best I can come up with.

"So, when do you want me to come down there? We can pack your things in both of our cars and head up to my place."

"Uh…well… I still have some work to do."

"That's okay. I'll come down and help you."

"No!" The word comes out fast and hard. "What I mean is…" I fake a cough. "I have a client's essay to review."

"I thought you were done with those."

"I-I am. I just need to do a final edit for one person. That's all," I say. "And Nick, I really don't need you to come down here. Why don't I just drive up to New Brunswick when I'm done?"

"Because we'll need both cars to bring all your things up here."

"No, we really don't have to do that. I have everything secured here. "I'll be…I mean *it'll* be fine."

"It's up to you, but I think—"

"Nick, everything will be fine here. I'm sure of it."

"Okay then." He pauses. "So, when do you plan to leave?"

"Well, let's keep checking the forecast, and then—"

"Jenny, no."

His words come out as an order, and an image of my father pops into my mind.

Jenny, no we can't stay here. Jenny, no I can't refuse to transfer.
Jenny, no you can't take that with you.

"Nick—"

"Jenny, please. Give me a time to expect you. Christie just announced mandatory evacuation of Long Beach Island and a bunch of coastal towns in southern Jersey. You're in danger. I want to come get you. Please. Do it for me. Please."

Jenny, no. I silently mouth the words. Nick is *not* my father. But still, I can't 'do it for him'. It's not *only* about my things. Sea Grove is my home, and I can't leave, not even for Nick.

"Okay, I'll be there after dinner," I lie.

My phone rings at six-thirty.

"Hi, Nick," I answer.

"Where are you?" He doesn't sound happy.

"I'm still here. I have a little more work to do on that essay. How about if I come tomorrow morning?"

"Tomorrow?"

"Yeah, in the morning. I'll get up early."

"Jenny, the roads are going to shut down tomorrow afternoon, except for emergency vehicles. And before that, the traffic will be horrendous. You need to leave now."

"Let me see how far I get on this essay. Then maybe—"

"No, Jenny. Not maybe," he says, and I hear him take a quick in-and-out breath. "Never mind. I'm coming down there."

"No, don't. You can't. I need to—"

"Good-bye, Jenny." And the call is disconnected.

I call him back. The phone rings and rings, then goes to voicemail.

"You have reached…"

"Nick, please. Don't come down here tonight. I'm not ready to leave yet. Call me back. Please. I need to talk to you."

I shove my hands into my back pockets and walk from one end of the apartment to the other. Back and forth, and back and forth. Plenty of floor space now. Nick's on his way. There's nothing I can do to stop him. But Sea Grove is not on the mandatory evacuation list. So, there's no reason for me to leave. He knows that. I can deal with a power outage *if* that even happens, and I have plenty of food and supplies. These storms are never as bad as they're predicted to be. After Hurricane Katrina, people are just overcautious. And looming disaster sells. This is manna from heaven for the media. I'll explain it to Nick when he gets here. Maybe after the storm passes and I put all of my things back where they belong, I'll spend a couple of days with him in New Brunswick. but not now. I need to stay here to make sure…

The door rattles with three sharp knocks. "Jenny, it's Greg. Let me in."

I fling the door open, banging its knob against the wall.

"What are you doing here?" I ask, blocking the doorway.

"That's what I want to ask you. I saw your car in the lot—"

"So?" I glare at him.

"So, you should leave. *We* should leave. I'm on my way to—"

"Have a good trip then," I say, interrupting him.

"Jenny, you're on the first floor. This place is going to flood. The whole complex is going to lose power, and I don't even know what else will happen. I was in the management office this morning. Mrs. Thornton said they'd be closed after today." He touches my shoulder. "Come with me. Just as friends, I promise."

I pull my shoulder back. "I'll be fine, Greg. No need to worry."

"Jenny, are you leaving? Just tell me."

"Yes, I'm leaving. Nick is coming in a little while. Okay?"

"Okay." He nods. "I just wanted to make sure. Take care, Jenny." He steps back, turns, and starts to walk down the hallway.

"Thank you, Greg," I call after him.

He stops and turns to face me. "I'll be back," he says in a bad Arnold Schwarzenegger imitation and smiles.

Shaking my head, I laugh and close the door.

Nick doesn't understand. He doesn't need to say anything. I see it in his face and the set of his jaw. He stands rooted in the center of the apartment.

"We don't have to leave tonight," I say. "Let's see what happens tomorrow. Forecasts change all the time. This is probably much ado about nothing. Remember the Y2K scare in 2000? Everyone thought all the computers in the world would crash." The words tumble out of my mouth.

Nick shakes his head, his arms crossed over his chest. "This is different, Jenny. Sandy is coming, and it's coming here." He points to the floor. "There's no doubt about it."

"Then why isn't Sea Grove being evacuated?" I don't wait for an answer. "Belmar is. Sea Bright is. Other places are, too." My voice goes shrill.

"I don't know, Jenny. Maybe it's because those towns have lakes or rivers. That's beside the point though," he says, his fisted hands pressed against his thighs. "Why doesn't it look like you've even packed anything?" he asks quietly.

I swallow and answer him calmly. "I've got everything off the floor except for the rug here and the one next door.

All I have to do is throw some clothes in a bag."

"So, you don't want to take any of your other things with us?"

"I think they'll be fine here," I say.

And so will I, I *don't* say.

"Then why don't you pack some clothes so we can get on the road?" Nick asks.

I walk over to him and lay my head against his chest. "It's late already, Nick. Why don't you stay here tonight, and we can leave tomorrow?"

He kisses the top of my head. "Jenny Gilbert, what am I going to do with you?"

I step back and smile.

I wake to the scraping sound of opening blinds, and a dull gray light washes over me. Nick stands at the window, peering out. "It's raining," he says.

"Rain, rain, go away. Come again another day," I singsong.

"This isn't funny." Nick leans over me, his face serious. "We should get on the road." He smells of soap, and his shower-damp hair glistens.

I stretch my arms over my head and yawn.

"I know." I lift my face to his and breathe him in. "You smell good."

The corners of his mouth turn up in an 'I'm not going to smile' look.

"Jenny—"

"I know. I know. I'm getting up." I force myself out of my nice, comfortable bed and head for the bathroom. At the door, I turn around, put my hands on my hips and stick my tongue out.

Nick laughs. Guess he can't help it this time. I close the door and turn on the shower.

Nick lifts the edge of the bed, and I pull the rug out onto the floor. We roll up it up and carry it next door where we repeat the process with the bedroom and living room rugs. Nick positions all three into a carefully balanced pyramid on my kitchen table. We do a thorough tour of the apartment. All is secure, and we head back next door.

I fill a bag with clothes and toiletries.

"What else do you want to pack?" Nick asks.

"Nothing." I shake my head.

"Nothing?" He tilts his head, and his eyebrows squish together. "But we've got two cars. We can take—"

"Nick, all my things belong *here*, and I'm not moving them."

"But we don't know what's going to happen here." Nick stretches his arms out, and he shakes his head. "It's definitely going to flood, and we don't know what else will happen once the hurricane hits."

I feel my body straighten, shoulders back, chin high. Military posture.

"Everything is off the floor, and everything is unplugged. Besides flooding and a power outage, nothing can happen. This place, my *home*, is ready." My voice is strong, calm. And so am I.

Nick shakes his head, his lips pushed together, and throws his hands up, then lets them drop.

"Jenny, I'm not going to fight you on this. I think it would be a good idea for us to take as much as we can, but that's up to you. My concern is for *your* safety. The rest is your decision."

"Thank you," I say.

He arches an eyebrow and stares at me.

"I'm not being sarcastic, Nick. I mean it. Thank you." I pause, wetting my lips. "Thank you for respecting my decision."

"Always." He nods and smiles. "So, are you ready to leave?"

I wet my lips and click my tongue. "I guess."

One more inspection of the apartment, and then, hand in hand, we walk out of the building.

Stepping into an angry wind blowing stinging needles of rain sideways, we hurry to the parking lot. The nearly empty parking lot.

"You know how to get to my house, but follow me anyway. I'll watch for you in my rearview." Nick pulls me into a quick hug, and we climb into our cars.

Wipers and lights on, I follow Nick out of the complex. The road is rain-slicked, and the sky is cement gray. Puddles pockmark the local streets, splattering our tires. When we reach the highway, we join a slow-moving caravan of cars, minivans, and trucks, all heading north or west.

I turn on the radio.

"…unprecedented damage. Public transportation in New Jersey will be suspended. Shelters have been established…"

I turn the knob sharply to the left until it clicks. Everything will be fine. Nick is right. I needed to leave. My apartments are going to flood, both of them. And Sea Grove will definitely lose power. Who knows for how long? I'll be safe with Nick. There's nothing to worry about.

But, maybe…Should I have…? Was Nick right about taking my…?

I shake my head, trying to dislodge the thoughts.

"My things will be fine," I say out loud.

I do a mental tour of my second apartment. Nothing on the floor, nothing plugged in. We rolled up the rug that was under my bed, and the comforter...my comforter! The blue and white cloud-patterned one, like the one I had as a teenager. It's hanging over the edge of my bed, not touching the floor, but close. Too close. If the apartment floods, the water will wick its way up the fabric. It'll be soaked. Stained. What if there's mildew? What if there's mold? And my toy hammock...It's filled with stuffed animals. They won't be able to survive mold or even mildew. And the books that I left on the higher shelves...What if the flood waters...?

And suddenly, I know what I have to do. Up ahead, I spot a white-lettered green sign.

U-Turn.

27

I slide my car into the best spot in the parking lot. It's just a few steps from the walkway to my building. Only four other cars are still here. I can see two buildings besides my own. All of the first-floor apartments are dark, but scattered lighted windows dot the second and third floors. I hurry into my building, slip into my apartment, and flip the light switch. Power still on, floor dry.

I pull my phone out of my bag, hesitant to check it. A barrage of text messages, missed calls, and voicemails fill the screen.

Where r u? R u behind me? R u lost? Call me!!!

My right eyelid begins to quiver as I press *Call Back.*

"Are you in your apartment?" Nick's question comes through fast and loud.

"Don't be mad. I had to—"

"Stop, Jenny. No more talking. I'll be there in ten minutes. I'm on my way."

"No, don't," I say. But he's already hung up.

I unlock the apartment door and hang my rain-soaked jacket in the bathroom. I catch sight of myself in the mirror.

Flushed face and messy hair. No matter. I shuffle over to the bed and sit down on its edge, feeling my shoulders collapse. I clasp my hands in my lap and stare down at them. Nothing to do now except wait.

Nick bursts through the door. I look up. His wet hair is pushed back from his face, and tiny rivers of rainwater roll down his neck. His jacket is wrinkled and soggy. He stands in the doorway, silent.

I force myself up, my body leaden, and walk toward him.

"I'm sorry. I really am. I came back for my comforter. I was afraid it would get wet. And then I started thinking. What if my things get mildew or mold? I'm sorry, Nick. I just can't…" My eyes start to fill. I blink and breathe in.

He nods, his face unreadable.

"Nick, I'm sorry. I really am. You shouldn't have come back. I tried to tell you." And then I am crying, my face hot and wet, my shoulders trembling.

Nick folds me in his arms, and I lean into the wet warmth of him. He strokes my hair.

"Shhhh," he whispers.

"You need to go," I say into his chest.

"No, I need to stay."

I step back, moving out of his arms. "Nick—"

"Wherever *you* are, Jenny, that's where I need to be."

He drapes his jacket over my desk chair and locks the apartment door.

28

The window behind my bed rattles as it gets pummeled by a crashing wind slamming storm-driven rain directly into it. I lift one of the blind slats and quickly drop it, shutting out the wrathful early morning sky. Next to me, Nick sleeps, his face pressed into a pillow.

Quietly, I slip out of bed, and carefully placing one foot in front of the other, I walk through the apartment. It's taken me years and years of searching and finding to arrive here to this place that is my home. I peer into closets and cabinets, silently open drawers, and take stock of the bins and boxes piled on my counters and desk. I scan the titles stacked in my CD tower and run my fingers along the brightly colored covers of the books of my childhood. My gaze sweeps over Barbie dolls, Beanie Babies, toys, and games. They've all been a part of my life. They *are* a part of my life. And I truly believe that they will still be here waiting for me after the hurricane has done its worst. But, in the end, they are *things*. They are *my* things, but still, they are *things*.

I tiptoe over to the bed and look down at Nick. The man whom I've lied to and kept secrets from, the man who came back *to* me and *for* me. And I know that I am home.

I lift my dreamcatcher from its spot over the bedside lamp, lay it over my arm, and carry it into the kitchen. Smoothing its feathers and strings, I wrap it in plastic and set it on top of my tote bag.

Moving back to the bed, I lean over Nick and whisper in his ear. "Wake up. It's time to go."

ACKNOWLEDGMENTS

Writing a book is a solitary affair. I am truly grateful to the people—all members of my 'writers' tribe'—who believed in me, supported me, and guided me. Perhaps most importantly, they showed me that I was not alone on the crazy journey that transformed the tiniest spark of an initial idea into the novel that is *Things*.

My sincerest thanks goes to Lynette Birkins, Sally Cohen, Melinda Colleton, Alyce Jenkins, Margaret Ksiazak, Arlene Novick, and Brooke Powell. To Jeffery Cohen, my longtime critique partner. I thank you for your keen insight, writerly wisdom, and patience throughout the long journey that has finally (yes, finally!) resulted in the creation of this book.

Thank you, also, to the wonderful and talented folks at Ant Colony Press. Jordan, the cover is even better than I had envisioned, and your business acumen is much appreciated. Colette, you have been a tireless and enthusiastic supporter. And Sarah, your editorial expertise and wise advice throughout the whole process that has culminated in *Things* has been invaluable. Every writer should have a 'Sarah'!

Saving the best for last, I am so deeply grateful for the three stars that light my way now and always—Mitch (my partner in all things), Jenna, and Michael. You are *my* gladiators!

ABOUT THE AUTHOR

Francine Garson's work has appeared in a number of print magazines and online publications. Her flash fiction received a first place award from the National League of American Pen Women in 2010 and a second place award from WOW-Women On Writing in 2013. She lives in central New Jersey, and *Things* is her debut novel. Visit her at francinegarson.com or connect with her on Twitter at @francinegarson.

Visit us at:

www.antcolonypress.com

www.facebook.com/antcolonypress

When Shadows Creep by K. Brooks

The Darkness comes, slinking out of the shadows in Flynn's new home, Freemont House. With Flynn's life in danger, his adoptive tribe—the other centuries-old Guardians—will do whatever it takes to bring him home. He reluctantly sheds the autonomy of his life by the sea and returns to Caldwell Manor, but the Darkness follows him, and threatens to unravel the Guardians' very existence.

www.antcolonypress.com

Unconventional by Scarlet Birch

Sam isn't supposed to be in love with Louis. She likes him. What they have is fine. But Love? When he drops the L word, she won't say it back, and she may lose Louis—the only constant thing in her life—forever. He won't give up on her, though, and as her life falls apart he is the foundation she didn't know she needed.

www.antcolonypress.com

In The House Of In Between by JD Buffington

Phoebe Backlund, who built her family's dream home, has no explanation for the events that take place there. She invites curious thrill seekers and notorious skeptics alike in the golden age of spiritualism to experience the house's clockwork poltergeists. Knocks, slamming doors, screams, and looming specters delight and terrify her guests, but answers are as elusive as the phantoms.

www.antcolonypress.com

The Editor by Luke Carroll

*L*incoln Larkin's most recent novels are so awful that they've pushed him to the brink of self-destruction. Now, those same stories are literally trying to kill him and everyone he gets close to. His novel Vriends is anything but a masterpiece and didn't land him on any bestseller lists, but the characters from this spoof are coming to life and draining innocent people all over the city.

www.antcolonypress.com

Made in the USA
Middletown, DE
13 September 2018